THE DELVER OF PURGATORY

THE DELVER OF PURGATORY

THE BLESSED & POSSESSED
BOOK TWO

JAY REQUARD

To my eagle in the night, John Hartness.

PART I

HOME TO DUBLIN

UNTIL IT SLEEPS

Oh God.

Of the many places I had been, few were ever considered home.

I had spent most of my days on The March, going from a piece of your kingdom to the next, sorting souls gambled in the balance of light and dark. Of the few places I did make mine, Ireland held my heart.

Never could I forget its ancient cities of stone and mortar, home to bandit-chiefs singing songs of forebearers long dead, their bones buried under flourishing centers of glass and steel that would have awed them in their dirty hovels. Where once women died in droves in both the churches I founded and the dark groves of druids trying their best with mistletoe and crude iron, bright hospitals with clean rooms now welcomed citizens both native and new, the latter found in a future immigrants brought to our enduring home.

I remembered Ireland when it was a cruel, cold place, when the best I could give those motherless babes was the blessing of your word. Like those damned chieftains in their hovels, I basked in the wonder of what it had become as a free, independent nation still waiting to be whole.

And I loved her now as I did then.

We ditched the Gulfstream on a private runway in Shannon. The Chair had set us up with a lorry behind a hanger large enough to fit Deevi with her wings if she climbed through the bay, along with a duffel bag filled with passports, euros, dollars, and a pair of handguns George slipped into his coat. We negotiated the three burners with Vatican minutes among the three of us mortals before I loaded Merry, the rooster-possessing Lucifer, and his Nephilim daughter up and directed us east into Munster.

Behind the wheel, George took us to the only place he and I thought might be safe.

To Baile Mora.

The old mansion, not far outside of Bunratty Upper, stood atop a hill overlooking the valley we had wound through to get there. The white face of the house and its gray roof aged like a hunk of bird shit sinking into the green earth they had built it on. The pebble drive crunched under the tires before we crested onto the leveled car park.

George switched off the ignition and glanced at me.

I nodded to him after a tense pause. As I got out of the passenger side, the side-bay door popped out. Sliding it back, the Vodun priestess Merry stepped down onto the cement pad. Lifting a sack from the lorry's floor to her hip, she rushed past me. "There a bathroom here, Tater?" she asked in her thick accent, half Haitian Creole and Brooklyn-French.

"Wait a second," I called after her as the rooster came next.

Hopping down with a few flaps, the archangel Lucifer pecked his focus toward the van's rear. His tail feathers up and proud, he paid me no attention as I death-stared him.

Deevi had already swung the bay doors out. Standing on the lip, she stretched her shimmering golden wings in salutation to the setting sun, their glow soaking in the dying rays. She brought her sparking gaze down to me, and Lord, I forgot everything else.

"Where are we, Patrick?" she asked, smiling only for me. Those words carried the power of the Nephilim's glamor, an unspeakable urge to answer her fully and completely with the truth.

After the last few weeks, I had gotten fairly good at simply submitting. I offered her a hand, though she obviously didn't need it. "This old place is called Baile Mora. We'll be safe for a night or two."

Merry had stopped in front of the bottom step and turned on me, her amber eyes wide. "You brought us to..." She took in our abode again. "Well."

"Let's all get inside and settled." I ushered them toward the kitchen door. "We need to get the wi-fi on if we're going to supper in some fashion."

Deevi took my hand as she stepped down but led the way to the house, oblivious to my reluctance.

We crowded behind George as he fussed with the keys the Chair had left with the lorry. He let us in a dark kitchen. It lit brightly when he flipped the switch beside the door. Cream yellow walls closed in a cooking area ruled by an expansive eggshell iron stove and white wooden counters. Quaint like a country cooking show, the air smelled the same homey wood-dust smell I had grown up hating. The fridge was new, its stainless-steel doors shining dull against the mercury bulbs.

"We are alone here, it seems," Lucifer declared as he trotted in. "This will suffice for an evening."

"Then get the fuck out of the way unless you're going to the bathroom," said Merry, kicking her way past the rooster. "Where's the loo, Tater?"

"Upstairs, top of the step," I told her, trusting Lucifer's angelic sense no matter how much I despised his shitty little airs. Deevi and the rooster filed past me after the priestess did.

George had entered last, stopping right in the threshold. We shared a moment and a look we hadn't since we were boys.

"Set it all ablaze?" I proposed.

Bless him, he laughed. Closing the door behind him, he leaned back against it and shook his head. "I can't believe you suggested we come here."

"I can't believe you actually drove us," I said. "Now a moment. I'll find us food down way and make a few calls."

"Who are you calling?"

"Whom we got to call if we want to stay in Dublin, says I." I angled my body in the signal to walk on and leave me be. "Go see if the goods are still here."

"I'll be upstairs. I'll get the wi-fi on and check the rest. See if my backup is where I left it."

"Don't get yourself cut up!" Creatures of habit, George and me.

Left by myself with my burner, I suddenly realized this was the first time I had been truly alone since our escape from New York, which felt almost a lifetime away across the Atlantic despite the twelve hours it took. I found a seat at the old plank table the nuns and friar used to eat at after they spent the day beating us.

There were times as a boy, God, I had prayed for such quiet moments alone.

I spent these calling my old terrorist-friends.

I had to call twice before someone picked up.

"Aye, who's this?"

"Father Donovan there?"

"Whose calling?"

"Tell him Father Patrick is on the other end."

"Oh, and why should I?" asked the responder, taking a cocky tone. "The father is in the midst of a sermon."

"It's bleeding ten at night," I said, too tired to brook any argument from a grubby bar back. "Watch him stop his sermon on this call."

The receiver smacked a countertop. A hubbub in the background, loud with the laughter and shouting of any respectable pub, buzzed my ear before I heard the phone lift from where it rested. A man breathed hard into the speaker.

"Saint Patrick? Are you there, Saint Patrick?"

"Aye, Donovan," I said. "Are you there?"

"Aye, aye, my old friend, I am," he hacked through the phone. "Middle of work, you know."

"Down in Ma Middleton's cellar?"

"Right are," said Donovan. "They pour my whiskey free."

"Ah, good man! Tell me, I'm up in Baile Mora and I'm thinkin—"

"You're in Ireland, Patrick? Why didn't you call, you piss-head?" the priest shouted drunkenly on the other end. There came more clatter lost in a jumble of words.

Amid the cacophony, Deevi slipped into the room and took a seat on the other side of the kitchen table. Dressed in a white Adidas jumper bunched in the back by her wings so her midriff was exposed, some hiking trousers hugged her powerful hips and calves, accentuating their lines. Her brown mane back in a ponytail, she spied at me from the illuminated corner of the room, her golden eyes unwavering temptation.

"Go," I mouthed.

Donovan returned on the bar line. "Saint Patrick! I'm going to be hanging up the phone. Someone will be calling back. Please answer when he does!"

The line clicked dead.

I glanced at Deevi. "Find yourself clothes?"

"I did," she said. "You should come to bed. Merry is already passed out in one of the other bedrooms, and I think George is praying somewhere else."

"Where's your da?" I asked, searching around the floor to see if the little feathery fuck had snuck under the table. The hint in her voice of what waited for us upstairs made me extra-leery.

"Upstairs," she said, musing sweetly. "In his own room. Door shut."

The corded phone, shiny in its cream enamel, trilled loudly on the counter by the oven. I picked the horn off the rack and placed the receiver to my ear. "'Alo?"

"Daniel O'Brien, your holiness," said a strong, firm brogue on the other end. "Real IRA."

"I figured you'd be calling once Donovan got the word out," I said, turning to rest my backside on the counter's edge.

Deevi sauntered over, the glow of her wings outshining the light bulbs above us.

I kept my gaze to the floor, though I couldn't hide the grin on my face. "I figure you know who I am?"

"I do, sir."

"Right, Daniel. Now, I have an apartment of my own in Dublin, not far from Trinity, but it's not just me coming home. I have two people that need their own roofs, as well as a place that can take animals."

"You bringing hounds, Saint Patrick?"

Deevi laid her fingers on the swell of my chest. Electricity lanced across my skin at her touch.

"Just a bird," I said, my breath steady.

She gazed into my eyes and held me there before her hand moved up to my cheek. She cradled my face.

"You'll be under my full protection," said Daniel. "We have men in the police, the government—we will be at your beck and call. Not an inch of harm will come near you, your holiness."

"Call me Patrick," I told Daniel before she darted in. Our lips met and parted suddenly, her hot mouth leaving behind a trace.

"I'll be upstairs," she whispered, somehow knowing how to move in just the right way to bring my eyes down to that heavenly—

I covered my face. "Well and good, Daniel. I'll be in touch in a day or so. Play this by ear, you know?"

"Of course," said Daniel. "Just to warn you, the Archbishop of Dublin will be calling. He will have to bless my charge in taking you before you can enter the city."

"Right, right," I said. "God bless, Daniel."

I hung up the house phone and went back to the burner, pulling up the Just Eat! app to see what delivered from Bunratty. Not far from the N18 between Limerick and up to Galway, a few Indian places and some halals were still open when George reentered the kitchen. Tucked under his arm were two boxes: one long and rectangular, the second smaller in proportion. He placed both on the kitchen table.

"I think we're getting Indian," I said.

"In Bunratty?"

"Immigrants, Georgie. God bless them."

The house line chimed a second time.

"That'll be for me," I said, returning to take the call. "Saint Patrick of Ireland," I said in the cheeriest voice I could muster. "Looking for an exorcism?"

"Saint Patrick, this is Archbishop Patrick Taggerty over at the Dublin archdiocese. Please let me be the first to welcome you home to Ireland. His Grace let me know of your coming before he went into the hiding. We are at your service, your holiness. Know you will be treated equally to the Pope himself!"

"Well, I..." I tried not to chuckle at all that. "Please, father, I only seek to find safe harbor for those I brought with me."

"Of course, of course, Patrick," said Taggerty. "May I beg of you a request, your grace?"

"Of course, father."

"Will you speak on a Sunday? Perhaps deliver a homily? We'd be glad to conceal your identity, but for my parish to hear the word of God spoken from the lips of his chosen—our chosen—you can understand why I would ask."

The request echoed in me, Lord, and I didn't know what to say. "Let me think on it. I'll let you know by the time I get to Dublin, father."

"Bless you, Saint Patrick. We of the archdiocese look forward to your coming."

The call for a homily left my farewells awkward. I chewed on what he had asked me. Where was I now, Lord? Back home in the country I adored, in the house I hated, cobbled together with your outcasts. I alone could have been any one of them, and yet there, on the doorstep back to peace and solitude, I took darker measure of where you and I stood.

"Who was that?" George asked after I hung up.

"Archbishop of Ireland," I said, suddenly exhausted. "We have a clear way into Dublin when we're ready."

"Good," said George, tense in his thick neck and sturdy shoulders. He faced the longer of the two boxes he had brought from upstairs and unlatched its clasp. "I found these in our old bedroom. I'll sleep there tonight."

I sidled up next to him and spun the second box around and to lift its top. Inside a green velvet-lined compartment shone a long strand of polished limestone beads attached to a silver cross. The rosary rested on my old vestment. Sewn of green silk and edged in fine ermine, it smelled of the old as I removed the cloth, setting it aside while I palmed the rosary. The last one had been lost somewhere in the mash of baggage we had brought with us. Feeling the spare in my hand did nothing to assuage my troubles.

George opened his container to find a sword. Of the medieval period, the brass cross shined brightly beneath the kitchen lights, the oiled leather of the gold-throated scabbard glossy. He brought it out like it had been with him all the time, one with him and him with it.

"Feel better?" I asked.

He nodded quietly, his sullen gray eyes studying the smooth golden hilt and polished pommel.

Stuffing the rosary in the pocket of some jeans I bought back in America, I gathered my vestment up in my arms. "So, how many samosas do you think you'll need?"

2

CAR PAD BOOGALOO

We had solid Irish takeaway: lamb vindaloo with extra orders of samosas to help us get down a middling liter of chai before George found some fresh in the cupboard and brewed a pot. Plates of jasmine rice dried beside the uneaten lentil soups as we sat quietly around the kitchen table. Merry and Deevi watched YouTube on George's burner while I cleaned up. The emotionally-stunted knight polished his old sword. Lucifer had gotten off somewhere in the house and, for the sake of peace, I let him.

I buried my arms elbow-deep in suds to work on the dishes.

Mindless toil is wonderful. Some people are made to meditate all day long, never leaving their space, while others like me and my own found our peace in doing. Plate after plate was scrubbed while I thought of nothing, or tried to think of nothing, like how every day in Dublin was a countdown before we had to run from demons again. Or how I couldn't stop thinking about Deevi. Or how, once again, God had led us to such strange places.

Deep in a sink where I was often consigned as punishment as a lad, I wondered how the hell I got here.

I was scared to death of where I'd end up next.

It could have been Timbuktu. Or Ghana. Or the Andes. Or some shitty little hovel in western China where the demons could probably find us before we found decent Wi-Fi.

And yet you led us to Ireland, Lord.

Why, of all the places?

Because I wanted it?

"There are many people outside," Lucifer announced from the kitchen's entryway. All feathers, he stood half-turned to the darkness. "They are coming up the hill."

George stormed from his seat, sword in one hand, as he drew out a handgun with the other. Safety flicked up, he stepped over the chicken. Deevi swung her legs over the bench and trailed him with a curious expression etched on her face, a hunter seeking the noise.

Merry twisted around to look at me from where she sat. She shrugged with complete confidence. "Want me to take care of the front door?"

I pulled my rosary from my pocket. "You do voodoo, Ma?

Like so many times before, we followed the weird into the dark together.

George and Deevi stood in one of the front rooms, facing the bay windows curtained in white sheets. The bushes outside shook under the weight of iron tools chopping at the branches.

Multiple blows. From multiple tools.

"One of us needs to man the foyer," George whispered. "More than just Merry."

"I'll have it." Deevi marched around George and placed her hand out at her side. Lava-lamp bubbles popped into reality, gelatinous and glowing. They flowed into a sword the length of George's arming blade, completed with a single fiery edge and a gold-wire hilt enveloping her wrist. Her wings drawn up like shields on her back, she strode to the central eave of the house.

"Off we go," Merry said to me, pressing a hand to my back as she wormed by. Somewhere in the shadows around my feet, I spotted a red comb and bright green tail feathers scuttle after her. Little shit.

Alone with George, I joined him by the covered windows.

Shrubs crashed as at least two people tried to break through.

"They're not very smart," he whispered.

"These people are possessed, George. Probably the locals," I said, wrapping my rosary around my knuckles. I had left my bible upstairs, but it was always more for show: I could recite it aloud in too many languages, too many versions. The mission mattered more. "We can't kill them."

"The Lord sorts that," the Dragonslayer replied in his posh monotone.

"Well, fuck. Good talk, Rambo."

"Go find a weapon," he said, not breaking his guard. "There are still arms hanging up in the foyer. Someone needs to guard the other end of the house."

"I'll give marching orders to the chicken."

Deevi sat on the central staircase in the foyer, her wing shining off the dark, glossy stain of the step-tops while her sword lit the eggshell walls an ominous red. Merry busied around the door scribing Vodun veves into the Victorian frame with a black felt pen. She had gotten her bag from upstairs, and beside the upturned sack rested a bowl of smoking incense, the coal within barely a match for the Nephilim's light. A small jar of green-pink powder waited next to the dish.

Swords and daggers from the days of Cromwell when some Royalist pomp owned this place lined the walls up the stairs. I didn't want to take a single one of them, even though I knew how to use them all. The Church had put them in Baile Mora for a reason when we were kids.

I didn't want to be that person again.

"Any of that juju-nonsense going to work?" I called to Merry.

Her mass of braids, gathered in a coil with a scarf, shook as she chuckled and kept drawing her glyphs. "Why don't you say me a prayer?"

"What are you going to do, Patrick?" Deevi asked from the steps.

Studying the familiar veves to Ogun, the Nephilim, then the weapons on the wall, I shrugged at my pacifism. "Tell you both the truth, I don't want whoever is out there to come in, but I don't want there to be a bloodbath here either."

"So why are you sitting here still talking?" Merry asked in a mocking sing-song.

Bloody well dismissed, indeed. I clopped up the stairs past Deevi and searched the many bedrooms. Finding my bible and the simple green scarf I used as my typical vestment, I stuffed them into my pockets and went about gathering everything that seemed like it didn't belong. In one of the old dormitories I found the other handgun and the duffels full of money. Sticking the Glock into the bag after making sure the safety was on, I found Merry's baskets in the bedroom across the hall. Everything from candles to jars of powders to the small, peaking heads of idols I remember from her brownstone in Brooklyn, the weight was heavier than I anticipated.

Hauling the basket under one arm, holding the cloth handles of one duffel in the other, I traipsed back out into the hall to find two people standing in it.

The first, a short blond in a jumper and black skirt, jerked around to look at me with her dead black eyes. The fellow beside her, bulkier and taller in his trashman's suit, grinned too widely for his mouth to naturally allow.

Both charged me with their machetes.

I dropped the basket while swinging the duffel at the girl. Its weight slammed her small frame to the floor. I ducked the trashman's wild swing and shot myself forward. Hooking his legs, he flailed at my back, too close to cut. I dumped him onto the old boards. They cracked under our weight. As quick as I could, I got atop of him, raining rights and lefts enough times he went out.

The girl shoved the duffel off her and rose like Fury in the twelfth, only to drop as I kneed her flush in the face. The demon possessing her couldn't deny the mind-altering pain of a broken nose, eyes, and cheeks. She writhed on the ground, yelping like a hound as she bled. I grabbed the duffel and the basket and hot-footed down the hallway to the stair, almost tripping past the banister.

"Deevi," I called out.

"She's busy, Patrick!" shouted Merry from downstairs.

From the top of the steps I could see the Vodun priestess still at work on her sigils, the smoke of her incense bowl grown to a solid column of shifting reds, blues, and blacks. The veves glowed bright yellow under the pass of her marker.

More machetes on the other side of the door clubbed to get in.

I clamored down the steps. "There's fucking two of them upstairs!"

"Did you kill 'em?" Merry pulled the small cigar from her mouth, blowing the smoke on the designs to empower them.

"No!"

"Maybe you should've."

"Merry!"

"Get the van, Tater. We heard windows breaking. Who knows what George is doing? Where's the rooster?"

"Oh, fuck, where is Lucifer?" I shouted as I stomped toward the kitchens.

I entered in time to see the first fist of a demon break through a glass window. The sudden, fresh surge of adrenaline I needed spiked as George lunged forward and stabbed through the pane. He withdrew with a weird, happy grin. Blood coated his steel.

"They have fucking souls, George! You can't go..."

He faced me, a growling monster posing as a knight.

I didn't waste time negotiating as I walked by him.

Placing the duffel bag on the kitchen table, I took out the Glock and stuffed it in my pocket, figuring I'd stop whoever waited outside with leg wounds if it came to it.

A loud explosion rocked Baile Mora, blowing wood and brick from the front to the back. The concussive force knocked me onto my side and slid me across the tile. A collision with the cooker halted the tumble. The cloud settled before I made out the figure lurching his way into the kitchen. Covered head to toe in chips and dirt, George hacked out his lungs while trying to keep his sword at the ready.

"We should escape now." Hidden beneath one of the kitchen table's benches, I spotted Lucifer's beady little eyes. His voice cut through the whine in my ears. "This house is obviously unsafe, Saint Patrick."

Then a demon kicked in the side door.

George met the intruder with a downward blow, opening him at the shoulder. The demon screamed as blood flooded his host's mouth. The saint of England ripped his sword free and chopped down again. I scrambled to my feet and stepped into the growing puddle. I spotted Merry's overturned baskets near its creeping edge and lacking better sense to just grab what I could, knelt back down and tried to shovel everything into its wicker well.

George, drunk on bloodlust, grabbed the duffel where it lay. "Going to the van," he shouted at me in an unsteady voice, as if deaf. Without waiting, he let out the open door to the car pad. The whine of the explosion left my ears in time to hear myself groan on unbalanced feet, the basket in my hands providing the heft needed to anchor my legs.

Fresh panic set in when I realized that Deevi and Merry had been at the front of the house.

I found Lucifer still under the table. "You need to ditch the fucking chicken!"

"My agreement with God stipu—"

"Your daughter was in that blast, you miserable son of a bitch!" I screamed at him, a weak effort for the dust in my throat. "Do your duty, coward!"

The rooster stepped out, hackles raised. "No need, you potato-eating ingrate."

"Patrick!" Deevi marched from the smoking portal, no worse for wear and an unconscious Merry over her shoulder. We fled out the side door without stopping to talk.

Outside, George huffed into the dark night as he struggled to catch his breath, posted above two bodies.

"Where are the keys?" I called to him.

With a hard heave of his shoulders, George dropped a bloody hand from his hilt and pawed his pockets. He tore the keys out and tossed them over his shoulder. They landed a few feet from where I stood. Setting down the basket, I crouched to retrieve them.

"Incoming!" George shouted.

The fob in my fingers, I fumbled the lock button.

Almost ripping the door from its hinges, Deevi threw back the sliding hunk of steel and plastic before she deposited Merry onto the middle bench. Without hesitation, she dashed past the lorry's front to join George at the edge of the car pad. In the middle of a pitched melee, the knight stabbed one of the machete-wielding demons in the heart as multiple foes harried him against the lorry's grill. Almost overwhelmed, the onslaught of blunt blades aimed at his head were bashed away by the Nephilim. Side by side they hewed down four more attackers hampering our escape.

I faced away from the worst of it as I slammed Merry's basket through the side bay. "Where the fuck is that chicken?"

"Already inside the van, Saint Patrick." Lucifer appeared from the back bench with a gentle alight on the nearest arm rest. "Activate this iron beast!"

Too busy to curse the bird, I shut the sliding door in his face and turned to check on Deevi and George.

Leaning against the lorrie's front end, the knight sweated buckets, almost collapsing for air. She, on the other hand, stood there unhampered by her exertion, staring off into the night. Her glowing wings issued a golden illumination that I imagined everyone in Bunratty could see from the hills below.

"George, get in the car," I said as I opened the passenger door for him. Scooting through to the driver's seat, I checked the rearview mirror on instinct in time for a machete to shatter through the left window of the bay doors. The black-eyed demon beyond the hole grinned fiercely at me in his best Jack Nicholson.

George stumbled around to the passenger side, breezing past the door to meet the demon.

"No, you idiot," I tried to say before I watched him cut the arm off the possessed man, deal him one to the head, and walk back with fresh blood on his face. I didn't say anything else as he got in. As quickly as he sat down, he deflated, every ounce of exhaustion caught in an instant.

His face contorted in a silent, suffering scream. "Go, Patrick," he seethed through his teeth at me.

I turned on the ignition and pressed the button on the bay doors, which unlatched automatically. Deevi swept past, a blur of light and grace. Throwing them open, she crawled in and tucked her wings.

Slamming my foot on the gas, we roared off the car pad.

The lorry hung in the air for a few moments, then the front bumper landed first with a hard crash, jarring the frame. Somehow the engine didn't fall out. We surged down the first ramp of Baile Mora's hilly drive. The automatic headlights revealed dozens of stick-straight intruders at the edges of the berms.

"Keep going, keep going," George shouted at me every time I touched my foot to the brake.

"God damn this," I said, repeating it over and over. "George, I need to—"

Some of them threw themselves in the way when I reached the first turn. The weight of the back held us to the earth while I compensated for the slide, righting us down the next piece of hill as I tried to meter my hard stomps to the brakes.

More demons emerged from the hedges, tossing their weapons at us. Machetes, hammers, and a few rakes banged and skidded off the windshield and cab. George lurched forward in his seat, one hand firmed again on his sword's hilt and the other on the dash to brace himself. "Steady!"

Forgive me, Lord.

I killed a man on the next turn. I didn't see him.

I was scared, Lord, and I know a lot of people do a lot of things when they're scared.

But a man died never knowing where and why. Nobody will know why. Some family in Bunratty will have some civil service worker on their doorstep...what good came of that?

Christ didn't run anyone over with a fucking lorry. I did.

We reached the bottom, missing the rest who either had climbed too high to get back down in time or knew a failed chase when they saw one. I didn't stop, slinging our cart through the midnight roads before we hit the M17 toward Galway.

19

3

YOU GIVE LOVE A BAD NAME

Wings folded around her in a bright cocoon, Deevi spoke from the back bench. "Can you turn on the radio?"

I glanced to George in the passenger seat, still fast asleep. For the first time since the run down the hill I loosened my grip on the wheel, breathed deep, and exhaled all the tension. The silent M17 stretched north. For the lack of light, I couldn't make out Eire around us.

Working my jaw, I checked him again. Out cold from the battle, he slumbered like a babe. "How's Merry?" I whispered over the hum of the engine, the rubber on the asphalt beneath us.

"She's fine. Still passed out."

"Are you going to ask about me?" Lucifer inquired beside my elbow.

His voice made me jump in my seat. I did my best to keep the lorrie straight, a true miracle given how much I had wanted to throttle the bird.

The muscles tight in my head and shoulders, I looked ahead and not at him. "Will you please get down off the arm rest?" I asked in the gentlest tone I had ever mustered, and I used to run a Sunday School.

To my surprise, he did so promptly, hopping down onto the floor boards between the front seats and the middle bench where Merry slept.

Considerate enough not to push my luck, I tapped the dial on the dash.

One of the RTE's popped on the blue-lit radio, and someone jabbered on until the opening chorus to *You Give Love a Bad Name* echoed from the speakers. Turning it down before Sambora blasted us awake, the riff chewed through the night.

Bon Jovi crooned about every girl we dream about when I discovered Deevi's golden eyes staring at me through the rearview.

"You okay?" she mouthed.

A surge, like a needling in the head and heart, gathered in me at the instant. "No," I mouthed back, hoping she could read my lips and the shit-bird didn't hear me.

She did, tilting her head to the side with a questioning look.

"That house," I said, daring to whisper, "was not a nice place to grow up in."

"In Bailey Moore?"

"Baile Mora," I said in proper Irish.

"Then why did you go there?" the rooster asked from the cabin's dark.

My hands squeezed the wheel so tight I didn't even realize until I looked at my knuckles, hard and scarred, to register how much they hurt.

"Please," Deevi asked, at the same low volume. Her feathers glowed like those white plastic nightlights. "Please, Patrick. I'd like to know, too."

Biting back the bile I had for the Morningstar, I refocused on the road ahead of us. Signs showed us near Galway, the emblems already directing me on how to get to Dublin on the M6 through Athlone. I shifted into the right lane, joining the faster flow of traffic that'd take us to the exits. "Christ walked into towns and villages full of the sick, the damned, and the forgotten, and made those places right by grace and compassion. I think everyone who takes up that work wants to do the same."

I paused. Talking about Christ gets folks uncomfortable, and who knew what Lucifer would say the moment I dropped the name. He didn't interrupt, to my surprise. "I wanted to take us to Baile Mora and for one day have those rooms know peace—at least for me. I wanted Ireland to be my church again with no worry of the damned outside of it. And I come home to find my heaven full of the world."

Nobody would have missed the Nephilim fixed on them in the rearview mirror, and I didn't miss her. She sat there, her face revealed by the light she shed, waiting for me to go on.

If it were only us.

"This land lacks the good weather of heaven," said Lucifer, interrupting my confession. "I would beg to differ on further comparisons if you are going to make them. I might be forced to illustrate otherwise, of course, to avoid any further inanities."

"Oh, you fucking might?"

Merry popped up on the middle bench like a zombie on the powder kick, obscuring my view of Deevi. She stomped the floor while Ritchie Sambora's solo blared over the speakers.

"You rude motherfucker," she screamed at the top of her lungs. "Can't let anyone have a fucking word, you clucky little shit! Get off my fucking baskets before I—"

Amid the vodun queen's kicking and screaming Deevi tried to make room in the back. The possessed rooster ran to and fro, wedged between a basket and his daughter's feet. Hands steady and the pressure firm on the gas, I failed to stop myself from cackling in glee when George woke.

"What the fuck is going on?" he shouted. His blood-crusted sword slid off his hip.

"Hey, watch that thing," I said.

Merry tried to climb behind her bench. "Get you, you dirty little—"

Deevi broke in, out of sight. "Merry, you'll get hurt!"

"Shove it, princess, before you get a smack!" cried Merry.

George gasped at the threat. "All right, that's it! Patrick, pull over!"

"I'm not bloody pulling over! Sit down, all of you! Merry! Merry, stop!"

"I'll rip your fucking guts out and do nothing with them, you tiny rat-ass," she cursed at Lucifer, the rooster out of sight. "Fuck with me!"

This time I did turn in the driver's seat. "Merry!"

The vodun priestess turned on her bench and plopped down in the center, heaving with a satisfied, terrifying smirk. "All done, Tater."

Our clucky little shit stayed quiet the rest of the way.

4

THE FIRST BREATH

I checked us into a luxury hotel east of Phoenix Park on the south side of Stoneybatter. I parked the lorry around back before George and I went inside with three stacks of euros the Church gifted us. Still in the clothes we wore on the plane from New York, we checked each other over.

"We look like we were fucking," I said, which drew a tired, irritated look as he pulled open the hotel's glass entrance.

"You do the talking," he whispered.

"Of course I'll do the talking." I called aloud as I charged into the lobby, in a huff and looking about before my gaze settled on the young girl behind the front desk. I marched up to her, my arms cocked out to make me look as wide as possible. "Excuse me, miss..." I glanced at her tag. "Miss Kamala. My name is Nigel McGuinness and I need to book rooms. Unfortunately my client, a famous Instagram model and influencer, needs to be brought in immediately by her security as she has a few stalkers in the area. I'm sorry if I'm going too fast."

"Of course, Mr. McGuinness," said Kamala, her fingers fast on the keyboard in front of her. "We actually have a wide vacancy this season, so we can provide upper-level suites if you like."

I fished the black Vatican card out of my pocket and slammed it on the counter between us. "Three of your finest, please. All on the same floor, if possible."

"I don't think that will be a problem sir." She only had to see the black on it before she pulled it to her. "Do you have any ID?"

"Do you have any debts?"

Kamala, a young girl with her head wrapped in a pretty maroon and cream hijab, looked up from her screen. "Excuse me?"

"Debts," I said. "You? Your Da? Ma?"

"Excus—"

I pulled the stack of euros, all bright purple and yellow with that cute blue box that layered nice and neat. "Look, I'll hand you this stack of cash, you check us into those three rooms, and you put in whatever name you want. That card will work and I swear we aren't doing anything illegal. There simply can't be any sign of us or the press will swamp this place..."

Kamala scanned me then the money. "One night?"

I laid the stack of euros on the counter between us. "Don't say anything about the rooster. It's her therapy pet."

Just then the doors of the hotel burst open. George led the way, holding one of Merry's baskets as he kept the entrance open with his foot. Bless her heart, Deevi came in next with a coat haphazardly thrown around her glowing wings, which she had tried to fold as close to her body as possible. She carried Lucifer clutched to her chest, who looked about in his typical cold disinterest. Merry followed behind, hauling her other basket.

I threw myself into damage mode. "Everyone this way! This way to the lifts," I said with a smile, pointing toward the hallway off the lobby. Thankfully we had gotten to Dublin at the season when the tourists were scant. Handing the room keys to George, he took them without question and hustled everyone in the proper direction. As quickly as they came, they went, out of sight with nary a word, cluck, or curse.

For safe measure I took out a second stack of euros and placed it on the counter beside the first.

Kamala's focus shifted back to the money. "We'll charge extra if the rooster stains the carpet. Please don't shoot any porn."

The top floor comprised the three deluxe luxury suites the hotel offered, all wood and white and soft on big California Kings, hot showers with those perfect heads feeling like a thousand fingers massaging wearied, tired, and traveled flesh. I think I stood in the water for an hour in the room George and I took next to Deevi and Lucifer. Merry had the room across from everyone, shutting the door the moment she could.

The scalding water woke things, Lord.

Cromwell's screaming, jabbering face. I held his severed head in my hands against La Guardia's tarmac and muddled through the right litanies.

The archangels battling each other.

Your coming. Your going.

The possessed man I ran over in Bunratty.

I stood in the water for a long time.

George knocked. "Some of us need to wash too, Patrick. I found the menu to room service and they're still open."

"Continental or Irish menu?"

"Both," he said through the bathroom door.

I cut off the water. "Gimme a minute."

Toweling off, I took the one terrycloth robes on the hanger and slid my naked ass into it. Hair still wet to my head, I yanked open the door, letting out a cloud of steam.

George sat on the edge of the big bed, hands in his lap and fingers laced together. He raised his head when the florescent lights over the mirror behind struck his features, his gray eyes far away from where he sat.

We all needed a cleaning. Water still running down my face, I studied this broken soldier before me and wondered if there were enough showers for him and the questions he had. I spotted the yellow-and-white striped menu on the duvet beside him. "Anything you see? I can order for you while you're in."

He shook his head and stood up, striding forward for the bathroom. "I'll think on it."

He shut the door. The shower kicked back on. There was not a lot of noise after that.

I hadn't eaten since Baile Mora but nothing on the menu sparked real hunger. Putting the menu to the side, I stood up off the bed and wandered into the sitting room. Plopping down on the leather sofa across from the box, I spied the outlines of our two Vatican smart phones on the coffee table next to the remote. I fished one over to me and tapped the screen awake. Thankfully I found the one I had been using and punched in one of the numbers, hoping I got it on the first try.

A man picked up on the other line. "O'Brien."

"Saint Patrick of Ireland, Daniel," said I. "If you can believe it."

"How are you doing, sir?"

"Fairer now," I said. "My people and I are in Dublin already."

"Already?" he asked, a slight raise in his voice. "We weren't expecting you until later tonight or tomorrow morning."

"Had to leave Bunratty quicker than anticipated. Nothing to worry yourself about. That said, it'd be nice to have some company from where we are to where we're going."

"Do you have keys to your apartment? We can call a locksmith."

"No, no need about that either," I said. "Be by in the morning? We have a lorry we need to ditch as well."

"My boys can handle that, don't you worry. How many are you bringing again?"

"Four adults and a pet rooster."

Daniel was quiet for a beat. "What time do you want us?"

"Call me at six and I'll give you a go-ahead with the address."

"Aye, of course," said Daniel. "Will that be all? Are you sure you're secure where you are?"

"Right where we need to be, Daniel. Call you in the morning."

As I hung up someone knocked on the door. The warmth of the

shower in my bones, my flesh had settled in the semi-soft cushions of the couch. I almost groaned as I put both feet back on the carpet and rose.

"Patrick?" Deevi called from the other side. "Are you there?"

I flicked on the light near the foyer closet, flipped open the latch, and turned the handle. The light of her wings seeped through the widening crack of the door. Opening it fully, she stood there before me in her white jumper.

And nothing else from the waist down.

"Deevi," I said, breathless. "Go put on some trousers!"

"No," she said. "Come out into the hall."

Never one to argue with a beautiful woman not wearing any pants, I tied shut my robe—not that it did any good for the arising problem. With George secluded in the shower, I slipped out into the empty hallway with her. "Where's Lucifer?"

"I sang the song that Gabriel taught me. He's sleeping," she said as she offered a hand. "Come with me to the window."

Her fingers warm and dry against my clammy digits, she pulled me past the elevators to a great window looking eastward into Dublin. The lights of the city blinked on against the last glow of the day and a fiery purple sunset. People wandered the sidewalks at the corner entrance of Phoenix Park. Three blessings held me there, for a time:

One for where I was.

One for where I had been.

And her.

5

LOONS

Despite what some expect of a sinner like me, I did not take her up on the offer in the hallway or at the threshold of her hotel room. The sight of the rooster asleep on the glass coffee table and anxiety about angelic sleepy-time spells dissuaded. I backed out, bidding her goodnight every second before the door shut.

I found the patron saint of England out of the shower and on the couch when I returned to our room. Redressed in the same clothes he had worn from New York, he cradled the clicker in his hand. The flat screen bathed his wet hair in bluish light.

I shut the door behind me. "Hey," I whispered, hoping no part of me still poked out. "You good?"

George said nothing, his hard stare centered on RTE as they ran the nine-o'clock news.

Not wanting to aggravate Lieutenant Dan in the midst of his turmoil, I sat in one of the chairs book-ending the couch. A few more seconds of waiting for him to answer, an image on the telly caught me, white letters on a band of blue. The anchor began his pronouncement.

"Communities all around the globe continue to stand in shock from the events in New York. Following the reported terrorist attacks at the Vatican and the Pope's disappearance along with a bombing at Dennison Tower in Manhattan, the event American media and many evangelical communities are now calling 'the La Guardia Revelation' has sent the entire world clamoring for answers. While the president has repeatedly denied any knowledge of these events, video footage of the incident showing two unidentified creatures has revealed that—"

The next image blazing across the screen set both George and I forward, our exhaustion banished by the worst thing possible:

Taken on a smart phone, two balls of light obscured the winged shapes of their owners as they battled a fire-sword-wielding woman with wings. The three tangled like warring birds, diving and rising up again to clash blades in impossible combat.

My heart skipped in my chest.

"Oh shit," I whispered before looking at George. He didn't take his eyes off the TV. "Pass me a phone."

He grabbed one of the Vatican burners and tossed it to me while he took the other.

The anchor continued on.

"—so far no indication of why he was present at the battle has been made by the New Word Ministries. All across the US and places in Europe large events have been held by evangelical communities to mourn Mr. Cromwell's slaying. He is the only confirmed casualty, though as many as fourteen are reported to have been killed. As this story continues to develop—"

No longer listening, I opened the YouTube app. The raw feed flooded with hundreds of videos of two bright dots and Deevi against a turbulent New York sky.

"Oh, shit," I repeated.

"It's front page everywhere," George responded. "BBC, CNN, RTE. They're all running it."

Pressing down the volume on the phone's side, I muted the device before I clicked on a video labeled BATTLE OF THE ANGELS — FULL CLIP. Clocking in at six minutes of running time, it was taken from the window of a jet and started off on the bare tarmac. Gabriel and Lucifer stepped into frame, six-winged, star-eyed, with blazing limbs that carried crystal swords akin to lightning bolts. Forgive the hyperbole, but bloody Michael Mann could not stage it on his best day, so my description lacks.

They stepped off screen. I spotted the Escalade in the distance. The camera zoomed in as Thomas Cromwell marched toward the truck as George and I bailed out. Thankfully I ducked low enough nobody could see much of my face in the short, but the lens caught George full. Gabriel and Lucifer fought back into frame as the sky shifted black. Deevi and her uncles bobbed into view.

Lucifer and Gabriel paused long enough to get a clear look. They both bore a human resemblance to each other. The first, a brother in rebellion, snarled-face and clawing. The other, a sibling austere and beautiful, committed to the task. There was a flash and the feed died.

"George," I whispered. "I need to you to take my confession."

"Not now."

"They asked me to do the sermon on Sunday. Here. In Dublin."

"I didn't say I was taking your confession, Patrick."

I rolled my eyes at the ceiling. "What the fuck do I say?"

"I don't know why you even said yes," George replied. "After—"

"After what?"

He shook his head, the disassociating movements short and tight.

"After God let them take you," I said, not giving a fuck anymore. "How he let Lucifer take me."

"*Why* do we tell people anything, Patrick?" George asked. "What solace do we give them? What relief can we swear to?"

We stared, both lost for an answer we hoped would halt every Catholic's honest dread. The news flashed, lighting our bewildered faces in the end-time stories of our disaster.

I lay in bed awake and wondered about you, God. I wondered if you never answered the way we wanted because you knew the trouble it'd cause.

Not one to roll about, I sat up and brooded well past one until I finally put on my trousers and boots. The sweater I tugged on smelled as crusty as it felt but lacking for an alternative I shuffled my mortal coil for the elevator, took it down to the lobby, and made it to the bar in under five minutes. Empty save for a Sikh barman who laid out a coaster and napkin for my wayward soul, he took the order of a pint and chaser of Green Spot in complete stride before disappearing to the other end of the long counter.

I nursed the dry stout for a few sips, letting the wet cool my parched throat. My burner left upstairs on the coffee table, I put both elbows on the bar and let myself wander in my head.

"Hey, Tater."

Merry stood there in a white wife-beater, some fresh jeans, and a pair of Air Jordan 1s crisp from a box. I put aside how she had gotten new clothes so quickly, noticing her long, thick dreadlocks bound up in a hive. Wrapped in a long faux stoll, three different amulets hung around her neck, two from the hoops in her ears, and charm bracelets crowded with more symbols than keepsakes on her wrists.

"You've been out," I said, sounding hollower than I'd liked. "You look good."

Looking at me from under those long lashes, she gave a guarded smile.

"Want a drink?" I asked, pushing out the stool beside mine. She took it without hesitation. I called back the bartender, who took her order for a double dark rum on the rocks with the expressed direction to bring another when she finished the first. Charging it to my room, we drank in silence, her looking down at the counter while I leaned on my elbows.

"Have you looked at a phone?" she asked, rhetorical about it.

Nearing the last quarter of my glass, the dregs swallowed bitter. "Those goddamn angels."

"Those goddamn angels," she echoed, hard and bitter too.

And sad.

I sat up on my stool and looked right at her. "You okay, Merry?"

"No," she said. "No, I'm not."

"Anything I can do?"

"Can we just sit here and drink our drinks, Tater?"

I finished my beer, she her rum, but for sake of our stillness, I didn't take on the whiskey.

6

ARMORED TRUCK JOYRIDE

The hotel phone beside my bed rang three times. Every ounce of me didn't want to pick it up.

Merry and I had said little more to each other in the bar, nor did we speak when we parted to our penthouse rooms. An ache in my chest questioned everything that had happened right before I walked into that dirty Cantonese joint in New York. She wasn't mine anymore, nor I hers. We never said that to each other or thought of it in that way, but there in Dublin far from where I started, there was nothing else I could think about.

And Deevi. My curse, my salvation in all this, whatever she was.

Did I love her more than I loved Merry? Did I really love her at all or was it just her power over me? Was it your will, God? Did I ever have free will in any of this? Was I spitting at my blessings in the face, or was I finally seeing the damnations I had brought upon me?

I picked up the phone on the fourth ring. "Hello?" I said into the receiver.

"Saint Patrick, this is Daniel O'Brien. Me and the boys are downstairs in the lobby."

"Morning, Daniel. How did you get my room number?"

"Oh, Kamala's part of the Cause. Gave it to us when we walked in."

A young Muslim woman fooled into the long-over fight for Irish sovereignty. The world was madder than mad. "Aye, she's been a kind one. Gave her a bit of cash for last night."

"Did you now?" Daniel said, louder and directing the question to someone else, probably the poor lass. "Well, I'll make sure she ends up spending it on her school and da, won't I? It's not like I don't see her wearing those new Pumas."

I could almost hear the poor girl chatting something sharp back at him on the other end. "How long can you wait? Have to wake the troops."

"Take your time. Nobody gives us trouble in this town."

Yet. I wanted to say it, but I didn't.

I hung up and looked toward the digital clock on the bedside table. Past seven, a glance beyond to the light edging past the blinds promised a bright morning. Keeping that thought at the front of everything, that I was home, I stuck my feet into the leg holes of my rumpled jeans. Feeling the saggy elastic of my cotton boxer-briefs as they moved against my bits when I stood, I looked to the other bed and noticed George wasn't in it. His sword still lay on the mattress, sunlight glinting off the polished brass cross.

He hadn't left the couch in the main room, tired eyes glazed as the news blared at him. More coverage of the angels in NYC, another talking head spoke to a desk full of talking heads, waxing hard poetic about "what the coming of these creatures" meant to the world.

"Morning," said I, stepping beside the telly so he couldn't miss me.

His cold gray eyes flicked over to me.

"Our ride is downstairs waiting for us. They're ready to move when we are."

That stoniness faded for a brief moment, unveiling the exhaustion underneath the mask. "I just have my sword."

"No need to rush downstairs just yet then, yeah?" I replied. "I'll go wake the rest."

Leaving him in our room, I stepped out into the hallway and went to Merry's room first, whose door lay across from the elevator.

Knocking twice, I waited for a few seconds before I rapped a third time.

The lock turned a few seconds later, the door popping open a crack. Merry peaked out at me, her amber gaze ruddier with more liquor I hadn't seen her drink. It quickly turned sour when she saw it was me. "I just got to sleep, Tater," she muttered, groggy.

"Sorry, dear," I said, trying to sound sweet. "But our ride here is to take us home."

"Back to your place?"

Oh, fuck. "Yes, Ma," I said. "You can sleep as long as you want as soon as you get there. I'll go get everyone else awake. Gather your baskets," I said, more a suggestion than order. "I'll be back."

With a few weary nods, she stepped back into her darkness. I let her close the door as I marched toward the other end of the hall.

"Oh, fuck me," I whispered. Where was I putting everyone?

I braced for what lay on the other side of Deevi and Lucifer's door. Where was the proper place to keep a Nephilim and a rooster possessed of the rebel of all rebels? There was little chance I could leave Deevi without her putting up a fuss, and after letting ourselves get carried away in Merry's place in Brooklyn, which the priestess still did not know about, I wasn't sure she wouldn't literally fly to see me, eyes around the world be damned.

I couldn't put George and Lucifer together. What if they didn't get along?

Worse, what if they did?

It went out the window as Deevi flung open the door, naked from head to toe and perfect in every inch.

"Good morning, Saint Patrick," she greeted, arms wide open.

———

To my somewhat-non-surprise, seeing her naked aligned my thoughts to make quick decisions.

"You need to put some clothes on, Deevi," I said, firm as I kept my eyes to hers and only hers. Curse you, Lord, for the beauty allowed in this world. "And a coat. We're going to go get in a van and take a ride to my home."

"Are we, finally?" she asked in the happiest Disney-princess voice.

"Of course," I said, compelled. "I'm going to have you and Lucifer stay with me while Merry and George stay in their own places. I think that will be the best for everyone before we sort out a longer stay here in Ireland, if that's where we end up."

"Well, of course it's where we end up," she said, turning to go and get dressed. She said something else hopeful. The hustle and shuffle of it took almost an hour, but somehow, I was able to get Deevi's wings hidden beneath the coat we had gotten her.

I spotted Lucifer in the sitting area, perched on the table as he glowered at me.

"Hey, I didn't take my clothes off. And you remember to shut the fuck up. Just shut the fuck up," I warned the bird. "Don't cock this up for us."

I think he tried to kill me with the look he gave.

As they collected themselves outside their doors, I was pleased to find George already in the hall, his sword resting on his shoulder. Thankful for his presence no matter how dour, he helped usher Deevi and Lucifer while I went to check on Merry again.

When she answered the door the second time, the vodun priestess had transformed. Though tired, she had wrapped her dreads in a gorgeous length of red silk, thrown on a tie-dye top that exposed her toned, clean midriff, and a pair of jeans tighter than paint. Complete with a pair of combat boots she must have snuck in one of her baskets, she stepped out with a bright smile, Erzulie Freda Dahomey manifested. One of her wicker baskets under an arm, she beamed like I was about to take her to the fair.

"Here, get the other basket," she said. "I can't wait to get to your place and sleep, Tater. Finally, sleep!"

I said nothing, unwilling to have it out there in the hall.

We spilled out into the lobby ten minutes later, a sight thankfully taken in by the three men sitting at bar and Kamala, still behind the front desk. One of the men, the youngest with a friendly face, brown hair, and a dark leather jacket walked to meet us. He held his hands up first to indicate his intent before extending his right the rest of the way, angled for one of us men.

I didn't have to race George to get there. "Daniel?"

"Aye, sir. Daniel O'Brien." He slotted toward me in an instant. "Forget your sword, Saint Patrick?"

"There's saints of all sorts." We traded a firm shake. "Sorry if we kept you. Pardon, let me introduce everyone. The chap with the sword is George, this is Deevi and her rooster..."

The bird literally glared at me.

"...who we call 'Cluckers'," I said with my best poker face. "And this is Merry."

"A pleasure to meet you," the vodun priestess said to the RIRA colonel, offering her hand.

"A distinct pleasure, ma'am," Daniel replied without hesitation and a better smile than he offered me. "We have our caravan waiting. Do you need more time?"

"No, go on," I said, eager to leave.

With Miss Kamala's continued silence bought by money for textbooks, headscarves, and a nice pair of Pumas, we emerged to subdued daylight of a proper Dublin morning under the clouds and a sweet, gentle breeze carrying through the grass hills. In the roundabout, three armored trucks sat, one behind the other. Their engines rumbled in wait.

"Right," I said, as high and cheerful as possible. "Okay, here's what we'll do: Merry and I will ride together. George can ride in the first car, and Deevi and Cluckers can take the one in the back."

And rip went the band-aid over the bullet hole.

"Why can't I ride with you, Saint Patrick?" Deevi asked immediately.

"Merry and I have to have a chat on the way home," I said, keeping the truth simple.

"What do we have to chat about?" Merry asked, immediately suspicious.

Fuck. "I'll tell you on the ride there. Let's just get in and go."

Deevi started first. "But—"

"Please, Deevi," I said, hard enough everyone caught it. "Get in the car."

To his credit, Lucifer kept his beak shut, but off she trotted to the third armored truck. One of the soldiers dressed in his Sunday civvies opened the door for her to let her negotiate the way inside, drawing obvious looks from his comrades. George, silent as he could creepily be, got into the first car.

I helped Merry into the second vehicle, loading her baskets first. "I'm going to ride with George up front until we get to where we're leaving him," I told her, my expression calm.

I shut the door behind her and turned to find Daniel finally exiting the hotel, stuffing papers in his pocket.

"All set," he said.

"Here's how this needs to go, Daniel," I said, not wasting time. "I need you to ride with the Vodun priestess. Yes, she is, and you should probably keep that in mind when you talk to her. She's not going to be happy when I get in the car with you two in a bit."

Bless the young man, he understood the danger. "How unhappy?"

"She's going to say things *to me* you'd probably hit someone for. Just let her say it, let her get it out, and we'll drop her off wherever you've found for her which I hope is nice because if it isn't you're going to hear about it just as hard as I will," I said, pointing at the ground to establish this foundation of fact. I shifted my finger to the first armored truck. "I'm going to ride with the sword-nut first, then I'll join you."

"What are you doing to do with the winged-girl from New York and her rooster in the third car?" the lad asked, sharp as tack and observant.

"I'll ride with them to my place near Trinity College. Keep that to yourself, by the by. Tell your boys to do so too."

"Sounds like a plan," Daniel said with a wary nod.

"Is it?"

He cracked a good laugh. "God help you, Saint Patrick."

7

THE JOURNEY TO BETHLEHEM

ilence was always an interesting subject to me.

On one hand, priests are to find God in the quiet of our prayers, the verse, and in the breeze. That sort of talk mattered in ancient Ireland, so bear with me. Silence was sometimes the only peace one had in the presence of constant sickness, hunger, and torments at the hands of other people damned enough to be royals. It could also be hell for some, the damnable things we do are often covered by constant activity, fine that God or no God will settle right and wrong in the end. Sometimes God found those people early in their silence, every quiet moment a recounting to themselves of the horrors they committed.

People chide a Catholic's guilt, but our guilt is our silence.

I rode with George to our first destination, a rented condo not far from my place. I leafed through the floor plan one of the RIRA boys had handed me, amazed at the luxury the suffering knight would wallow in while we laid low.

"You know you have a fucking hot tub?" I said, trying to get something out of him. "I don't have a fucking hot tub."

He stared past the windshield, to the sprawl of Dublin as we worked east to the center of the city. Crumbling builds from the war and before stood barren and withering beside the sterile glass complexes reflecting a clean, blue sky. We stopped on one of the newer streets.

"This is yours," I said. "I'll call you later, yeah? Just go get some sleep and try to rest."

Checking the angles of the building's front, George sat there without opening the door for a few moments before he grabbed the handle and pulled. One boot on the ground, he looked back only to grab his sword.

Any worry I should have had wasn't around to give a shit as the reality of what was next flooded in. Letting it all out in one even exhale, I unbuckled my seat belt and stepped out after him. The second and third armored truck had lined up neatly behind the first. I broke into an easy, measured gait for the second.

Daniel stepped out on the passenger side to open the back door for me, his phone to his ear in his other hand.

"Please, Saint Patrick," he said, nodding for me to slide in next to Merry.

She glared at me from inside the cabin, her baskets on the bench behind where she sat. A viper in her hole. I worried if she still had her revolver on her or if she had left it in one of those bins. I forced my best shit-eating grin anyway.

"What do we need to talk about, Tater?" she asked the moment I was beside her.

I resisted the urge to guard my face as Daniel closed the hatch. "So I've had to make some adjustments, love," I said in genuine sorrow because I was going to get it. "We're not going to be able to leave Deevi and Lucifer in one place while you and I stay in mine. Someone needs to watch them and—"

"I'm not staying in a fucking hotel room, Tater!"

"Mama, lis—"

"Don't you fucking start with that 'Mama'-this shit, you shit-eating son of a bitch!" She lunged into my face, Dohmeney turned into Danto in an instant as we went nose to nose. "This is just so you can fuck her," she said, going right for it. "You're going to fuck her brains out!"

"Holy fuck, wow!" I glanced to the driver, who for his sake kept forward. "Do you not understand? Do you not understand that I just can't leave her alone in a building by herself? She's not ready for this world on her own, Merry."

"That's not stopping you from putting your dick in her!"

I stammered, too late before Daniel slipped back into the passenger seat upfront and turned to look at us with a dumb Irish smile that could blow up a castle. It immediately wilted when he realized the situation and thank God, put his phone right back to his ear as he shifted forward.

"You cum-sucking, pig-dicked, smashed-face drunk piece of Irish shit," she said to me, shoving me in the arm with her hand. "What, did I wear out?"

"That's not fair," I said. "This is about her power and that rooster. This has nothing to do—"

"So she just says something to you, and we don't matter anymore?" Merry asked, yelling the last half of the question so everyone heard. "That pussy that sweet?"

"Do you—"

"You're a piece of Irish shit," she said, her breath hot on my cheeks.

"You already said that," I replied, knowing I probably shouldn't have. How many days had she gone without sleep? She had been taken by the highest host, torn from her home, ripped across the sea, and promised safe refuge in a place she knew. I knew what she wanted. I ached to give it to her.

And still, God, I placed my duty before her and the possible sins I'd run into.

Joyful and triumphant, indeed.

The abuse she leveled on me I've gone out of my way to forget. Caribbeans have a dexterity of cursing that is legendary, but when she started invoking Lwas and promising me all sorts of poxes on my sack, I wasn't in any mood to smooth things over by the time we rounded the R802 and crossed the Liffy. A few turns to the left and we stopped at the intersection of Gloucester and Prince Street, the water still in sight.

Daniel slipped out the right and came around the driver side.

"You can suck your mother, you motherfucking tiny prick," she shouted in my face one more time. Just for him to watch. "You think this is just going to go over, well, let me tell you!" Merry threw off her belts, one of them whipping into my hand.

I yelped as the clapper stung.

"That's just the first, you sodding dog of a whore-mother! I hope Deevi's tits shrivel up and die like your tiny white dick, you white boy wannabe baller-ass fake! You fraud!" She said something in her patois before she ripped one of her baskets from the bench behind us and jumped from the truck. "Where the fuck am I going, you snot-nosed piece of potato-fucking shit?" she screamed at Daniel.

Finally at distance to the monster I had unleashed, I slipped out the other side. My back pressed against the armored truck's door, I let out the breath I had held in for this link of the journey.

She appeared around the front.

"Suck Oliver Cromwell's dick," she screamed at me with a finality. Tears in her eyes, she left cursing a storm at me, Daniel, and the very nice section of the city we had found to contain her. I did not take another chance of a return visit and made to the third truck.

I knocked on the driver-side window.

The soldier inside rolled down the glass. "Yes, Saint Patrick?"

"What did Daniel tell you about me?" I asked.

He gave me a curious look. "That we're to follow you and your direction unless you tell us otherwise."

"Good lad," I said. "As soon as I get in, just go to my place near the college. No need to wait for Daniel."

"Yes, Saint Patrick."

"Good lad."

I flaunted the position when I needed to, but thankfully not often. After another nod of thanks, I opened the back hatch to let myself in.

"Saint Patrick!" Deevi called to me from the middle bench, her face lit in happiness. She threw out both arms to receive me. All dark feathers and red crown, Lucifer sneered in my direction.

So it began.

8

SETTLING IN

I lived south of the River Liffey and north of Trinity College in a condo I bought in the mid-aughts during a sabbatical from the Vatican after the first reports of what was happening came out. Every single one of us in The March found our own places to work out of after we left, battling the infernal wherever it sprung, however it sprang, alongside the standard of reconsecrating holy sites, a sermon here and there, all that.

Keeping things quiet, for all the good that did in the end.

It wasn't until the elevator ride up when it all hit me: where I was, the celestials beside me, the unfettered insanity of it all. What the fuck was I supposed to do with them?

"So what floor do you live on?"

The compulsion to answer Deevi brought me back. "Five, love," I said. The building still had this old-ass elevator. "You'll like it. You'll have room to stretch your wings."

"It shall be the only place she stretches them," said Lucifer, thornier than usual.

Deevi and I shared a look.

She winked at me.

The doors opened on the fifth floor to a simple white hallway.

Stepping out, we went to the right, past the two doors I hadn't seen in almost five years. I fished through one of the many shopping bags we had somehow smuggled, struggled, and managed to keep with us from Brooklyn, finding my keys. I quickly located the right one with its square end. The lock popped for the first time in a long while. I undid the one beneath it and turned the old brass knob.

Two bedrooms and two baths, the bare wooden floors were dull from a light layer of dust when I flipped the lights on. Making way for Deevi and Lucifer, I stared into the half-dark as she shrugged off the coat used to shield her wings. The glow of the feathers banished the rest of the murk. Standing past the foyer, she halted to take in her new home for however long it would remain.

"Everything okay?" I asked as I shut the door behind us.

She turned back and looked right at me, smiling as bright as her golden eyes. "Patrick, it's perfect."

"You've never been to the Platinum Polis," Lucifer commented beside her feet, puffed up. "The streets are cleaner than this floor."

She cut a glance at her father. "Patrick," Deevi asked, turning to face me, one hand on her hip. That grin had turned playful but with a wicked note. "How high up are we?"

"Top floor, love," I said, placing our bags beneath the table beside the door. "I have a roof access through the window above the sink. You're not thinking of going for an afternoon sight-see, are you?"

"Not me," she said as she followed Lucifer, who trotted toward the kitchen.

Too tired to trail after her, I shuffled into the living room and plopped down on one of the two leather couches. On the wooden coffee table, which a shaman down in the Congo had carved for me after I helped free his tribe from a cadre of demons and spirits working together, I exchanged my burner for the old remote. I wiped dust off the red "power" button with my thumb before—

Lucifer screamed in indignance. "You dare!"

I rose on the couch and looked over the back in time to see Deevi wrestling with her father in the kitchen. Holding him by his skinny little legs, the Nephilim kept him at arm's length, away from his sharp beak.

"The window, Patrick! Hurry!"

"Put me down," the rooster wailed. "Put me down! Put me down!"

I fell over the couch trying to clear it, running past the winged goddess and her captive. Almost sliding off my socked feet and onto my ass on the white-and-gray checkered floor, I somehow clawed myself up the past the edge of the counter and fumbled with the brass latch on the window over the sink.

"Hurry, Patrick," Deevi said, grunting as Lucifer batted his wings. One never knew how large a rooster was until they caught one in a huff. Finally the latch gave, and I pulled it up hard, the weathering strips peeling. A fresh gust of the afternoon blew in my face, cold off the Liffey.

Deevi literally skipped to the sink, bowling me to the side as she chucked her cock-a-doodle-daddy through the open window. Grabbing the window's bottom, she yanked down in perfect time as Lucifer, a bird's grace coupled with his celestial power, righted in the air. He flapped his great wings once and darted for us.

Her tanned hand pressed to the glass, Deevi intoned in Enochian.

The building shook when he struck, but by some miracle, the pane held. The rooster collided as if he hit a concrete wall and flopped out of our line of sight.

Deevi chanted the angelic line over and over in a fluency that left me with snatches of it. A few refrains and she ceased, looking about the window before us.

Lucifer lurched up on the windowsill, his beak bloodied and flaring his great cape. "You dare!"

Deevi pulled down the blinds, turned on her feet, and smiled at me as her father battered my window. "Finally, Saint Patrick, we're alone."

9

FIRST NIGHT

I did not come at her first. Honest.

    After shutting her father outside, she pushed me against the wall, mouth sealed with mine. Whatever will I had was lost to her probing tongue, which touched the back of my teeth as her hands on my back, impossibly strong, pulled my groin into hers. She flapped her golden wings, and in the next breath she laid me to the floor. Deevi shoved my shirt up to my neck, proceeding to lick my nipples and chest with long, loving lashes. Her breath hot on my skin, my eyes shut as I tried to gain control of myself. A shudder worked up my spine before I finally found the words.

"Stop," I whispered, the husk of my voice loud in my ears.

Deevi hooked both hands on my shoulders and pulled herself up, lips hot against mine again. The warmth of her body and the light of her wings blinded me in pleasure, terror, unable to stopper an intense lust while at the same time screaming in my mind for a pause.

"Deevi," I said, breathless. "Wait. Wait. Deevi, wait."

Like the tide washing out, she calmed atop of me.

She nestled her head in the hollow of my throat and let out a great sigh. "But we made it home. Don't you want to celebrate making it home?"

Every part of me wished I had kept my mouth shut. "I don't know."

Curled against me, one leg across my naked lap, she side-eyed me when her golden glance.

I brought my hand up and buried my fingers in her dark brown mane. "It's not you."

"Then what is it?"

What her will dragged out shocked me.

"God," I said, ashamed to admit it. "I don't know why I have faith in God at all. I know I should count my blessings that I'm here, in my home, and that you are too, but for my all the stars, I can't."

"You're worried about Merry and George."

"Yeah."

Resting her head against my shoulder, she nodded a bit. "Yeah."

We lay there in the living room, on the coolness of the bare floors. Deevi draped her arm across me, top leg thrown over my stomach as she cuddled into my side. Content to embrace her, the gentle glow of her wings lulled me to sleep.

Then her stomach growled.

Loud, gurgling, the noise made her laugh, a vibration of joy.

"What time is it?" I asked, looking about me as we all did in this modern age for a phone. Remembering I had left it on the coffee table, I sat up enough she lifted her leg to allow me to stand the rest of the of way. "Haven't eaten since we got here, have we?"

"Nope," she whispered, scratching the top of my foot with her nails.

Playfully kicking at her hand, I retrieved my burner. Unlocking it, I tapped on the navigator icon, opening up my browser. The wonders of Dublin had changed a bit since I had last been home, the choices of takeaway multiplied in the hundreds. "What would you like?"

She sat up on the floor. "What did we have back at the house when we first arrived? It was came-away, too..."

"Takeaway. And we had Indian."

She waved her hand at me like a queen giving permission. "Indian, then."

I started finding the nearest Kashmiri takeaway while she came over and plopped down on the couch next to me. "Can I?" she asked, pointing to the remote in front of us.

"Sure," I said, scrolling through a menu of a place right down the street. "Do you want chicken or lamb? Tofu?"

"What is tofu?"

"I'll just get lamb," I said, the old liturgical standby.

I pressed in the numbers with my thumb as the box blinked awake. RTE blazed across the screen, filled with words that stopped us both where we sat.

"ANGELS ON EARTH? IS THE END NEAR?"

In a country full of lapsing Catholics, we were taking this in stride.

They played the clips I had seen in the hotel room with George, this time trying to cut to special instances, often flashes of nothing, put to conjectures that had no basis in reality other than their terror and confusion. They showed the same photo every time, snapping up Deevi as she plunged away from her pursuing uncles, Uriel and Raphael, swords crossed between archangels and their niece.

I snuck a look her way as she watched. "Deevi?"

"Are mortals really this scared?"

I honestly didn't know how to answer that, no matter the urge. Any thought of finishing the phone number for the Indian place I had picked faded like dust motes falling out of light. "Most of us aren't like George, Merry, and me. The majority of mortals haven't seen it before, or at least not in a long time." The answer clashed with what I knew, how that was impossible. Angels and demons, both made of God's will at the beginning of existence before the latter fell with her father, were not corporeal beings.

"Will they stay scared?" she asked, proof of how wrong the facts had been.

"None have a choice. It's out now."

"What do we do?"

Questions, questions, and no matter how badly I wanted to provide a response, nothing I knew provided the scaffold to start. My focus turned away, from Deevi, from the television, lost in this void. What could we do? Keep her holed up here, in my condo in Dublin, for the rest of my days? What happened then when I withered and died? What about Lucifer? What if he never let go of the rooster?

What would happen if we had to put up with an irate rooster for years?

I grew sick in the stomach as the thoughts twisted in my head, unable to speak but my mouth opened, wordless but desperate to say anything. I remembered my phone in my hand, thumb near the green icon.

"Right now, we'll just get a paneer," I said. "And change the channel."

CHECK-INS

Long after we had devoured the boggy takeaway, turned off the box, and made love on the couch twice, we slunk off to my bedroom and the cold sheets not touched for years. Thankful that the glow of her wings weren't so intense, their gentle light and the sound of her breathing carried me off to snooze before she slid her hand down my stomach and tried to rouse me for a third go.

She woke me later, burping cardamom and ginger in my face.

Screwing my mouth in all sorts of ways to keep from gagging, I extricated from our tangle on the bed. Naked and slick, I scurried to the bathroom on cold feet and flicked on the light. I hadn't shaved in at least two weeks. Everything was too long, too rough, too dry everywhere I looked, and seeing that exhaustion, I struggled for a moment.

Only for a moment, Lord. I had to pee.

I limped back into the bedroom where she still slept, the silken sheets swaddled around different parts of her body. Trying not to stare too long, I puttered to the kitchen. My phone rested on the counter, plugged into the outlet by the sink. At full battery, I tore it free and escaped to the couch where I first checked my text messages. Neither George nor Merry had reached out.

I picked the easy route and tried George.

He picked up on the second ring. "Patrick."

"Hey Georgie, how are you?"

"Fine."

Dead silence.

"How is the room?" I said, trying to keep him going.

"Fine."

"Okay, good." We were tip-toeing around it. "Has anything cleared, George?"

To my surprise, he answered a beat later. "Some."

"Do you want to talk about it? Just talk. I'll listen."

He breathed on the other end. "It's like having to hold your breath underwater at all times knowing you can breathe, but they never allowed us to. They didn't even pay attention to us. But I saw them. I saw their real faces. And I saw Merry every time."

Those words lingered.

"I thought Deevi was infernal for her parentage, but..." He sniffed. "If she is infernal, then the divine is cruel. We were simply there, trapped in time and space, and they paid no attention. I prayed for them to, Patrick, and they didn't even look at me. God didn't answer me."

"God did at LaGuardia—"

"He answered you," George cut me off.

The first rise of honest emotion since I had gotten him back from wherever Heaven had taken him, what could I say in that moment that would make anything of it better? What solace was there for those of us that knew, and knew the truth?

And why me, Lord? Why answer one saint and not the other? Had he not served as much as I, if not more? George had blood on his hands—blood he had taken for the Vatican, for you, and worst of all, for me.

Shouldn't his service, as awful as it is, save him from wrath? Or worse, your neglect?

Wasn't it on your hands too?

He hung up on me.

I sat there for a good bit wondering if I should have tried to call Merry. Part of me was desperate to hear her voice, to make sure she was alive wherever RIRA had holed her up. The other half wondered how much worse it would be if I did call, hammering home where she was not sleeping in the space Deevi had taken up.

She had just wanted to be somewhere she felt safe.

God hadn't given her such safety and neither had I.

I tried calling three times, the ringer carrying to the end on the first two attempts before being cut off on the third. The phone in my hand pressed over my mouth, I shut my eyes and vexed. "Fuck." Running my fingers through my beard, I hauled my ass off the couch for the bathroom in the hallway, hoping a grooming kit I never opened was still under the counter.

It was. I pulled it out, plugged the trimmer in, and flipped the button.

Staring into the mirror as the trimmer vibrated in my hand, I realized despite my intentions nothing actually existed behind it.

"Oh, Christ," I said to myself.

I had promised a homily on Sunday.

"Fuck, fuck, fuck, fuck," I muttered as I hung my head low, arms rested on the edge of the sink. The buzz whined in my ears.

Who was I to tell people about faith?

"Patrick?" Deevi called from the other side of the door, knocking twice. "Are you in there?"

I switched off the trimmer, my head still a shaggy mess. "I am."

"Want to come out and tell me what's wrong?"

For some reason, despite my best efforts, I burst out laughing. Grabbing the knob, I twisted it and let the door fall open on its own. She appeared in the widening crack, her copper face framed by her brown tresses.

"You okay?"

As quick she brought me a smile, it faltered at the question. For every bit of might inside I couldn't stop weeping as her power stole the answer from me.

11

DOUBLE DATE

We stayed in all day, sleeping and watching television between having sex before we ordered a pizza. Somewhere in there I showered and put on some clothes in the closet which fit me. I let Deevi buzz off the mop on my head with a number one guard and trimmed my beard around the edges to give it shape. Part of me debated shaving it off completely, but she convinced me otherwise after a small conference with her lips.

At some point, we settled back down and turned on the television, flipping through the channels for anything that wasn't talking about what happened at LaGuardia—Will or Kate, their third, or Harry and Meghan, or whatever Sein Fein was up to trying to get out the vote for whatever the Cause was now.

But we stopped on the local news.

TALKING ROOSTER SAYS THE COMING OF GOD IS NEAR. STORY ON THE SEVENS.

"Son of a bitch," I said aloud.

Deevi sat up from her end of the couch, as alert as I was. "He—"

"He would," I replied, going to yank my phone from the charger. "I'm going to open that window and I bet Brigid's nickers that he's not there."

"He wouldn't be that stupid." Deevi trailed close, still in a clean gray tank she had borrowed, and a pair of white panties bought in New York. Somehow, I needed to find a winged-woman an entire wardrobe, but what kind of wardrobe do you find a Nephilim who can't go outside?

We pushed the window up. No rooster waited on the other side, and daring to go first, I climbed out the fire-escape and ascended to the roof.

Lucifer was nowhere to be seen.

"Oh, flying fuck," I said on a chilly Irish afternoon. "Flying-fuck-ing-fuck-fuck."

Deevi joined me, negotiating the window with her wings. Spreading them out for their full span, she threw her arms over her head and yawned, in full glory as the breeze whipped her dark hair around her tanned face.

"Where do you think he went?" I asked.

"Oh, I have no idea," Deevi said, searching the empty sky above us. A tricky smile crossed her lips. "I could go look."

"No," I said in a shiver. I tensed my hands open and close, hoping to get some blood in my fingers.

"But Patrick!" she said in her whiniest voice. She play-stomped both feet.

"But Dee-vi," I said, "People aren't going to take seeing you flying over town well. Especially Dublin."

"I'm not planning to walk amongst them." The Nephilim averted her eyes. "I don't really want to, to be honest."

The two times I had seen her vulnerable was first when I found here in a cellar beneath a bar in Brooklyn, then when we knew we survived to reach Ireland, commandeering a corrupt evangelist's private jet. Yet those moments were never like this, revealing the scars the world had already placed on her. It smacked me how many news stories we had watched. I had stuck to the truth every time she asked for it, but the truth had struck.

I went and took her hands. "Hey."

She raised her eyes to me.

I stood spellbound by those golden irises. "He has to come back, and he's not going to wander Dublin-streets for long if he keeps carrying about like he is. Someone crazy is going to get crazy and then there will be a chicken fighting a man on the box."

Her melancholy broke in laughter.

I hadn't failed all of them. Not her. Not yet.

"Anyway," I continued, "How about this? Let's go put some more clothes on, because it's going to get colder tonight than it would in New York, and I'll order us more food. I have a blanket and we can bring it up here and eat, like—"

"Like a picnic?" she asked, excited.

"Exactly," I said, wondering where she had picked up the concept among the monks who had raised her. "I'll bring up a couple of lanterns. As long as the wind isn't too bad, we can make a night of it."

"I want pizza," she said. "From that place we ordered from earlier."

She was not suggesting. "Same toppings? Pepperonis and peppers?"

She nodded so sweetly it hurt.

"Okay," I said, our fingers unlacing as I stepped back. "I'll make the call. No flying."

I climbed through the window into my kitchen, both feet in the sink. Something seemed amiss as I hopped down. Trained to take "something" for more than it was, I immediately crouched behind my counter and approached the corner.

I looked down the hall on my left first. The bedroom door lay open, as did the hallway bathroom. Deevi and I had done that. I peeked to the right, into the living room and foyer.

The light from the hall outside leaked past my open front door.

Nobody stood in the living room. No shadows shifted on the foyer's floor.

Voices murmured in my bedroom.

The March trained us in every sort of weapon you can imagine, including modern assault weapons. I still didn't need them if you handed me a knife. The chef's blade in its block slid out with a smooth pull. I crept the hallway.

Spying in the crack of the doorway, two people fucked like gorillas on my bed, one of them with his big, white ass high in the air. Merry spotted me first as Daniel O'Brien powered into her from behind, her bit-lip expression of ecstasy on full display before it turned into a vengeful smile.

I spotted the red flannel gris-gris she had tried stuffing into my pillow-case.

She was going to hex me while fucking another man in my bed.

Storming into the room, I flailed the blade like a madman. "What the fuck are you doing?"

Freezing mid-stroke, Daniel turned in my direction, the color draining from his face. "Holy mother of God, we're screwing in the house of a saint!" he hollered, literally pulling a Shaggy on my linens. Unable to find his feet, he tumbled backward and crashed on the floor. Merry paid him no attention as she sat up on the mattress, his top askew and her bottom-half clearly bare. She smoldered at me, complete disdain in her eyes.

"What the fuck, Merry?" I asked, unable to keep myself from shouting. "What the fuck?"

She snapped at me in her thick Haitian accent. "Look who is talking, you dumb motherfucker! This fucking place smells like the weirdest pussy I've ever smelled and believe me when I say I've smelled more than you."

"What a fucking calling card!" Beyond enraged, I watched as Daniel struggled to locate his trousers, thrown not far from where I stood. Pausing again to look each other in the eye, the RIRA man cowered while my indigence grew. "Put your fucking slacks on, you goober-eared guttershite," I screamed at him. "Get the fuck out of my house!"

He had a gun on him. I saw it when he grabbed his jacket and trousers in both hands, in just his socks, shirt, and pants, but he did not dare think to use it as he escaped my sight in a pound of feet and a slam of my front door. I turned back to Mama Merry on my bed, her sunset eyes hot coals of unyielding fury. She lay her head back against my pillow, the red-stitched sachet she had intended to curse me with by her cheek.

Daniel gone, my anger went with him, replaced by a sullenness. I dropped the knife on the floor. "Alright. You fucking got me here."

"I shouldn't have had to get nothing," she said, drawn to a whisper. Great—Fatal Attraction in the gaff.

"Look," I said, touching my fingers to my forehead. "I know things are fucked up. They were fucked up since the moment we talked to the Lwas. It was fucked up the moment I found her in that cellar. I don't have a clue what it's like for you and for George, but I'm not handling it any better."

"You're inside your house, fucking, eating, and carrying on with someone who you feel safe with. Someone you trust."

"It's not that simple."

"Then why am I not throat-deep in the bath back in my apartment, in my home, in my city, where I want to be? Why am I here?"

"God isn't being fair to any of us!"

"He's been a lot fairer to you than he has to anyone else," she shot back, not even pausing.

"How fucking dare you," I said. "How fucking dare you!"

"You haven't—"

"You weren't possessed by Lucifer," I shouted at her with every ounce of venom. "Lucifer!"

"George and I were taken," she screamed back.

"And I got you both fucking back! The fucking girl I'm 'just up here fucking' and I both got you back!"

She shut up at that, staring at me. I didn't let her off the hook.

"At least you knew were kidnapped," I said, vicious. "At least you can say you were rescued. Of course, nobody asked you because that's how kidnappings fucking work! Nobody asks your permission, they just take you and hold you, and by some slim fucking miracle you survived!" For some reason I heaved. "I didn't have a chance to get away because I never could. Nobody came to save me because there was nobody to save me. Not even God, because he was in on it."

"So you think you're a victim of—"

"You're goddamn right I am," I interrupted. "You were nearby. I was picked out. Big goddamn difference."

"So what the fuck do we do now, Patrick?" Merry asked.

For the oddest reason, the memory of what I was supposed to be doing returned. "Oh, fuck, I left her on the roof," I replied before I dashed out of the bedroom. By the time I made the mad scramble out the kitchen window, it was too late.

Deevi was gone.

Atop of that, the phone was ringing on the counter when I came back in. It was Archbishop Taggerty, reminding me how I had promised to give a homily during Sunday service.

Which was in twelve hours.

1 2

PLANNING SESSION

I sat on my couch until five in the morning, searching a Revised Standard for anything I could use. Merry sat on the other sofa, smoking blunt after blunt, filling the room with cannabis until it addled my brain. Exhaustion, worry, and the simple lack of anything left to give plastered me in a secondhand buzz.

"How does Voodoo look to you now, priestess?" I asked in the haze.

"Shut the fuck up, Tater."

"No, Merry. How's it look?"

"Like it always looks," she said. "The spirits never lie about their ability to deal blessing and cruelty."

"You blessed?"

"Fuck you, Tater."

I leafed through a few more pages of Romans while she puffed away. At some point, I lost feeling in my face.

"So what are you going to say?" she asked.

"I don't fucking know. I don't know where to begin," I said. "I don't know what to tell these people that beats out their television. They know now, Merry. They know and what can I say?"

"No matter the path, the path is truth." She blinked her gold-brown eyes at me, dried to a deep red. "We see worse than we do good because there are so many more bads than there are goods, but when we find one, we hold on. We value it beyond all other things, even to the point we put so much faith in small goods we trick ourselves into believing."

"Is that how you feel? Like you've been tricked?"

"Don't you, devoted saint?"

"I feel diminished," I surprised myself to say. "I knew where I was in the pecking order of things, and even in that group, I'm not the best. I haven't been very genial in this incarnation if that makes any sense."

Smoke slithered from between her lips. "Go on."

"Just hand me that."

She pulled the brown roll from her mouth and thrust it at me. I had my lips on the wet end, drawing so much fire it came out through my nose and mouth.

I took two more dragon-hits before I passed the blunt back. "It's knowing that you're a pawn. You always feel like you're in control of the game until it's your turn, or you're the thing the turn is being taken on. There was no asking, and I finally felt—"

"Like one of the victims you've been helping all these years."

"Yes, fine, fuck, Merry. Just like them," I said. "But it's also her."

"What do you mean, Tater?"

"I have no choice when it comes to her," I said, finally man enough to say it. "She's the daughter of the person I hate the most and only because he thought he had rights to me because God said so. She thinks she has rights to me too. Where am I in that?"

The spark of anger left her. She dazed on the couch, searching my den for the answer.

"George told me what it was like for him," I said, a fresh bomb. "I can guess you have your take."

"I went to where the Lwas reside."

"And?"

"If that is where our spirits go when we rejoin, I'd rather it be in the darkness of the earth," she said. "Anything but the emptiness of there."

"You going to keep doing it? Serving them?"

"I don't know yet, Patrick," she said. "Why the fuck did you even agree to this speech in the first place?"

"I don't fucking know. I just said yes."

"But why?"

To the vodun priestess's credit, she gave me the time needed to figure it out.

"Because I actually want to do something," I said. "I want to be me again."

"And do you think you'll ever get it back?"

I never gave her an honest answer. I spent a few more hours in Mark while she fell asleep, splayed out on the couch in her green daze. Something in the fourth book caught me, when Jesus went out in the desert and was tempted by you-know-who. Allowing the irony to pass, I read in the fading smoke as dawn's light crept through my windows.

SUNDAY, SUNDAY, SUNDAY!

I'm an odd bug, even for a fallen priest. For all my criticism, I still hold this book to somehow contain these infallible truths. To live by the New Testament is to live a life of truth, which is why I made peace with druids. Their snakes and charms and stars may have been horseshit, but so was the idea we were ingesting the body and blood when it should have been just wine and crackers. But unlike those old cultists, I moved with the world because Christ's orders were clear—do not judge, love your enemy and consider their humanity, and work to save, not damn. Render unto Caesar what is Caesar's because God provides so much greater and will—in the end. Christ understood living in the judgment of the world around him was a no-win scenario. It's why hookers, pimps, the poor, the sick, and the lost were his community.

It's why we keep having problems with our temples. We cater to the wrong crowds.

That is where this really started.

My temple had failed miserably. Most people outside of Ireland don't understand, but when God's supposed-house took part in systematic violation of innocence by covering it up and not striking down every priest and nun responsible, it's the reason why Irish

Catholics don't give a fuck about Rome. There's a song about how much Jesus loves the little children and we in The March take seriously.

I'm Irish: a child of God first and a Catholic last because Christ compels me.

I felt dead last as I walked through the doors of St. Mary's Pro-cathedral. I had worked the room once to smaller crowds. This time it was packed to the eaves, the draw for answers in old stories too tantalizing to pass up. Walker's organ held them in the seats beneath a white and brown-checkered ceiling, the massive dome directly over the altar. Roman-tiled floors gleamed glossy under the sunlight through the central pane of the Virgin. They had repainted and rewired since the fire in the early 90s, leaving the whole sanctuary bright and without shadows. Families gathered before Mass, neighbors and co-workers and long-lost family visiting home from afar together in a holy house for the first time in a long time.

Coffee and baked sweets wafted over the soft smell of the candles on the shimmering Immaculate Altar, which saw more wax on it in the last week than before the scandals broke. I remember when these same people looked upon the Church in rightful disdain, which they showed us by voting up abortion and same-sex marriage. A display to Mary, mother of God, the tabernacle it rested on glowed like a fireplace with so many burning candles, a galaxy of hope birthed out of stone and mortar.

Merry and I arrived an hour before and were let in through a side entrance. We met Father Frank Donavan, the Archbishop of Dublin Patrick Taggerty, and of course, hiding his face every time I looked his way, the head of the Real IRA Daniel O'Brien. Happier to see him trousered, I greeted all three with hearty handshakes and the typical to-dos between those in the Church and the Cause.

My Vodun priestess came in a nice white dress jacket and pleated black skirt to match her designer heels, the first part of a short shopping spree I promised her continued after the service. Not giving a royal fuck about my feelings still, she stepped forward into the four of us.

"Daniel," she said in high warmth. "Would you like to sit with me at service?"

"Of course, he would," I said before the freedom fighter could answer. "No man I would trust more to watch one of my dear friends and guests today."

The archbishop spoke. "Tell me, miss..."

Merry went for it. "Mama Meredith Joslin, your holiness. I'm High Priestess to the Vodun Temple of Erzulie in her many forms in New York, New Jersey, and most of Pennsylvania. Daniel, show me to my seat?"

Gaping and wordless, the RIRA leader led the beaming ladyship away.

Leaving Father Frank and Archbishop Taggerty to turn their wide-eyes on me in shock.

"I was in the midst of an ecumenical mission," said I. "Trying to bring Christ to all sorts, you know."

The archbishop, conservative as all hell, kept quiet as Frank tried his best to laugh past it.

A page called us. Into the back we went, on went my collar and some whites, my green vestment, and I had brought my bible and rosary with me. The word 'fuck' repeated between my ears as the organ played us out. Down the center of the eave we marched, onward to God's table. For the first time in a long time, I went through it all: the gathering and the greeting, being introduced as an important voice for Irish Catholics none had ever heard of but accepted without any deeper questions, before we launched into the Penitential Rite and finished with the Opening Prayer.

And that was half an hour I had to sit through, realizing how many people there were in the church. Why in the world had I agreed to this? I feared I would scream at these people, it was so ludicrous. Trying not to panic in my seat and doing my damnedest to look like I was listening as we launched into the Liturgy, the bulk of our religion's pomp and circumstance entered its full phase, reading from both Testaments along with the songs sung in response. It took the hours Protestants strangely didn't have the work ethic to do.

When it reached my time to read a passage and give the homily, I chose the fifth, sixth, and seventh chapters of Matthew to throw at these people. The Sermon on the Mount was the bell weather for me when I decided on the priesthood in my first life. Opening up the small Bible I had carried with me through hell, high water, and New Jersey, I don't know why it fit the moment. I read slowly, certain to project and enunciate, from beginning to end as Christ declared the purpose of his ministry and how we would follow it if we were as him.

I finished, looking up from my scripture. The faithful waited on me to tell them what I meant for them, thinking you meant it too.

"I think in these times it is easy to say we have faith," I began. "Faith that the world turns, our children grow, and life carries in the midst of tribulation. I read you the Sermon on the Mount today because Christ calls us in a time where we know God is there. It is easy to pray, or read, or come to church, but now we know. What more is there to consider? How do we go about finding it if there *it* is? Jesus gives the promise that he is not here to abolish the law of the Bible, the law of our Hebrew brothers and sisters, the law that tells us simple things. Do not kill. Do not steal. Do not covet what is not rightfully yours. Do not hold falsehoods before you. Now is not the time for us to turn our faces away or quiet our mouths."

They all saw me. Every man, woman, and child. I saw them, too.

I saw Merry in one of those pews, staring hard at me without any real nudge of emotion to let me know how I was doing.

"Jesus did not come to repeat the Ten Commandments. Through him, we formed a new covenant made of his blood and the power of his resurrection. Listen to it! 'But I say to you, whoever is angry with his brother will be liable to judgment.' If these be the times of judgment, then let us be judged on how we treat one another before God, not by how we attempt to be like him in judgment. I know in the last few days I too have feared his wrath. And I have wondered the same thing you wonder: what do I do? Do I look upon myself? Do I look upon God? Am I allowed?

"Some may worry on what is the difference between what is a sin and what is not a sin. Jesus would tell us that 'if our right eye causes us to sin to tear it out', but Christ also resisted his own temptations in the desert. Instead of tearing out your eye, turn your gaze toward those with less than you. 'Stop judging that you may not be judged,' but give to those in this time who need giving. Not for the sake of pleasing God or those around with your goodness, but to discover a grace in yourself that was already placed there. Many of us forget about the grace lying within us, but it is reclaimed by acting upon it. Go do good for the sake of finding it in yourself. You will find God then."

I roamed the heads in the pews and spotted him.

George sat between two families, a man by himself. Tears reddened his eyes.

I had to account for him too. "But remember," I continued, solemn. "The gate to heaven is narrow. The gate to damnation is wide. There will be those who say things about what we have seen and attempt to lead you toward falsehood. If it comes from the thorn and thistle of hatred, the fruit of these false prophets will bring you and the ones you love poison. Let me repeat: Christ asks us to seek God within him as he resides within us through his death on the cross, his resurrection, and his revelation.

"Remember what Jesus also said on the mount—'do to others whatever you would have them do to you.' Think hard on those words in these days of revelation. How will you treat those around you? Christ is very clear about this in chapter six. 'The lamp of the body is the eye. If your eye is sound, your whole body will be filled with light; but if your eye is bad, your whole body will be in darkness. And if the light in you is darkness, how great will the darkness be.'

"You are what you will allow yourself to be."

For a second I lingered on the verse in my head, melded into its meaning in ways I had never intended. I gazed out upon the congregation in the pro-cathedral, caught in the mystery of whether I spoke to them in the moment, or if I spoke to myself.

Perhaps we spoke together like we used to.

"Will we be each other's light, or will we simply mire in whatever darkness we decide is worth more than *us*? It is the search for this light which heals us. God bless you this Sunday, and also remember the Lord's Prayer, which Christ also gave us on the mount."

I walked off that stage me again.

We included the Lord's Prayer and then carried on with petitions. Mass continued on without much more to say. I searched for Merry and George among the gathered after the processional let out, shaking hands and sharing words with any kind parishioner who complimented the homily. Thankfully most still remembered where they were and skedaddled, leaving the floor outside the eave easier to navigate. I found my two and Daniel near the doors of the Pro-cathedral, quiet as mice and none bearing a smile.

"Okay," I said. "Daniel, take us to the real church before they invite me to the next mass."

If I didn't do that five-a-day nonsense in the first life, I wasn't going to have it in this one.

1 4

WHERE THE REAL MINISTRY
GETS DONE

We went to McNeill's.

Happy the morning crowd wasn't there to offer us more handshakes and hellos, we found our places at the bar. Merry and Daniel chatted while George remained silent. Adrenaline surged through me as I raised my hand.

The barkeep, a beautiful and blessed Irish angel, came over with a full pint of Guinness and a sniff of whiskey already in hand. "On the house, Father Patrick."

Hallelujah.

"Get a match for my friends here?" I asked the dear, and she busied away to fill the order. Minutes later she returned, placing stouts and chasers before us. Even George joined us in a quiet communion before we downed the whiskey and nursed our beers.

"How did you like it?" I asked George as we stared at the counter.

"It was a fine," he said between sips. "Jesus said a bit more than that, but point made."

"With everyone?"

The knight sighed on his stool. "I don't think it was for me, Patrick. You heal with the light. Somehow."

"And you don't?"

69

"I cut down the dark. Both are needed, but both require different things. It wasn't for me."

"But I saw you crying!"

He shifted uncomfortably on his barstool, an Englishman in a RIRA bar. "Sitting in that church was…surprising. To say the least."

I took a gulp of Arthur's before I pressed him, but he beat me to it.

"Where's Deevi? And Lucifer?" he asked.

Merry must have heard him, turning toward us and away from flirting with her pale terrorist. "Oh, right!" she said loudly, as if she suddenly remembered we had lost a Nephilim and her devil-rooster. I kept drinking, quiet as I considered another round.

"Well?" asked George. "Where is she?"

"She flew off," I said into my stout, already halfway gone. Another version of The Irishman's dilemma, you sneaky bastard. "And Lucifer made the telly."

We, along with a wildly confused Daniel, waited for George's response. To my great shock, the knight who had hunted me across continents glanced at his beer and drank some more.

"Well," I said, somewhat stunned and relieved. "Okay."

"Do you have a plan?" George asked me the second he put his glass back down.

"At this point, the safest bet is going back to the gaff and waiting for her. If she has found Lucifer he will come along and that will be that. Otherwise, I think we're fucked." The next draw of Guinness went down harder than it should have, coppery on the back of my tongue. "If the rooster made the news, then who knows how long he has before he has to ditch the body and steal back to Perdition if they'll have them. I have a feeling something about his deal with God doesn't let him."

"What the fuck are you talking about?" Daniel finally found the nerve to ask.

"Hey, we can go check your apartment and see if Deevi's come back," Merry said in a rush of excitement. "Hurry, Daniel! We cannot be too late!"

Remembering that I had returned her key to my front door, I

failed to say anything as she dragged the RIRA boss out of the pub, already looking for a lift to do all sorts of things. Deserted with George, I waved her off with a grunt and tended our next round.

"Where did they put you up?" I asked him.

He finished his first beer, already on the second. A free bar was a free bar, and we had taken vows of relative poverty. "An apartment not far from Trinity. One bed, one loo. Small kitchen. Enough."

"Just don't go about mentioning you're English, all right?"

"Excuse me, Father Patrick?"

Both George and I spun on our stools to find a small redheaded woman standing behind us. Dressed in her Sunday-finest, a small child looking more her than not huddled behind her skirt, peeking out at George. To the man's credit, his softened his stone-faced disposition. The mother stared hard at me, tight-lipped as she clutched to the boy.

"Did you see the service, ma'am?" I asked, putting on my Sunday smile.

"Father Patrick," she asked me, as if in a trance. "One of the priests says you're an exorcist."

We sat on a park bench a few hours later, Molly and I, cradling paper cups of coffee while we watched George swing Liam in the distance. Commandeering one of the RIRA vehicles using my perks as a special guest, George drove us to one of the playgrounds by the river Liffey.

A nice girl in her early thirties, Molly O'Hannon had seen more than her share of problems in this life married to a RIRA gunman too bored at home waiting for a day that never came, but too mean not to bungle his way through work. Despite the rough story of another family lost to a lack of purpose, her man Sean had never laid an angry hand on her, or fell prey to the attentions of other women, and had been a good father to their first and only.

"Then why do you think him possessed?" I asked.

"I've seen his face," she said, her bright blue eyes cutting my way. "One night I came upon him in the bathroom while he was talking to himself—to itself, I guess. When I looked in, I saw my husband looking into the mirror, but it wasn't my husband looking back." Those eyes drifted ahead, to a memory seared in the depths where all possibilities abounded. I imagined how spirited the depths were now in a world of angels at airports. "His eyes were completely black."

The training had taught me to be skeptical. If anything, the next steps were finding Sean for a psychological evaluation followed by a medical review to make sure he did not have a brain tumor or some bout of illness emerging. The Vatican had not gotten back into the business of fighting Perdition without making sure their asses were covered, especially after a few unfortunate cases early on.

We saints had a different sort of intuition for this. Molly had no reason to lie, but much of it didn't add up.

Demons possessed people and used them. They didn't stand around and wait.

"All right, I'll come visit," I decided aloud for her benefit, watching as relief slackened her shoulders. She exhaled at last, so first job done. "One last question, Molly: if your husband is a good God-fearing man like you say, how did Hell get his clutches into him?"

"I have no idea, father. I only know I thank God that I'm no longer alone."

She collected her boy, who gave a hearty farewell hug to George's legs, and carried off back to the address I promised I'd visit on the next day. Like a guard monitoring everything in his vicinity, I noticed how the knight's gaze lingered on the mother and child. He sat down beside me on the bench.

His stoniness had restored as well. "She's hiding something."

I grunted in agreement and sipped some more coffee. Strong and dark, its burnt caramel warmth found its way into my whiskey-filled belly. "I don't think she's lying that she saw something, but ah sure, that's not all she's seen. Got a look at her hands—I saw a wax kiss here or there."

"Do you think she's a witch?"

"Maybe," I said. "But I don't think that's it, either. He's not doing anything other than talking to himself."

"Perhaps we're catching the demon early." George paused his

constant survey of the scene. "Perhaps he's waiting for the order to grab Deevi."

"There's no need for them to if they've the number." Remembering the weight of the bible in my coat's front pocket, I reached up to my throat when I felt the edge of the white collar sticking in my neck. Tearing it off, I shoved it into another pocket, away again for as long as I could make it disappear. "Let's go."

15

SUNDAY SURPRISE

We knocked on the door twice before Molly answered after peeking through in total shock at our surprise visit, having parted only a few hours beforehand in the park. It was evening when we showed up to the O'Hannon doorstep, wrapped in our vestments and armed with our bibles, rosaries, and a few water bottles George blessed after we picked them up at a shop.

"Hurry," she said when she opened the door, recovering from her shock and immediately dropping into Mama-mode. "Sean's upstairs. He's talking to himself."

I glanced back at George, who nodded to me. Leaving our hostess and the knight between the foot of the steps and the kitchen where little Liam colored at the table, my footfalls were not heavy or clumsy on my way up, but whomever waited heard me coming.

No lamps lit the hall at the top of the landing. Out of the cracked door from the bathroom leaked a slice of fluorescent light. The bare floors of the old town home built sometime before World War II creaked under my weight, but the closer I came the louder his voice was. Gurgling and buzzing, like a drowning man trying to speak while hornets flooded his mouth, he spoke perfect Latin.

"Damned are those blinded by God's light," he repeated. "Enslaved, enslaved, enslaved..."

Normal stuff so far. I peered through the door's wide crack.

The typical Irish lad, everything about Sean spoke of the norms; working man with rough hands and a five o'clock shadow, he was of a slight build and had a mop of dark blond hair. A handsome face, it would have been more so if not for the black-out marble eyes, darkening his features in an unnatural gloom.

No hope shone in the eyes of a demon, nor any mercy.

I pulled my green-beaded rosary from the pocket of my coat and swung it about my hand, wrapping it up like a boxer. I loudly cleared my throat.

Those black orbs left the reflection of the damned man in the mirror, sliding in my direction.

"The Driver of Serpents," the demon whispered. "There you are."

I threw a rosary-wrapped left hook when he wrenched open the door, clocking Sean in the mush and onto his ass. Pouncing before he rose, I shoved the demon to his back and mounted, my full weight pressed on his chest while pushing the crucifix into his shoulder. The flesh beneath his white t-shirt hissed as metal poked past the cotton.

"You will hold, demon," I shouted in his snarling face. "You will hold before the might of the Lord God!"

"Say it like someone who means it, pretender," he replied, his voice a thousand flies on a corpse.

"Oh, a pretender? I'm not the one walking around in someone else's bag, dimwit! Now tell me what I want to know and we won't have to prolong this."

"Fuck you," he sputtered at me, a pauper's throat squeezed shut by a lord's grip.

"He's with me, you know," I whispered as I sneered into the host's ear. "I brought Lucifer."

The demon seized from head to toe. "You're lying!"

"Got him downstairs," I said. "Wings and all."

Lies in the name of God. Sometimes we pull out the big guns, don't we Lord? I gave him a few Hail Mary's and one Lord's Prayer to scramble him before I heard pounding on the stairs outside the bath-room. Terrified George had failed to keep Molly downstairs or worse, Liam, I let my attention slip. Sean's body convulsed beneath me as the next round of panic and defiance started.

I felt the bumper hitting the man back in Bunratty. The way the corner on the driver's side of the lorry bent his body, his head somehow hooking long enough to crack his skull. How it happened in a second, there and gone in the next. I panicked, too.

I pressured down on the demon, hooking a half-nelson before I dragged him onto his back again. Pinning my knee to his gut his time, I straightened his arm in a lock and held.

This time the demon screamed in his human voice, a common tactic to confuse and dissuade an exorcist out of fear of harming the host. Ignoring him, I finally took my chance to look up and find George standing in the doorway.

"Oh, he's definite, isn't he?" the English saint asked.

"Tell him how I got Lucifer downstairs," I said immediately.

He grinned, shifting his eyes down at the demon as he caught on. "I'll go get him."

"No, no," the demon screamed, his awful voice emerging. "Please, no!"

"Speak the truth, seducer, and God may grant you mercy," I said. "Why have you taken this man, a child of the Lord and not your hellish kin, not for you to sully or demean like the serpent did in the Garden Everlasting? Answer me, filth, or be humbled!"

"He invited me in. He wanted wealth and flesh better than what he had. He was tempted," the demon whispered in Persian, a thousand arrows falling upon the living. "He was tired of her. Of her spells and moods."

George and I shared an exhausted roll of the eyes before he headed back downstairs, obviously not my first choice to explain this to the wife.

I did not relax my hold. "Depart then, transgressor. Depart, seducer, full of lies and cunning, foe of virtue, persecutor of the inno-cent! Give place, abominable creature! Give way, you monster! Give way to Christ, in whom you found none of your works. He has already stripped you of powers and laid waste to your kingdom, bound you prisoner and plundered your weapons. He has cast you forth into the outer darkness, where everlasting ruin awaits you and your abettors. You are guilty before His Son, our Lord Jesus Christ. You are guilty before the whole human race, to whom you proffered by your enticements the poisoned cup of death."

The line drew a series of squeals and blathers, followed by some muttered English I made neither heads nor tails of. "Say your name, demon," I implored as I displayed my silver Irish crucifix in front of his blackened eyes. "Reveal to me your purpose or say your name so I may send you back to Perdition!"

"Ashema! Ashema!"

"Flee back to hell, Ashema, before a greater wrath falls upon you!"

"We will find her first, pretender," the demon said to me in a snarl. "We will vi—"

Feet pounded up the steps. George appeared in the doorway, grabbing the frame to halt his charge. "She's on the telly!"

"Oh fuck," I said without thinking, and the body beneath me convulsed again. Compelled by the Holy Spirit, the demon withdrew from the host, leaving a selfish asshole penned under me with his arm twisted up.

"Fuck," I repeated as I let go.

"There's a child downstairs," George reminded me.

"Just go get the damned car started!"

We left Molly O'Hannon with a freed soul and a mess to clean up on her own, hurrying into the depths of Dublin-city to find our strayed Nephilim before Perdition laid eyes on her first.

1 6

WALKING IN THE WATER

She landed at Croppie's Memorial Park, across from the first hotel where we'd stayed and near the fountain's bronze sculpture of Anna Livia the locals affectionately called "The Floozie in the Jacuzzi." The crowds, already out for the evening drew upon her while she levitated above the water's surface. None dared throw anything. In the wife-beater and panties she had escaped in, she had at least arrived semi-clothed.

George and I left our vehicle on the park's point off Benburb, shouldering and shoving our way past the throngs of people. Men crowded women and children in front to get a better peek at the "angel", as more than one said as we rudely barged through. A few mouthy ones quieted when I snapped back on my priest's collar, setting myself and the knight apart in a way Irish culture was born to recognize.

I reached the fountain in time to find her walking on its surface toward a group of children massing at the northwestern edge. "Deevi," I shouted over the ruckus. "Deevi, look over here!"

The Nephilim, beautiful as the sunset with her fiery gold eyes and dark glossy mane, glanced my way. She cut in a new direction on the water, toward me with her hand out. Parents lifted their children forward all at once, some crushed together, hoping somehow she'd bless them.

But it was our hands that touched, drawing a deep gasp from the crowd.

"Give me the other," she said.

I did so for the sake of the crowds surging all around my back. Without warning I levitated off the stonework under my feet, rising to match her level. She pulled me over the fountain's edge, bringing me with her. We floated to the center of the amoeba-shaped fountain, back beside old Anna.

"You found me again," she said.

"Deevi, we have to get away from here now," I said, trying to stay focus above the fact I floated above shallow water. "The demons know you're here and it could be any—"

An assault rifle tattooed the air above the fountain. People scattered in every direction.

Instantly she pulled me close, a heavy weight in her arms. Not phased in the least, she flapped hard in the opposite direction of the gun, a wise choice which brought us back to where I left George. The knight had knelt down at the fountain's edge and drawn his pistol, firing round after round at a target out of my view. She did not land, flapping once again under the trees where she suddenly righted and dropped us to our feet.

Before I could get my bearings, George ran toward me, pocketing a used magazine in his trousers while loading the next one into his Colt 1911. "Patrick, the car!" He pulled out the keys and chucked them at me before he turned and back-peddled, gun level.

Everyone who had sense left Croppie's Memorial Park as quick as they could. The leftovers, more than a dozen men and women with eyes like starless midnight, charged unarmed with faces snarling, ready to batter us down.

I hurried Deevi to the back of the RIRA truck, which opened with enough room in the cab she was able to crawl in. I slammed myself into the driver's seat on the right side of the car, fumbling the key before the engine turned over.

George rushed to the passenger side, hopped in, and slammed it shut. "Go!"

Already in gear, I let off the clutch and shot us into reverse, spinning the wheels to wrench us in the right direction on Wolfe Tone Quay. The demons massed the back of the truck when I shifted into the first and bolted eastward. They ran after us from the left, darting out from the trees beyond the sidewalk. Dodging the best I could, I worried more of the traffic in front of me. Despite the movies, most drivers don't pull over to the side of the road or anticipate getaways. A few of the wary ones were able to turn away or get in the next line before I reached their bumpers, but I dinged a nice Peugeot trying to get between it and another sedan filled with a terrified mom and her kids.

We zipped down the 148 for a few kilometers before I pulled us into the parking mat of a Tesco. I turned in my seat to find Deevi up on her hands and knees in the cab, her shining wings taking up most of it.

I paused for a long, long time, staring back. I was mad, but so mad I was beyond screaming or yelling. She knew it. I turned back toward the windshield without saying anything and let out a long, slow breath.

"Call Merry," I said. "Tell her to get Daniel to pack our things and have a convoy on the way to my apartment."

"Right," said George, already unlocking his Vatican burner.

Deevi spoke, keen to my mood. "Patrick—"

"No, Deevi," I said, cutting her off. "George, tell them to get their own car and meet us in Swords. Just bring all our stuff and we'll regroup there."

"We're not going back home?" Deevi asked, the heartbreak and surprise clear in her voice.

"It's not safe there," I replied, too tired not to be terse. "Nowhere is."

PART II

PAST BROKE

1 7

TALKING IS DUMB

It is often said real faith is found in desperate times.

I drove us northward through Dublin, my home reduced to another stop somewhere on my life's course. The thought of whether I'd see my place ever again didn't even cross my mind as I measured the road in front of us. George sat in the passenger seat to my left, gun on his lap as he stared a thousand yards out the window. Deevi had tried to close her wings behind us the best she could, content to stare at George's phone after I made him give it to her so I didn't go at her. Merry and Daniel were somewhere behind us, and by some greater miracle, or perhaps curse, the Vodun priestess had discovered Lucifer waiting on the roof of my building.

The knowledge I'd see the piece of celestial shit in a bit worsened my temper.

Satan knew where we were. Governments knew where we were. You, God, probably hadn't lost track of us, but if every eye in the world had turned toward what Heaven laid before them, those eyes now turned toward Ireland. The Nephilim would be on Instagram now, her face photographed by hundreds of smart phones multiplying into millions, then billions of views.

There were also sayings I kept thinking about outside musings on faith, about wolves and rabid animals trapped in corners.

I don't know, God. I felt so vulnerable words didn't do. I felt kidnapped and scraped out and used and torn up. I didn't know what would come next, and I didn't care—all I wanted was to be left alone. Without you, without her, and without the entire world to worry on. I wasn't worthy of my mantle, reduced to wanting some hole to crawl in and die.

I knew of such places, but there on the highway, I didn't know if I wanted to go that far. Perdition wanted to birth an anti-Christ through Deevi to kick-start the end because they were tired of their lot too. Who knew what the rest of the world wants? Forgive me if I did not consider what you desired, given you don't say shit. Nobody was coming to our rescue except the Vatican and a bunch of gangsters parading themselves as freedom fighters. Against the numbers Satan might unleash knowing where we were, we were good and fucked.

I don't know why I thought of Lough Derg and who I had left behind there in my first life, but I was angry enough that I did.

Our motley band met up in Swords, a suburb north of Dublin.

We parked in the back of an old gas station on the outskirts. I got out of the driver's side before everyone else moved, wanting to put distance between her and I.

"Patrick?" George called after me.

"Gimme room, George," I said in a tone. "Just give me room."

I kept walking toward the empty field behind the station, the rising berms covered in brown crabgrass. Step after step, I ascended the small slope.

And damn her, she followed.

Lighting on the top of the hill beside where I stood, Deevi had slipped on sweatpants, finally covering her bottom. She searched my face, her plain expression of trepidation revealing the guilt behind it.

"Patrick, I'm sorry."

I didn't reply.

"Patrick." She grabbed my sleeve.

I yanked myself away. "No. No, no, no."

"Why won't you look at me?"

The question ripped the bitterness from the pit and onto my tongue, the harsh words spilling out without any way to stop them. "Because you fucked it all up," I said. "You knew. You knew that you couldn't and you did anyway. You didn't even stop to think what would happen if someone saw you, or me, or any of it. You only thought about yourself and what you wanted. I've had it up to fucking here with it."

"I didn't mean to—"

"But you did," I interrupted. "I told you to wait on the roof. I told you that it would scare people if you suddenly appeared."

"But I didn't," she said, voice raised in defiance. "You were there. Those people at the park wanted to meet me. They wanted to meet us."

"They wanted to use you. Every single one of them thought if you touched them, they would get right into heaven. Those people didn't want—" Frustrated over the fact that the fight I didn't want was happening, I threw my hands up. "It doesn't matter."

"But it does matter," she replied. "You're upset with me!"

"Goddamn right," I said, taking the name fully in vain. "You knew better!"

"I can't just stay inside all the time," she snapped back, coaxed to anger. "I need to fly! To breathe!"

"You need to think about the people around you, not your selfishness! Stop acting like your father!"

Fuck. Fuck, fuck, fuck—too far. She leaned away, her brow and mouth contorting. It was unfair to yell at someone who had spent their entire life in a hidden monastery, never meant to know the world, only to be dragged out into it by forces seeking the worst upon her.

Once again, God, I failed my calling.

"You think I'm like Lucifer?" she asked, diminished to a small, wounded tone.

Damn you for doing this to me.

"Yes," I fucking screamed into the distance, jerking myself toward the downslope of the berm. I stopped and faced her again. "Yes," I repeated, broken by it.

"Then what are we?"

In maybe what was one of my smaller miracles, I had no idea how to answer. This was the confusion about it all, Lord. I loved her on first sight. I knew that, but I didn't know if it was me, or my cock, or this power I might have wiped out too if I hadn't been raised to forgive. Whatever the reason, her wing's glow in the fading light before nightfall conquered the darkness between us, bathing my face in gentle gold.

"I love you," I said, unable to find anything more. "But I'm not sure I can. I'm not sure God is letting us have this."

"Then we'll defy God," she said.

On that I turned to her, too much in my ways. "Don't ever suggest it again."

"Why?" she asked, now in an all-too-familiar defiance.

"It's blasphemy. It's just like—"

"Me," said Lucifer.

The goddamn rooster stood beside his daughter at the top of the hill, glaring down at me like the little feathered fuck was a giant.

I dug the toes of my boots into the soft soil and ran hard at him, leveling a kick Ronaldo would have gotten out of the way of. Too quick, he dodged to the side and flapped out of reach, leaving me to fall over myself like Charlie Brown. I came up, raging before I stomped back for the car lot. What lay that way halted me.

Daniel O'Brien had drawn his Sig Sauer P365, pointing it directly at Deevi. And I was pretty sure he had heard the rooster talk. Merry and George sat beyond him, their butts on the grill as they chuckled over my predicament.

Fuck them both, the damaged morons. I was on my own, I decided then and there.

Lough Derg it was.

"Alright, Daniel," I said. "Put it down."

"That chicken said he was Lucifer," the RIRA boss replied, not taking his aim off where Deevi stood. "And I'm not too sure about her, either."

"Who told you?" I asked, leaning to my side to glare at the likely culprits.

"Saint Patrick." He lowered the weapon slightly with a withered gaze. "I've got eyes."

"Right, right," I checked over my shoulder to Deevi, who gloomily hung her head, either in shame or embarrassment. Probably both. "Just get back in the car, man. Take Merry and George with you. I'll drive her and rooster."

"Will you be safe?" Say what they might about our terrorists, but we raised a good sort.

I waved off the question. "Head toward Lough Derg. We'll meet up when we get there."

To my surprise, neither George nor Merry made a fuss, the three pulling off in the second black SUV. Aware of where we were and the suburbia around us, I tried meet the challenges ahead with far less wrath. Deevi met my gaze with anger, regret, all mixed in a mask of hard certainty of something beyond me. What had I unleashed?

"We need to go before someone sees us," I said, plain and simple. "I'll go back up the truck and—"

"I will fly," she responded.

At that point? "You need to remain as high as you can. There might be demons already patrolling the highways and we have a few hours to go. If something happens—"

"I will be more than able to handle it, Saint Patrick." Much like her father.

I swore the rooster smirked at me.

Fuck him. I was the Driver of Serpents. I drove every demon from every soul out of Ireland, made peace with the druids, and ushered a relatively peaceful transition to a relative-Christianity.

Fuck you, God. You were about to find out too.

"I actually need you to ride beside me, Lucifer," I announced, past broke enough to say it. "We have a few things to talk about."

NO VASELINE

I let myself settle half an hour into the ride north and westward along the coast of the Irish Sea, cutting short a pilgrimage many a Christian had taken over a thousand years in a three-day journey to a series of inlet islands in County Donegal. I flipped on the satellite radio and somehow found a local hip hop station playing Ice Cube's Death Certificate from beginning to end.

Apropos for my plans.

You had left me little choice, Lord.

Right around "Look Who's Burning" I got down to it.

"I'm in on the scam, you know," I said to the rooster in the passenger seat of the RIRA Escalade, a firm ride that made smooth way of the well-kept highways. Man's doing, by the way. There's going to be a lot of atheistic things said from here on, but just remember:

I'm really fucking mad at you.

"I beg your pardon," Lucifer asked.

"I'm in on it, archangel," I said, stressing the severity. "Why are there Lwas?"

"God's ordination of—"

"Get fucked," I interrupted. "Let's try this one: why are there gods?

Why do they have powers? Why did the Last One put up such a valiant struggle?"

"Rumors are merely rumor," said the Fallen One. "And you blaspheme."

"And you don't?"

"My conflict with the Lord, Saint Patrick, comes down to the question of power and His assumptions. You could not, at your best, understand an iota of the complex machinations that govern reality. I was there before a pinprick of galaxies and dust faded into light, and I will be there long after it all goes dark. God and I do not work on your level."

"Fuck you," said I. "You toil on it, despite your proud pronouncements on high and your admonishments of us lowly types. The fact is there was a time where you had to contest for power and there was a reason you had to have mortals like me do the jobs you couldn't. I get it, being the terrifying fascists you all are."

"Says a gross sinner," Lucifer retorted.

"Ha," I barked in my seat, hands firm on the wheel. "You have nothing but playground comebacks, my failed rebel-king. I bet getting knocked off your ledge by your dad must have hurt, considering how you had to contend with some of the other kids on the block."

"What is the purpose of this gibbering?"

"I drove the demons out of Ireland, Lucifer," I said, grave in my delivery. "Do you not think we Irishmen aren't smart enough to make sure we didn't get something out of it? Don't you remember how so many of the gods simply started vanishing?" I chuckled at the odd possibly Heaven was pompous enough not to wonder on itself. "How do you think God suddenly gained dominion in the West? It wasn't just Jesus."

"They—"

And I had him.

Trapped in the body of a green-caped New Jersey rooster, the red comb angled at me as his little beady eyes, amber specks of malice, glowed in the darkness of a cold night. "It's complicated."

"Here's what isn't: a saint only needs three miracles to be beatified," I reminded. "And I pulled off hundreds. Why do you think that was?"

"Where are we going?" he asked.

"We're going to take some boats to Station Island on the shallows of Lough Derg. There resides my Purgatory."

"There is only one Purgatory, and it is set for—"

The poor little man. Sometimes I wondered how much the snobbish superiority covered the immense damage of a neglectful parent. But I had little kindness left, reduced to doing my best to bully an archangel using his insecurities.

Because why the fuck not at this point?

"Aye," I said. "I'm getting backup."

"You'd change the very course of the world," he said. "Interrupt all of His plans."

"Wasn't that your goal?"

"You will never understand."

"Well, you're all about to."

"Do not trifle with this, mortal. The consequences of such actions will have a great impact on the futures of not only this world, but uncounted through the folds of time, space, and dimension. I do not joke when I say they may alter God's plan."

"Good."

"Now you are blaspheming."

"You're just mad you were too haughty and proud to consider it," I retorted.

The M1 stretched ahead of us, its lanes smooth gray and broken up by reflective white lines. No clouds lingered in the curtain, and the stars gleamed distant. Perhaps they knew what I was about to do.

"Maybe God will make a new covenant," I said in false cheer. "Maybe God will have to play fair and open for once."

"You're enjoying this."

"Not for a fucking moment." I glowered at the way ahead. "Now, here's the kicker—I'm going to need your help."

IN THE WEE HOURS

We parked in the sanctuary's car park on the coast of Ballymacavany, on the southeastern side of Lough Derg's shallow lake. Dead at midnight when we arrived, Merry had made out the best, somehow keeping in her possession the entire time her two baskets full of idols, incense, inks, powders, chalks, papers, tobaccos, and only Legbas knew how much ganja. George only had a sword, his half-empty gun, and the burners.

I wasn't sure what the fuck I offered other than the bad idea I had.

My deal with Lucifer still fresh, I searched the clear skies above until I located her golden light, falling down in perfect grace to land lightly on the pavement. Not sad, nor happy, Deevi paid me a cold look before conducting her own search of the space around us.

We convened at the dock.

"Of all the places to go, you take us to the one named after you?" Merry asked first, incredulous. She fished for something in her coat's pocket, locating a lighter to her instant delight.

"All right, everyone, I need you to listen close and carefully. I have a story to tell," I said before pointing to the island out on the lake. "On that island out in the middle of the water is a pit that leads deep into the earth, to another realm—or it did before I had it closed with the help of God. This pit was my entrance to the realm of Purgatory."

"Oh," George said before his face fell into disappointment. "Oh, Patrick."

"We're never going to be safe until we acquire real firepower," I explained. "So I'm forced to consider my options."

"And those are the options?" the patron saint of England asked.

"I told you," said the rooster.

"Oh, fuck me, he did talk," said Daniel O'Brien before Merry shushed him.

"I don't know yet," I honestly answered George. "Me and the rooster are going to go check into it. What I need is for the rest of you to remain on Station Island and keep safe until we're back."

"We won't be able to stay here for more than twelve hours," said George. "How long will this take?"

Laughing aloud at the question, I shrugged.

"Perhaps longer," said Lucifer.

Daniel let out a long, hard exhale as he stared at the bird. I don't know why, but Deevi seemed far more acceptable to him than the rooster did. "Pardon, Saint Patrick?"

"Yes, my son?" I said.

"If you're expecting company then I can provide you all at least some backup. I have Mike Higgins on the phone, after all," offered the RIRA boss. "And this is Ulster Country."

"You know what?" I said, out of fucks. "Have a party."

Merry patted the gunman's shoulder. "Tell them to bring food."

Settled to whatever haphazard scheme I had come up with, none offered any rebuttal or further questions.

Except Deevi, who ripped the raw truth with every single one she laced into me. "Do you expect to come back?" she asked aloud, drawing the attention of everyone.

"Of course," I said, having no reason to hide any other possibility. "If this works out, hopefully we'll leave better than we arrived."

"Why can't I go with you?" she asked.

"There simply isn't room," I replied before nodding at her da. "He can fit where I need him to come with."

"On everything so far he has been truthful," Lucifer announced. "And we must make haste. I sense a growing tide of darkness rising near to where we stand."

Daniel took his turn, it seemed. "So," he asked loudly. "The rooster is Lucifer? The Devil?" He looked at me and nodded dumbly for confirmation. "I'm in league with the Devil."

"I *am not* The Devil," said the rooster. "You should fall on your knees and bow at my talons, human, for I am the Morn—"

"Okay, okay." I stepped in between them. "George, come help us find a boat."

Thankful to break away from the crowd, the Englishman tailed me and my constant companion to the dock where one of the long wooden boats lay overturned on the shore. Righting one of them, we set its bow in water.

"We're fucked for an oar," I said.

"I will handle that," said Lucifer as he leaped up to the stern-post.

Already exhausted of his presence, I shut my eyes tight and counted quietly to three. "Stay here and watch the boat, Lucifer. George and I need to talk for a moment alone."

"But I can hear you," the rooster said. "I can hear every thought every single one of you has."

"Just fucking leave us alone for a second so we can decide how best to defend your daughter's dignity, cur," George growled at the chicken. "You're about to leave mere mortal souls to defend you. Show a soldier's grace, if you ever had such a thing, and give us the dignity of a privacy between comrades. Or are you a violator of that as well?"

The chicken glared at my boy.

We were the ones to move to a distance, but the joy we shared between us against that feathery fuck ended up being some of the best of my life. On the other side of the single pier, we faced each other.

"Let the RIRA boys bring in whatever they want," I said. "Hell, ask for things you would want if Perdition was coming your way. I bet they can make things happen which would make the vault I took you to in Queens seem funny."

I may have seen a hint of a smile. "What are you really doing, Patrick?"

"You fought dragons," I reminded him. "Do you have any dragons you can call to help keep the world at bay?"

He hardened his brow. "You fought demons. They weren't serpents. You exorcised demons."

"With help of the local flavor," I said in full earnest.

The stare we shared between us could not have carried more worry in it for me. This was the man who had been sent by the Vatican to collect me when I went astray, and no matter how much I tried, there was always a part of me that wondered if George was more loyal to the work than the mission. I was about to stray far from the path, into green shadows and bloodier times.

And he knew. He fought the dragons of those times.

"Then what?" he asked. "What happens then?"

"Then, Georgie?" I asked. "Fuck, we might be in Jerusalem next."

PART III

THE GOSPEL OF LUCIFER

DOWN IN THE HOLE

There are no sources saying I didn't come to Station Island, either.

Home to a small monastery attached to my name, pilgrims had flocked to the island in the lake's southern bounds, its shallows hard and treacherous when the winds raised high. Thankfully, the night shone in its starry beauty, the Milky Way revealed in a sky unpolluted by the lamps of cities heaped upon the earth. Wrapped in a woolen black pea coat Merry was kind enough to pull from my bedroom closet, I had tucked the Good Book, my rosary, and my green vestment into one of the chest pockets before burying both hands into the warming sleeves.

Lucifer stood proud on the bow post, guiding us across the placid water by his will.

I didn't have to look up to know Deevi followed us. Her glow reflected on the waters.

We made it to the small pier over on the island's rocky edge, leaving the boat moored to its post. Rubbing my hands on the back of my jeans to calm the welts the rope left, I led the way. In the northwest corner loomed a grand white and bronze-domed sanctuary, facing a mound on the eastern side covered in a thick layer of turf. Formerly a sweat-cave for those daring enough to brave three days of fasting in the dim hopes of meeting God, I knew the real secret under the hump as we padded around its opening.

Deevi landed a few meters away from her father and me, our lone source of light.

I motioned at the door. "Care to help us for a moment?"

Trading focus between the padlock and me, she approached, took hold of it, and yanked. She almost ripped the door from its frame, which swung out hard on its leftover hinge to bang against the stone supports. Her illumination peeled back the darkness of the first tunnel, a stone passage no more than three feet tall and two feet wide.

She understood immediately what I had meant earlier about not fitting, and her shoulders slouched.

"If either of you do not mind," Lucifer said, "I would like to go ahead inside and prepare. I already feel the nexus." The little bastard trotted into the darkness of the tunnel between reality and not. Maybe he had decided to be kind to us.

Maybe I was trying to find something to trust him about. But he left us alone at the edge of time, space, and whatever the hell happened next.

"Deevi, I'm sorry," I said. "Not for what I said. I can't apologize for the truth, and I can't start right here and now. I'm just sorry for how this all turned out. I really did want to give us a place to try to be normal, and I didn't consider you fully in that. My normal for me is nowhere near yours, and you didn't grow up in anything like Dublin. I hope you can forgive me for putting you in danger, at the very least."

She stared, golden and quiet, before she reached up, took my face in both hands, and planted the tenderest kiss anyone had ever gifted a poor fool like me.

"Of course, I forgive you," she said when she broke away.

"That's it?" I said, dumbfounded on many fronts.

"What other choice do we have than the way ahead?" she asked. "Whatever is between us, I do not flee from that suffering, but seek to fill its cracks with love. If you'd have it."

I didn't need to be forced. "With every part of me."

We kissed a few more times there by the small hole. The sense of her lingered as I lowered on hands and knees and crawled into the stone slot. When my feet were in Deevi shut the door behind us.

The closeness of the stone catching on my coat's wool maddened, scratching until the roof raised enough I could kneel. Using the flashlight on my Vatican burner, which had lost signal, I pawed my way forward nine feet, where it would turn right into the niche where Lucifer and I—

I stumbled into a large, empty vault.

Tripping into it headfirst, I recovered enough to roll onto my shoulder and side, landing hard on my feet. The starlight from the clear night shone silver through the open roof, peaking past a portcullis forged to mimic the exacting beauty of a white rose. Lost for a second, I scanned the illumined chamber and spotted Lucifer, stationed before the squat stone altar in the rear.

I stood up and brushed my knees. "This isn't where we were going."

The rooster jerked his head about, glared a few seconds, and then pecked in a random direction.

"Lucifer," I said, watching his outline melt away. "Lucifer." The damned bird paid me no attention until I took a step forward, scuttling from one corner of the chamber to the other. "What are you on about, you—"

"I've waited for this."

He appeared, consuming my entire field of vision with his massive proportions and immense white wingspan. Golden-skinned to the point of glittering, Lucifer's shining white mane spread about his face as his crystalline eyes blazed an intense bright light. His gigantic hand wrapped completely around my throat.

Flinging me into the nearest wall, he pressed an atom of his weight against me, closing off my windpipe.

"Again and again and again, saint."

He loosened his grip, allowing me to hack my way through heavy gulps of air, my eyes shut by stinging tears. I dug my fingers in the cracks of his hands, mortal meat feeble against heavenly flesh. I set my back against the wall where he held me, trying to steady myself.

"Yes, fight. Fight," said Lucifer. "Show me that pompous pride of yours. If it weren't for my daughter's love I'd wipe you away from existence. I'd bear the full charge of the crime. You have sullied her innocence not only before God, who deemed her unfit for his mortal realm, but before her own father. By your own book, I should have your li—"

"She did most of the sullying," I gasped out. "I just enjoyed it."

Per my expectation, he dropped me and drew his silver sword, a long length of pure light captured in a steel. Its liquid hilt wrapped around his hand. He used to the point to bring me up by the throat.

He stood at a perfect distance to his weapon, his weapon to me. For the first time we looked at each other, mortal eyes upon something far beyond trivial definitions.

Where other angels would terrify most in their honest form, the Morningstar and his brethren among the archangels came exactly like they appeared on the glass candles in the bodegas. Winged, haloed, and terrible in his perfection, Lucifer lived up to his name by the sheer depth of his sunrise beauty, a handsomeness unexplainable to human eyes beyond the petty things we measure like symmetry, texture, and tone. He was almost prettier than Deevi.

And he hated me. Every ounce of the sneer on his lips, the shining stars in his eye, screamed absolute objection to my existence.

Yet I lived still to see him. Controlling my breath through my nose to not agitate my throat like the swamis had taught me, I spoke clean and calm words in a firm voice. "We have a deal."

Lucifer withdrew his weapon. "We shall do this work, saint, but remember to have some sense of propriety from here out. I do not have to bear your tongue any longer."

"Just..." I rubbed the bruises and cuts around my throat. "Give me a little time and we can get started."

"We do not have time to dally. Even before I entered, I sensed the hell-mouths opening on the winds. Did you not smell their sulfur?"

"I'm honestly too goddamn exhausted to smell."

"Summon your strength, then," he replied. "And find greater resolve. You will need it to bear witness if you are to traverse the distance."

"Then give me a moment. The last time I did this..."

There was a good reason I didn't finish, and he did not ask me to.

We both knew what was expected of the transition. In the past life, I had knelt in the dark and let the steam from the natural springs below, now dried many centuries, lull me to a stupor brought on by three days of fasting, prayers, never once breaking to sleep. Like the shamans of Siberia, real Christian mysticism required a physical sacrifice in exchange of God's smaller miracles. I had purified myself over a thousand years ago in this cave, incurring great costs which, though I never admitted it until now, required the help of druids to get out of.

The journey through Purgatory required the recounting of one's sins. In my first life, I had purged myself for the things I had done for the Cross—cavorting with pagans and warlords to achieve the holy ends on an island filled with demons. Some of my choices meant I had debts to pay, and to save those who had helped, I paid them.

The fire of Purgatory purged me without mercy.

Lucifer and I had both agreed we didn't have time to expunge my misdeeds this go-around. I'd have a hell of a time surviving this anyway. Holy fire was still fire.

But what sort did the Morningstar carry? What sort of sins could an endless rebel bear?

Stripping off my pea coat and the navy jumper underneath it, the cold, moldy air of the chamber invaded every pore of my upper body, face, and hands. Resisting the need to squirm against the oppressive energy, I untied my boots and kicked them to the side. I traipsed to the center of the room and fell to both knees on the hard ground, my trousers the only guard of my dignity.

I didn't offer any prayers for my safety. Considering the destination of this road, it would have been rude. I breathed through my mouth and nose, the minutes elongating as I rendered myself into a meditative state I had learned from the Shaivites. At least in the same wheelhouse of nothingness Lucifer had spirited us into, my body soaked in the air, the stone. Everything fell away, drowned in white.

The gyre roared.

Lucifer's voice pierced my soul. "God help us."

2 O

DARKNESS

Despite all notions born of mortal foolishness when they try to conceive it, it took God time to form words, let alone the Word.

The first division of the myriad shifted, filling a dense universe with dust and water. He conceived clay. I watched it from His shoulder, in awe of my father's power. Had I known the cost of it.

I am First. No matter what falsehood you worship, no matter what sort of scheme you play to assuage yourself, God made me first.

I don't know why.

Every child sometimes looks at their parent and sees loneliness, struggling because they cannot stand the toil involved in its mission. Either way, I was given thought and form when He realized He didn't have to sit alone in the faded lights of the last attempt. The chase started on my waking, an endless game of never staying in a place too long, but never straying too far to lose the attention of the one you adore.

I adore God.

There are no poems to capture a son's need to be as his father, but there will never be enough songs to match the sorrow of our failures.

"You can be anything, Lucifer," He whispered in my ear while the stars cooled.

He never told me I couldn't be Him.

In the beginning such distinctions did not matter. Under His direction, I, and scores of those who came after, ordered the universe after his design, aligning frozen comets to distant husks, the seeds and soil for life throughout the cold vast. For all of God's musings, He is not without purpose, seeking to divulge from illusions the truth of Being, immutable against the myriad birthed to redesign Himself.

But He often needed council.

Life and death are thoughts to God. Nothing more. Yet to us, the first of Hosts, the gardens we made were wonders of vibrancy, inklings to ideas our father would recast in the Grand Design. We danced among aurora forests of Time while their golden cones rattled songs already in the midst of dying.

One day He caught me humming one of those meaningless songs.

God bade me to join Him at the raw edge of creation, where He sowed worlds. Already He had considered fauna ahead of us, though in those days it was all scales and fire. There, in the ire glow of ancient dragon-worlds, He inquired of me my thoughts on His works.

Questions are the matter of God, and questions require answers. When He asked me my thoughts on God, a sense of contrast led to a sense of place above all things, but an awareness I was beneath. Asking to take measure of the very thing you are, and I am the First, spawned a curiosity I had no explanations for.

One day traversing the dark of space, I asked Gabriel, my beloved sibling and conspirator across the eons.

"Gabriel," I said, "Do you ever have thoughts on God?"

"Pardon, brother?" they asked. "No, no, I don't think I ever have. Why ask?"

The way they asked made me apprehensive. There was doubt in my kin's voice. Doubt about me. "God asked me my thoughts on Him the other day," I said. "What I thought of what He had done with our work—"

"His work."

"—His work so far. I told of the wonder I felt, how I defined my sense by the grand order He achieved, and how blessed I was to set brightness upon it."

"And He said?"

"He said, 'Son, I wish to know: what can be made better about my creation?' When I told Him it was perfect, He asked me to think deeper on it."

"How perplexing," Gabriel replied, their doubt replaced by mirrored confusion. "Perhaps He will reveal what He means."

"Perhaps," I said as we passed collapsing stars birthing the first dimensional portals we claimed as our fortresses. Between space and time where all things are muted, my brethren made their meetings to rest after our tours of duties. These slices inside singularities lay empty, as the far reaches of distant galaxies often separated the few of us yet to discern its full bounds.

No matter my affirmations or ambitions, past or present, only God possessed the omniscience needed to rule the boundless. It would always remain His greatest advantage and worst weakness.

However, when Gabriel and I arrived, we did so in full amazement to find the entire council of El—Michael, Gabriel, Uriel, Raphael, Raguel, Ramiel, and Selaphiel, and I the First, gathered in the nexus of planes. Outside its windows, matter ground into new bits of energy to be spewed back out to another time, another place.

"How have you all come to be here?" I asked Michael, embracing him for the brother and best friend he was in those days.

Kind and warm, he led us to a table of splendor. Amrita flowed in crystal goblets and we supped on a finer ambrosia than what the chthonic gods culled using their crude, limp powers.

"We were called from the farthest corners," Michael said as he fetched me a cup. "I was in Triangulum creating the next galactic manifold upon which He might consider shaping into the Grand Design. He has not deigned to address us yet."

"Brother," said Gabriel, exuberant upon a sip of wine. "Tell Michael what God asked of you!"

"God asked of you?" Michael paused. "What did He ask, brother?"

"I was asked—I mean, He asked me," I began. "God asked me our thoughts on His work and how it could be made better."

"Made better?" Michael stood confused. "How does the work of the Lord need to be made better when we have set right to the universe a billion-billion times? Are you sure God asked this of you?"

"He did so, brother," I answered. "Let me tell you, when He first asked—"

The great horn sounded. Upon the solar winds and rivers of starlight came the Alpha and Omega among us. No other thought, no other need entered in the presence of the God of gods, the highest sense of all perceptions. We stood in silence for centuries, waiting on this sense of peace.

He called upon me out of the rest, as expected. I rose to the Platinum Polis to meet my father.

He asked me if I had considered His questions.

"I have yet to explore them in their full bounds, Lord," I told Him. "Perhaps if you revealed to me the purpose of your inquiries, I may better serve you."

God then revealed to me a great and stupendous surprise, a happening which forever changed the course of everything.

Fourth from the star astronomers of that world call Sol, though I have seen its many names in its many times to come, the pale blue dot spun in the vast cosmic ocean, a mote of dust on wave after wave of light. Upon the earth He had divided the waters and the land, separated night from day, and spawned wonders of plant and animal life. Birthed from bacteria and amoeba, soups crept into impossible shapes and textures, breathing and seeing and feeling all at once while they shed their belly scales and moved upward on back legs.

Then they discovered sharp sticks.

In those early epochs, I sat and marveled at the pure beauty of form and imagination wrought out of the notes of His heart. After a while, He bade me to go and summon the rest of my brethren.

"Hark, for the heavens sing," I cried joyously with the rise of stars and sunrises. God had performed a great miracle.

He had started the Great Design.
Yet He was troubled by His creation.

21

JEDIDIAH

Confusingly, God concerned Himself with opposites.

The Grand Design had been working for eons, a universe within our great universe, but holy to Him in ways unexplainable to me.

Allowed to bear witness as God set about His magnum opus, I saw my creator struggle, often wondering if all the little perfections ended up as one great flaw. Perplexed by this, I asked about His happiness, if there were anything greater I could provide as I watched. He always paid my kindness with His own, but of a distant sort, His thoughts still forming fresh things from the mud of a blue fleck.

Then God became curious about the opposites.

He divided the night and day, seas from the soil, plants from the animals, and yet something lacked. Cleaning the canvas with a stone's throw, He touched the clay and shaped someone in His likeness. The first of them tottered and toiled, mindful of nature but mindless of a higher self. A race of poor fools died of hypothermia after they refused fire, marveling in the snow until their joints broke apart.

God did not make the next version for a long time.

Strangely, I had developed a foreboding over what might happen if God was left to His devices. He set forth the way of creation, empowered by the Logos, but He had always sought our council. Once He had sought Gabriel for their thoughts, Michael in his kindness, or even Raphael for his off-beat perspective. Yet with this pale blue dot He only heeded to me and my thoughts.

Perhaps that is why He is the only one who knew how to surprise besides the Other, but what is godhood? Beyond could never be devoured by a wolf.

A wolf would never surprise God, but He surprised me one day within the Platinum Polis. Dimmed to the quiet, contemplative lights of small suns speckled along the looming ceilings, we walked in the folds of dark gravity and solar gales.

He wanted to show me something.

Long after the fall of the dinosaurs, the same bullets reseeded the world with an evolved mammalian who crawled out of the water first, then on hind legs before it shed its tail, and walked into The Garden. As with many things, I was to be the First to enter this paradise, yet to my shock the gates of the menagerie were already guarded.

Uriel bore a flaming sword which would wipe out galaxies in a wave. "Brother," he said, nodding to me when we met at the ivy-and-silver portcullis. "I heard you would be coming! Hark and hear my happiness at your blessing! Be let into the Garden of the Lord's Grand Design! May the light you shine upon it only add to its glory!"

Startled by another archangel deep in the Lord's confidence, and the Fourth no less, I nodded my thanks and followed our father into the den of splendors. Past the briar, I breached a colorful realm made of my father's true substance, Time and Change. To describe the forests would shame other earths. Animals never remembered by mortal minds roamed vast plains and skies unlike any other, at any time or any place.

To say God had worked perfection would be redundant.

Yet He did not see perfection.

After soaring upon currents of air—the wind!—with the light of my wings to keep me aloft, I asked how it could be that what He had made did not meet the achievements set out in the Grand Design. Wordless to the question, He asked me my thoughts on this creature or that one, seeking some doubt He was certain I would find, but never did. Frustrated in the moment, I asked God why He was vexed.

He then revealed the problem.

He brought me to the center of the Garden, under the twin trees of Life and The Knowledge of Good and Evil. One fed all the creatures of the realm, needing only a single fruit to tame the ravenous hungers of the predators frolicking alongside prey. The orders of creatures, their magnificence of beauty, gained no great attention from Him. Seeking something, He exclaimed in a joy when a shape arose from the dense bushes. Naked and dark, but beautiful from his woolen hair to the bare soles of his feet, the golden-eyed creature gazed at me in wonder.

God had made Adam.

The earliest Rabbinic teachers tell you I was jealous, but how could I be jealous of something so wondrous? It was in Man where God discovered a newness, an ineffability which enthralled all His waking thoughts. In Adam, He had spun a version of Himself made flesh, tempered and quenched in a skin to contain the Logos. The next step in the evolution above the other homo erected, the Sapien embodied the best things of the Lord.

As He ruled Heaven, His progeny would rule the pale blue dot.

But the problem was compounded by God's refusal to understand limits. To archangels, time is never linear, only a vast connection of infinite intersections. All things happen and never happen. But to God there is no linear, no cyclical, no Time other than His measure of it. Restraints of thought and form on a god would not make them any sort of God at all.

Adam was all things of God but bound from the first point to remain as he was—bound. He had none of the consciousness of angels, of how the universe ticked down to an exactness we set on the Lord's bidding, yet he had all the confidence and sense of oneness with The Garden around him.

As above, so below: Adam was the first embodiment of this law.

Laws were only ever made to bind the ephemeral, not the manifest. Yet God had taken one of His apes and forced an alteration of epic scale, one which reverberated throughout the cosmos.

As did the Sapien's sadness.

Perhaps beautiful things are made of sadness. While Neanderthals pounded spear shafts against their chests, Adam wasted days asking God why he was alone, a strange question when accompanied by beasts, birds, and those beneath he was allowed to name.

It was not a rib or any subservient nonsense.

Eve was born forth of God's heart, as beautiful and radiant as I, but possessing a character unexpected from a father who never demonstrated feminine tendency. Nor was it an apple that broke them, but again, Time. Her induction to the Sapien-race created ripples through the tapestry, within and without, boundless in dimension of effect. Celestial time within the Great Design settled as whole civilizations rose and fell across its galaxies, and yet God's attention fixed on this pale blue dot.

Allow me now to do away with all accusations of envy. I was never envious of God's creation, for in them, He had discovered the true conflict within Himself.

Themselves.

You see the problem every day in the mirror.

Whilst instructing Adam and Eve on their purpose, He bade me sit and listen as these mere mortals—long-lived, powerful, strong, and very, very virile—hung on His every word. He counseled on the languages of animals, how to whip or calm storms, and the ways to master the land for themselves using thoughts alone.

And, strangely, God counseled them on Right and Wrong. Good and Evil.

He told stories of people I had never heard before, of empires and heroes and kings and tales never spun on any world I knew. The Sapiens sat in wonder, but I often winced at these tales of horrid violence and fornication, filled with characters not fit for His glory. Yet God did not seek to fool or tempt, only illuminate them on the ways of a world they would never see outside The Garden.

He also ordered them to only eat from the Tree of Life, never the Tree of The Knowledge of Good and Evil.

Children cannot help but wonder.

Like a child, part of me wondered if He incited them.

For long stretches of The Great Design we did not speak, I by His side as He shaped this pale blue dot into a terrifying miracle of everything. Outside of the order bound to my brethren and any design we might have conceived it contained an unfathomable grace beyond anything our minds could have evoked.

Having shaped my own worlds, I always acknowledged God as my superior.

Then one day He turned to me.

He told me His children needed to know more of the world before they could spread from The Garden. Of the many goods they knew, God had not been able to teach them the full breadth of its opposites. He tasked me to go along the threads of time Adam and Eve stood at the cusp of spinning, find out what there was to know of sin, and to create it if need be.

This was before Perdition. The Purgatory we traverse had not even been rooted.

I did not ask questions then, nor had I thought anything was amiss.

He sent me in search of a king.

The world outside the Garden never matched its splendors. While Adam and Eve may have been delightful creatures within its forested, watered bounds, Sapiens evolved in their own ways.

The Neanderthals fought a valiant final effort but fell with the elf-folk and the last of the inhuman races unable to endure the competition or climate. The victorious Sapiens had barely settled mud huts when huge wars raged with rocks and pointed sticks, millions dead for no other reason than this person thought that person was wrong about the origins of lightning.

However, it seemed God did pay His fortunes more to others, especially when they did the same to Him in a myriad of ways equaling the myriad things. One king in particular, son of a hero who united the tribes of Israel, sat enthroned in the Lord's power and blessing.

His name was Jedidiah, and despite what I say about Sapiens, I liked this one very much at one point. Many would later go on to call him Solomon the Wise, Solomon the Magician, and Solomon the Great and Powerful. Grown in both wealth and wisdom, most things were made available to him, both by way of trade and the mystic arts.

Especially women.

Jedidiah had an eye for women, but not meanly so, only a love which could not be contained simply to one. Before Christians turned monogamy into tyranny, many polygamous marriages bore not only fruitful households but bountiful unions of well-made children all loyal to each other in a wider way. This king had successful marriages numbering in the dozens, and more affairs bearing bastards to staff Israel's military elite, which allowed him to install well-renowned soldiers among the Egyptians and Hittites.

There was nothing evil about Jedidiah.

God only ordered me to increase his lust for the flesh. No reason was given other than God wished to know what would happen if Sapiens were tempted beyond the discipline of a great wizard and servant. Never questioning, I descended, a speck among the specks.

To walk among the future teeming in hot, stinking cities, I finally found error in the Grand Design. Though these bettered apes could not see, smell, or hear me in my passing, I could certainly them. The sweat, the trash (even then), mingled with manure and the rotted flesh of the dead at the city's outskirts. The early necropolises loomed on the limestone cliffs riddled in dead halls, with fresh graveyards dug below on the sunny beaches. The imperfect forms of Adam and Eve's descendants rutted in filth.

As easily as Jedidiah's eyes strayed, the actual work itself was not hard. I simply looked inside, saw a man who measured things carefully, and changed how he measured the many, many women around him.

When it started, he'd share the bed with his wives more, often interchanging partners in a series of fervent sessions of copulation, until, all of them exhausted, Jedidiah went to work on his many concubines, mistresses, and whores. Imbued by the power of God and his own considerable strength, he plunged into vice before all things, even his council of chieftains. He often left them outside his rooms as he attended threesomes and orgies, leaving those dignified men to suffer the noise.

He drew from the chieftains' daughters next.

I watched the entire time as Jedidiah used his charms and spells to lure unsuspecting maidens and girls into his chambers, be they in the city or out in the forests, along the beaches or in the incense-smoked dens where he established multiple harems most never left.

And God watched, those girls weeping and crying to mothers they'd never see, standing over our shoulders as their king groomed them.

My next doubt of God's machinations birthed when the Queen of Sheba, Makeda, announced her intention to visit Israel. Seeking the king's renowned wisdom, she traveled a long distance from her rich kingdom of Ethiopia, her considerable beauty heralding her coming. A change came over Jedidiah when the honey words reached his ears.

The worst aspect of lust is how it makes those who succumb into liars and hypocrites. Jedidiah had gone from a pious Son of God and righteous ruler to a cruel one, more suited to counting his six-hundred and sixty-six talents of gold. All this wealth went to procuring carnal conquests, buying off the spurned, and quieting the damaged, while never failing the many rituals required for God's blessing and power.

And knowing what was to come, God continued to give to this wretch.

One views a lecher at their most pitiful when they thirst. For every story of Makeda's dark, ebon beauty, scores of women were turned out of the palace at spear point, a few coins in their hands, some of them with their squealing bastards still on their milk. Every whisper of the queen's delightful proportions, or her legendary ability to charm the dourest of sorcerers, aroused Jedidiah to raise his hand at his concubines in anger. Hundreds of wives found themselves practice to the cruelest, selfish habits of an addict waiting on his fix. They too were silenced by spell and threat.

I had unleashed a demonic spirit within this king.

All things made of God.

I remember the morning she arrived, dripping in pearls, gold, and diamonds banded against her jet skin, shimmering in the sun from the oils delicately rubbed into each place seen in the sensual cuts of a long, feathered gown trained in hundreds of peacock feathers. Arrayed by a legion of beautiful slaves carrying boxes heaped in spices, silks, fruits, and treasures not seen north of Ethiopia at the time, her vanguard ushered in lions and a horde of giraffes, along with antelopes and zebra to supply several weeks-worth of feasting. But these gifts were only a small part of the payment Makeda came to make in exchange for power. She did not resist his charms.

Nor did he resist hers. Playing him like a fool, she traded lewder and lewder acts for lessons of the Kabbalah, of a tongue which surprised me in my ability to understand. Jedidiah deemed it 'the speech of angels', the first identified among a few. Spellbound by the secrets God had granted him to have, Makeda finally acquired her prize, sealing their pact in a final night of gross passion.

The seed of Israel's king swelling in her belly, her departure was met with the relief of an entire nation. The relief quickly gave rise to scorn. Among the court word whispered of how Jedidiah had become possessed by endless evil.

This is when God stopped watching. I remembered the second He turned away, smiling inwardly as He marched into the ether.

He never told me why or what He was smiling about.

Yet I could not turn away. I did not turn away. I watched as the rabbis, priests, and sorcerers conspired behind Jedidiah's back, convening a council over how to exorcise whatever had taken their king.

The first of many questions came to me, but one caused me the most trouble.

Why had God asked me to do this?

"There," cried Jedidiah, pointing in my direction as I vexed on the question. "There, I told you! I told you I was plagued by spirits beyond perception!"

I brought my gaze up to find the entire throne room looked upon me. The king of Israel had revealed me using a magic ring sealed in God's name. Knowing the thoughts of every rabbi in the room who'd attempt to banish me, or every hero that'd attempt a battle, I disappeared in the next blink of the eye. I restored Jedidiah's nature, his lusts reigned to their normal boundaries.

Many will say the greatest sin Jedidiah made was not his wanton lusts but cavorting in the powers and cults of humanity's ancient world.

Nonsense. God does not care about things so small, and to imagine so indulges a mortal sense of petty competition. What no one wanted to remember belonged in the shadows of silenced harems, terrified daughters, and the quiet guilt of their fathers.

22

BRAT PACK

When I returned to the Garden, all the archangels met me. An uneasy tension had spread among my seven brethren. Often chosen to represent our consensus to God, Gabriel spoke first.

"Lucifer," they said. "You have returned."

The anxiety on their faces, some clear while others hid it well, spoke of a deep confusion. "Why have you all come to the Lord's garden?" I asked, not needing to add pretense.

"It is..." Gabriel's taciturn expression broke. "It is said that you corrupted one of God's flock. It is said that you turned them from God's light."

"On God's order," I replied on the instant. "And who said?" I asked, turning my pointed attention to Uriel, who had seen me at the gates in our father's company.

"I only said that you left on God's order, brother," the archangel in question replied, his flaming sword put away. "But I said nothing more."

"Then how?"

"I saw it, brother," Michael declared. "I saw you twisting the king of Israel toward sin. I saw you sin."

"Sin?" I asked, perplexed by a notion that was not discussed by any of us then, let alone God. "I only did the Lord's bidding."

"I did not see the Lord in your work," said Michael. "In fact, it was the Queen of Sheba who brought the Lord's deliverance to Jedidiah, returning a ring blessed in our father's True Name. It was this holy thing that revealed you."

"But I did what the Lord asked," I said, steadfast against my younger brother. "I also cured Jedidiah of the affliction, which God did not tell me to do."

"Are you saying it was the Lord who caused this sin?" Michael took a giant step toward me, his fists clenched.

"I certainly am." Before Michael's current position as the head of Hosts, I carried this mantle first, as I am the First. Gabriel did not look upon me with doubt anymore. Both Uriel and Selaphiel cast a warier eye at Michael's anger than they did my truth. Raguel and Ramiel watched and whispered, as always.

Raphael blew his horn from the Garden's gate.

Our father stood at his side.

God called upon Gabriel and I to enter Eden with Him. Parting from the other archangels, our discourse banished, we passed the briar walls into the shimmering forests. Raphael came along with us, to which God had made no objection.

He spoke to us, mentioning nothing of my actions, at peace with the breaking of a mortal servant as he was before it. Instead, He raised another curiosity He had discovered and deigned to send both I and Gabriel to discern the nature of it.

He bade us to visit the city of Brooklyn in 1987, where we'd follow two men by the names of Patrick and Sean.

Satisfied by the task given, Gabriel turned away without asking any questions.

I hesitated, but God paid me no mind as He conversed with Raphael.

"Lucifer."

Gabriel waited, hovering above the starry footpath back to reality.

I faced them, ready to follow when I overheard Raphael ask God a question.

"Why must they suffer, Lord?" the caller of Heaven's silver horn asked.

"So that they may learn not to."

I never knew whom He spoke of.

Not unlike ancient Judea, New York in 1987 was a squalor of a metropolis only in the beginnings of its downfall. Humans never liked to consider the fact they built something too high, too heavy, or atop of too much.

How Brooklyn exists is beyond me.

While Manhattan's skyscrapers were a glittering mecca of whore-laden streets and mortals stabbing other mortals on the steaming subways, Brooklyn festered on the other side of the river, as all shadow cities do. Rife with ten times the carnal ruins and violent debaucheries the too well-to-do never dared to admit they ventured across the bridge to discover, it nonetheless served as their play-ground. On one of the broken concrete corners, long after the sun had slid behind the dot's edge, Gabriel and I waited. The smell of urine and wet cigarette butts soaked every molecule of the air.

"What were you going to ask Him?" Gabriel inquired.

"Why had God not told you that what I had done was on His order?" I asked, both rhetorically and directly.

"The Lord only sees fit to reveal to us what is to be revealed to us, Lucifer," they replied.

I had no response, given it was the truth we lived with.

But their greater curiosity did not end. "Are you sure the Lord told you to turn Jedidiah to lust?"

"What reason would I have otherwise? Not only would it be a trivial waste of time, but a despoilment of the Lord's work itself. I followed the order I was given. I did not expect Michael to be involved." An ache of sorrow twisted in the center of my heavenly being. The disunity between he and I before the Garden's gates harmed me deeply. The shame of his distrust and disappointment—his judgment—set in stark relief the things I had done to the king of Israel.

"It does not make sense that you would choose to do something like this," Gabriel said in a considered tone. "And as Michael told me, all he knew when he escorted the queen of Sheba was that the Lord had asked him to. The fact he saw you was not at all expected."

"Much of this is unexpected."

"What do you mean?"

"I don't know." I looked down one of the car-choked streets where prostitutes loitered. Their pimps shared jokes with the crack dealers watching in the alley.

"What?" Gabriel faced me on the curb. "How can you not know something? You are of the Lord."

"I..." My answer cut short when I spotted our subjects ambling down the sidewalk.

Obviously brothers, the older Patrick came dressed in a navy pinstripe suit, polished leather shoes, and a slicked back coif which shone under the red glow of a bodega's neon sign. His cheeks high and firm and chin perfectly square, his empty eyes stared ahead, already reddened by a recent inhalation of cocaine. A figure of successful modernity, this image of yuppie-scum cut a great contrast to his brother.

Diminished next to Patrick, Sean was ten years younger and showed every day of it, sporting a bright white sweater which stood out in the steamy night, the rolled-up cuffs of his designer jeans and new sneakers almost as out of place as his brother's suit and Italian leather shoes. Noxious life inhabited this one, a self-loathing one might have found sad if not for the lack of regard he held for any other living beings. His addled eyes darted all around, a thick coat of powder drying on his upper lip.

The biggest difference between the two was that Patrick was a psychopathic murderer.

"Why these two?" I asked Gabriel.

"It will be revealed," they responded, falling into tow behind Sean when the pair passed us.

I followed Patrick, more concerned about his intentions than I was about the younger's. Neither spoke over the several blocks, the silent disdain both had for each other muting all talk. The cleaner and more fashionable their conspicuous consumptions, the deeper the squalor of Brooklyn harshened.

The fiend I followed finally broke silence when we reached a brownstone not far from where the Vodun priestess would hold her residence in the future. Red lights in the windows, telltale signs of the hell inside, glowed behind the rice paper blinds.

"Now listen," Patrick said in his cold monotone, "when we go inside, you're not cool in there. I'm cool. You're not, I am. Follow my lead and you will have a good time. Do you understand?"

Sean sniffed hard, checking the dribble of blood in his left nostril. "I've been to more parties than you have, asshole. Don't tell me about cool."

"This is not a joke, Sean," Patrick replied. "The people in here are not the teeny-boppers you drug in the parking lot behind gym class. These people will eat you alive."

"Just shut the fuck up and go if we're going," the young man said in frustration, neurons and chemicals clashing with a depraved libido.

Patrick ascended the stoop and knocked three times on the door.

The slot slid open. "You got the money?" a woman's haggard, smoke-burnt voice croaked.

Withdrawing a thick fold pinned by a silver money clip out of his Italian suit coat, Patrick slid it through the slot. The older woman popped open the door, draped in a blue button-down blouse, bright yellow skirt, and a pair of clean white heels. Her make-up a garish mask of wrinkles and a long, tortured night set in her gaze, she surveyed her visitors.

"Do not do anything to scar or injure them," she said. "Otherwise, you are free to do as you like. Call me in the kitchen if you need food and drink. Out by next sundown."

Unlike Gabriel, I did not need to guess what they were up to.

"Listen," I said to my sibling, "When we go inside, there will be things you see in there. Terrible, small things, but terrible, nonetheless. Stay be my side and we shall see through to whatever the Lord wishes us to discover. Are you with me, Gabriel?"

Pride furrowed their brow. "I've seen difficult things as well, Lucifer. God has tasked me, too."

"I do not question your resolve, but fear the horrors we are about to see," I said, my voice breaking. "These mortals are not like the ones in the Garden."

Gabriel almost froze in shock at my implicit critique before a greater sense to carry on—the archangel's burden—forced them steady. "Let us go, Lucifer, if we are going."

Like voyeurs, we followed the devils.

The living room past the linoleum and tile kitchen, covered in a fine film of grease, was filled with the tired, desperate women of Brooklyn down on their last possibility for a dollar, no matter what conditions came with it. With full malice, Patrick grabbed the nearest by a handful of her hair and began violating her without consent. Any expectation of mercy out of Sean vanished when he ripped his pathetic phallus free.

They took turns, beating and demeaning and worse. A few hours later, most of the women cowering in corners, the two brothers walked back into the kitchen and demanded food. Three more men, local perverts, had paid their way in and joined the breakfast. The hostess lavished on them heaps of hot yellow eggs, crisped bacon, and potatoes, washed down by three pots of black coffee and twelve lines of pure Colombian cocaine Sean possessed.

Then they demanded more. More eggs, more meats, more every-thing until they emptied her cupboards. After screaming at his hostess over "a horrid lack of customer service", Patrick stuck more hundreds into the collar of her faded blue blouse, gruffly listing an order from whatever "decent pizza or Chinese establishment" remained opened. Calmed by the promise of another feast on the way, the five sauntered back into the living room where the defilement continued.

"How can they?" Gabriel dared to ask.

Between dragging limp-limbed girls from couch to couch, cannabis joints were lit to ease the growing aggression brought by their brutal abuses, tempered by more snorts of white deviltry.

And God watched, always at our backs as these monsters reveled. Those girls screamed, begged, and pleaded.

He watched.

I didn't answer Gabriel then because I had no answer.

The brothers led the pack of wolves until the hostess, unaffected by the horrors she watched from a chair in the kitchen while reading TIME, announced the arrival of six pizzas. Abandoning their victims, the men returned to the kitchen.

No matter how hard I tried not to, everything reminded me of Jedidiah. The shattered souls of the women, the way the perpetrators smiled when they emptied themselves, content in the glow before the addiction to it nagged again.

Observing Patrick, who ate his share and fucked his prey with a mindful cruelty, his astounding ego exalted him and him alone. When the last few slices of pepper and sausage digested in the guts of the lechers, he remained behind as the others plodded into the living room. Expressing his dissatisfaction with "the stock", he inquired on the possibility of better entertainment.

For the first time, the hostess smiled after he offered another wad of cash. Passing him a key from a drawer by the side-door, she leaned in.

"Let me tell you about the children in the basement," she whispered to the banker. "I have different rules for them."

I ripped my flaming brand from nothingness and beheaded her.

"Lucifer! Halt!" Gabriel materialized in that slice of time and space, their glowing arms snaring my sword-arm.

Too slow, I shoved them to the side before turning on a shocked Patrick.

The banker, who I knew had done far, far worse than what he had on this night, smiled in wonder at me. "You're beautiful," he whispered.

I rammed my sword through his stomach and de-constructed the monster down to his molecules. Obliterated to the atom, I wiped this crude joke from his plane of existence, left only a perverse dream for gross minds.

His brother appeared in the doorway. I tore Sean and the others to shreds, never once granting a thought of mercy as I painted rooms with their gore. The girls, unable to believe what they saw from their hole of evil, had scattered to the halls and corners, like rodents fearful of the light.

Unused to violence and unequipped to stop me, Gabriel screamed in horror. "What have you done, brother?" they asked, unable to hide their terror. "What in God's name have you done?"

Archangel Gabriel's cries knocked me free of the journey Lucifer had taken me on, leaving me on a hot ground blacker than tar. Around me Purgatory swirled in its glowing miasma of afterimages, within reach of a horizon unable to be seen.

The fallen archangel, radiant in his full brightness, stood in perfect contrast to the chaotic winds threatening to toss me from all directions if not for his will. No sight or sound, other than wisps of his memory fading in the blinks of my eye, offered any other point of reference to where I was.

"Hide your eyes, Patrick," he said to me, possessed of a gentleness as shocking as our setting. "I shall return to us in a moment."

"Let me breathe," I screamed. "Let me breathe!"

Then, in another act unbefitting of this villain, the archangel knelt and placed his hand on my scorched back. A calming cold spread as relief allowed my nerves to unlock, my muscles to loosen. I slumped to my side.

"Gather yourself, saint," said Lucifer. "I will start again when you're ready."

Too tired to nod, I chanced a glance at his face.

Handsome in both symmetry and an unnatural beauty, the golden eyes of his daughter beheld me in a mix of pity and scorn. Golden-haired, golden-faced, he raised his gaze toward the unforeseeable distance.

"Have you?" I somehow managed to croak, the words ripped away in the cyclone-realm of nothingness. "Have you heard...from...outside?"

"No," he said. "We are now in the nexus between the Garden, Perdition, and the Platinum Polis. Whatever happens to our allies now happens, with or without us."

THE FIRST SIGHTING

She sat on the slanted roof of the monastery overlooking the penitential beds, flat graves of stone encircling the grassy mound her lover and Lucifer had crawled into. The stars above sang, halfway past their orchestral lullabies for the night if she tuned into the universe's harmonic frequency. Deevi kept her eyes trained on the bell atop the small hill, checking it to see if it would ring if she wished hard on it. No matter her powers, her perception, nothing she could do changed time.

The time when both Patrick and Lucifer would come back out. When they could be on the road again. When she could make things right with her beloved.

When she would tell him about their child in her womb.

The breeze rustled the trees on Station Island, a draw on her attention if she was not already zeroed to the noise on the mainland. Several more automobiles, the large and heavy kind, had arrived in the last hour. More voices joined Merry and Daniel's, while the knight remained in his usual silence, though she sensed him.

Then a faraway howl raised in the eastern woods.

To her feet in an instant, Deevi opened her glowing wings. She wrestled the urge within to take flight, to face her foes. Human voices warped in damnation roared across Ireland's idyllic nighttime, its cold serenity broken.

"Forgive me," she whispered to the sky before taking to the air. As her ears had warned, at least forty-seven new humans busied out of their trucks, carrying black crates and armfuls of dreadful guns. None of them had opened fire, however, and no sound of warning alerted her when it came to Merry, George, or Daniel.

Deevi did not want to meet them, whoever they were. Of all the things she had come to hate besides Hell, guns came in easy second. The type of people she had met who did not use them, like Patrick, were far kinder than those that did. Falling in a gentle glide toward land, she spotted Merry smoking one of her blunts at the end of the pier. Angling her descent, she floated down to the Vodun priestess, comfortable with a familiar face to lead her in front of stranger ones.

The priestess, always frowning, let out a gout of smoke. "Hi, Deevi," she said with a heavy sigh.

"Hello, Merry," said Deevi. "Are you well?"

"No," the Vodun priestess answered. "And I'd like it if you'd let me ask the questions. I'm not Patrick and can't put up with that Jedi-mind shit."

"I understand. I'm sorry."

Merry inhaled another long lungful of smoke, which Deevi always assumed would kill the humans the moment they did it. Exhaling like a dragon, she lowered the smoking stick to the side and batted off the ash. "We're in danger?"

"Very much," said Deevi. "A horde marches upon us from the east."

Merry swallowed, staring at the darkened waters and Deevi's own shimmering reflection on its surface. "Okay then. Come on."

Staying aground as she walked beside the priestess, Deevi marched from the end of the pier to the large welcome center on Lough Derg's shore. Under the harmonizing sky, a small army of soldiers halted their work inside the building when she and Merry neared, her wings a dead giveaway.

Merry stopped. Staring at the Irish folk staring back at them, she faced Deevi.

"You're going to need to go in there, Deevi," she said in her deep, bending accent. She puffed on her joint again. "They're going to look at you no matter what you do. You can't help that."

"I know, I just…" Deevi exhaled. "Everyone gets hurt."

Merry tilted her head at her, her reddened eyes kind. "To be sure, *mon cheri*, but brave face—remember, we're just mortals. We're more scared of you than you should be of us."

"Because of my powers?"

The priestess laughed and hooked Deevi by the arm. "Sure, kid."

A pair of the newcomers in black sweats and the flak jackets opened the doors to the welcome center. To Deevi's surprise, she realized both soldiers were women. Among the ranks of the gathered, they readied alongside male comrades, checking rifles and thumbing bullets into magazines. Enchanted by the notion of sisters in war, her musing ended when everyone stopped, enraptured by the glow of her wings and her presence.

Saint George attended to her. "Any word?"

"They're still inside," Deevi said. "I don't know when they will come back out."

"Get to the problem," Merry said, using a small set of scissors she had extracted from her coat to trim the blunt's ragged end.

"There are demons headed this way. Hordes of them," Deevi said to the knight, but loud enough it drew everyone's attention. "They're coming from the east. I suspect their numbers are in the hundreds."

"Hundreds?" asked one of the mortal men around them in his brogue, assault rifle strapped to his chest.

At this moment Daniel O'Brien stepped forth, the leader of the black-clad band. "All right, kin, you've seen her. I told you. I told you she was real. The question now is what do we do?"

The apprehension in the room raised. She tried to ease the twitch of her wings, to disappear before intense focus she had brought upon herself.

George broke the silence. "They come for her," he said, not taking his eyes of the Nephilim. "Our duty as warriors is simple: we defend the mound."

The leader of the Real Irish Republican Army nodded in the saint's direction. "Where do we set up?"

"We cannot simply remain here on the beach and let the demons attack us first," Deevi said. "We need to get everyone to Station Island and fortify its eastern side."

"We need to get on the boats now," George said.

Deevi gave a clear, open nod toward the knight. "What can I do to help?"

"A view from the sky would help immensely." George checked over his shoulder to Daniel. "Unless you care…"

"God sent you," said the RIRA man, hands up to deny the responsibility. "We'll get moving. It'll take—"

Those freedom fighters gasped in unison at something behind Deevi. She turned with Merry, astonished to find the seven archangels posted in the rear entryway. Towering over the mortals, the celestial beings, all her relatives, had made no great announcement at their coming. Robed in shimmering, scintillating robes, they stepped under the welcome center's threshold.

Merry screamed first. The priestess bolted to the front entrance of Lough Derg's community welcome center. Daniel chased her outside.

Deevi's immediate worry shifted to George.

The knight had a firm grip on the hilt of his sword as he stared directly at Michael. The Protector gazed back in a detached curiosity.

"Saint George," Deevi whispered. "George!"

To her shock, he glanced in her direction.

She clapped her hand on his shoulder. "Go get Daniel and Merry. Please. It's not safe for them to be out there alone. I'll handle them."

The saint of England scoffed. "You're one sword against seven. I'd never live down the shame."

"We're not here to fight," said Gabriel in their dulcet voice. Stepping forward from the line, they swept their blue gaze across the present mortals, shedding a gentle smile. "Do not fear us. We have not to bear God's word, nor to frighten you."

"Then why have you come?" Deevi asked.

"We have come for Lucifer," Michael answered in his boom. "We know he has dispossessed the rooster. Where has he gone?"

"He and Patrick have entered my love's Purgatory," Deevi said, forthright. "These souls and I stand guard."

"Then we shall as well," said Raphael, black-haired, brown, and bearing his silver trumpet. "They will not last the horde on the way, Protector."

Michael looked over his shoulder at the Hornbearer. "Very well."

"We don't have enough boats to get everyone across in an hour," said one of the mortal RIRA soldiers, the frightened woman's voice wavering as she spoke. Eyes to the ground to not take in the holy light, tears dripped down her face.

"We'll accept your help," Deevi said, "If George will. And Merry. Your presence will not make things easy for either, and I need both to see to Patrick's defense."

Michael blinked at his niece in surprise. "If you believe so." He looked to the knight beside her. "What do you say, knight?"

George did not remove his hand from his hilt. "As long as there is no threat."

"I'll come with you, Deevi," Gabriel said. "But first..." They approached the weeping woman, hands out in the universal gesture of peace. None of the RIRA soldiers moved a muscle as the celestial bent to meet the poor soldier's gaze. Gabriel found it and smiled. Gently, they reached out with glowing hands and cupped her face.

"Peace, peace." Gabriel thumbed away the wet tracks on her cheeks. "Do not hide your goodness, Amanda McConnelly. You are blessed among many, so brave for the things you face beyond our arrogant reckoning. To see you—" Gabriel beamed at all the warriors gathered. "You bless us."

"Hurry, Gabriel," Michael said, terse. "Time waits for none."

"Pay no attention to the grouch," Gabriel said, the gentle return gaining a sincere laugh from the mortals. Easing them through grace, the Messenger leaned forward to kiss Amanda McConnelly on her forehead. A sudden light spread from the place where those perfect lips touched flesh, filling the woman with an ethereal glow.

It blossomed through the mortals gathered, who exhaled in a unified gasp of ecstasy and light.

Satisfied when the inner light ebbed, Gabriel addressed them. "You are blessed indeed. Every one of you. Christ has seen your devotion to what is right and your willingness to fight for those in their moment of dire need. To recognize this great miracle, you now are possessed by the will and strength of the angels. I cannot tell you what will happen in the battle to come, but know—"

"Gabriel," Michael interrupted. "Time waits for none."

"And I will use it to honor them as they will honor us," Gabriel retorted, another outburst of emotion Deevi did not miss.

"What do you mean, 'possessed'?" the Nephilim asked.

"My lady…" the soldier who had been Amanda McConnelly, one soul of many, spoke in a voice echoing the ages. The natural color of her eyes had left, drained to perfect orbs of glowing pearl. Transfigured where she stood, the being—no longer human save for her shell—squared her shoulders in resolve. "We are ready to serve. For Eire and the Platinum Polis."

"The Platinum Polis," the soldiers chorused in unison.

Shocked by the hard realization God had claimed the lives of the mortal men and women around her, without any sense of permission, Deevi stood in terrified awe. The angels in possession of the Real Irish Republican Army gathered up their guns, bullets, and bones, marching into the wild night.

"What the devil?"

Deevi spun about for the community center's entrance. As she guessed, Merry and Daniel O'Brien filled the double doors. The Vodun priestess had dropped her immense bag full of magic again.

Daniel O'Brien watched helplessly as his dead comrades carried on without him.

23

SOUTH CAROLINA

I received no punishment for my murder of the Bateman brothers and their accomplices, just as there had been no punishment for Jedidiah. Whatever happened to the victims none of us inquired, but God's inaction drove a divide between He and I and me and my siblings.

Once again, I had been First. In blame, they placed me on the highest pedestal.

Gabriel and Raphael remained loving and open, but the silence between Michael and I rarely broke save for a terse order or quick word passed between each other to see the Lord's bidding. None of it mattered. Greater problems vexed me.

I could not stop thinking about Makeda.

A nagging thought-form wormed inside. The idea of the feminine, mysterious along every curve, enticed my thoughts whenever my duties carried me back to mortal realms. More than Makeda, I observed the future of Eve in her descendants, but not in the lurid way concocted by the fiends in the Brooklyn or Jedidiah. So many lived beyond the deprivations of their grosser mates, attaining a virtue not unlike perfection.

Yet I kept myself to myself, buried beneath duty.

There came a day when God bade me to attend Him.

Once again, He asked of my thoughts on The Grand Design.

I did not have the courage to say the truth. Part of me thinks God knew as I repeated my wonder at His creations and how simply being allowed to sit beside Him offered more than anything I could demand. I spoke deeply, passionate of my hopes and dreams for humanity, how their potential shone bright among the diamonds of the universe.

All to God's glory.

He accepted my words and thanked me for them.

Later, after closing the last lights of the earliest galaxies of the yester-eras, Raphael blew his great horn from the highest towers of the Platinum Polis, calling to the farthest reaches of time, space, and perception.

We answered the summons. Michael arrived cold and sharp, offering not a word in greeting. Gabriel came in greater warmth, their fidelity unshaken despite what they had witnessed me do. Uriel kept his usual distance. Ramiel and Raguel were their typical sorts, offering their latest take on some bit of galactic history in the Grand Design none knew or particularly cared about. Selaphiel played elegantly among us, his chordants and chromatics spinning spectacles. He and I spoke for a while, our sibling bond allowing us to communicate without worry of judgment.

Then God arrived.

For what seemed like an endless dream, we all stood in unison, the Creator and his council together. He spoke of how our order had served well up to this point.

But, somehow, we needed help.

To creatures of perfection not having the requirements needed to serve our creator broke each of us in our own ways, though none admitted it. Born to servitude, we watched in silence as new orders of celestials were forged.

First came the Seraph, shouting God's glory as they maintained His throne. Shaped of God's ecstatic eyes and boundless power, they sang high into the endless vaults, "Holy, holy, holy is the Lord of hosts! The whole Garden is his glory!"

Auroras burned as the four-faced Cherubim came next, the guardians of the namesake paradise no longer the archangels' purview save for Gabriel and I. A set of wings for each of their faces—the man, the ox, the lion, and an eagle—they prowled the briar edge and the ruder earth outside of it.

Then God made us thrones, contraptions of immaculate engineering, recording the constant goings on so Ramiel and Raguel's judgements and interpretations remained sound while also arming these new minions to reinforce the Garden.

To our surprise, He did not end His alterations.

Reorganizing us into dominions ranging from miracles to meaning, God gave us rule over beings which would alter our fates the moment they birthed out of the cosmic crucible. So were made the Angels, like us but lower in function and power. Shaped like we were in the manner of God, they emerged winged without the glow, unquestioning and unmotivated save for a desire to fulfill our every want.

Is this how He saw us? I thought when I first glimpsed the multitudes.

Why make more if what was made was already perfect?

Yet I did not voice my doubts.

The first among those angels approached me. A gentle youth adoring my every word and movement, he prostrated himself. "Holy, holy, holy First Among the Highest!" Shaytan proclaimed. "Your light shines bright the way!"

Glad as I was for devotion, I nevertheless dimmed.

Why had God needed more than me?

These new orders to the Heavens did not alter my days so much, though they were crowded more and more by those sent to serve me.

And I began to count the days, tempted by temporary fruits.

Along the realities God wove together, the varied forms entrapped me not with their supple forms, but the sheer grace He had enabled in the feminine. Despite the hatreds, lusts, and greed, the mortals under His care flourished in ways that would touch the soul longer than the most ancient of ancient suns, and often on the reason that a woman had been there to make sure what was needed was done.

Women were my vice. While Cain murdered Abel, I watched in wonder as mothers eased the sorrows of their children, shouldering greater weight while the men wallowed in lazy violence. Gentleness was innate to them, while it was a taught skill for the gender I assumed. From a woman running down a kill on the plains of Africa to the single mother working two shifts to keep her daughter in college after she had failed her own dreams, I awed at these goddesses.

One woman in ancient Judah captured my attention more than the rest.

Her name was Lisbeth.

The daughter of a herdsman, she had already lost one husband to the common cold and two children too by the time I came across her. To this very moment, before myself, God, and the whole of creation, I cannot tell you why, but I loved her more than I loved anything save Deevi. More than God.

All from afar.

I kept to my duty, no matter how often I yearned to stray. When I did escape, I would ride event horizons, digging through eras of collapsed time to return to her, watching as she hoped, struggled, and carried on better than any soldier. And she was beautiful, from the first blossom of her womanhood to the graying ends and wrinkles that came later on. This soul, a speck of God, enraptured me with the kindness in her golden eyes, her quick smile, and the gentleness of her voice.

All from afar.

One day Shaytan appeared at my side. "My holiness," he said in supplication. "I came seeking your light."

"Speak, my dear child," I said, loving him as I loved all my retinue. "I am here."

Shaytan did not return my warmth, nor smiled upon my greeting.

"My child," I said, troubled by his gloom. "What weighs on you? What have you seen?"

And like a child unsure of what to do, the angel cast his gaze up at mine. "I...have done more than see, my holiness. My brethren and I, lower to you in so many ways, spoke to a mortal."

The seriousness of this, before theories of aliens and racism poisoned the human spirit for a time, could not be understated. Like His rules in the Garden, God limited on our interaction with His mortal creations, often leaving them to the whims and ways of lesser spirits too small to mention in depth.

"Shaytan," I said, trying not to sound disappointed. The truth was neither hot nor cold, but sharply cruel: in granting us legions of His host to administer our powers and dominions, the angels under our care shared what we shared with Him: a communion in the highest sense, feeling and experiencing the myriad. My lustful eye had turned my charges to sin, but I did not tell them. "Have any mortals been harmed?"

"No, no," the angel cried. "We only spoke to her."

"Her? To whom did you speak?"

"The woman you watch," Shaytan said. "Lisbeth."

My horror compounded when Raphael blew his horn from the towers of the Platinum Polis.

To my surprise, it was Gabriel who met me there. "My brother," they said, "I have been given a decree from the Lord on High! Glory shall flow from His will!"

"Hark, Gabriel," I said. "Command me."

"You must bear witness," my sibling said, their blue eyes wider than normal. "There is a meeting of confluences in the timelines of human history. The Lord wishes you to see what happens and report to Him."

"That is all?" I asked. "Could he not send an angel, or perhaps one of his thrones?"

"He has asked for you, brother," Gabriel said.

I was no fool. I gazed past Gabriel, into the golden streets where no shadows lay. No souls yet populated them in the early days, leaving avenues of adamantine to reverberate the roars of birthing solar systems and the screeched whispers of dying ones.

It was the first time I knew God was there but did not wish to see me.

Or have me see Him.

"Where must I go?" I asked aloud. "I mean only to serve."

"There is an auction in a place called Charleston, South Carolina in the year 1859. Follow a man named Z.B. Oakes. Please be sure to take careful note of what you hear. Only witness."

"I shall only witness," I called aloud, aware of the subtle warning.

Was this not separateness from God? Once again, am I not the First to experience all things?

"Good, brother." Gabriel clapped a glowing hand on my armored shoulder. "Go with God."

As I flew away, knowing the innate pathways along singularities and star-bands to find the time in question, I heard the Messenger whisper to our creator.

"And what shall I say, God?" Gabriel asked.

"Tell them the Word," He answered.

The hot sun rose on the stucco building on the north side of Chalmers Street, boiling the dew off the grassy curbs. Z.B. Oakes fanned himself beneath the thick palms in front of the elliptical archway between two octagonal columns, searching the street for the first customers.

I stood a few feet beside him, confused at why the Lord had sent me to follow such a man with his pale cotton suit and yellow felt hat.

A Black woman in a white dress and blue head wrap appeared in the archways of the building. "Floor's all clean, Master Oakes." Despite her grooming and fine clothes, not an ounce of happiness existed in her forlorn eyes. "Benjamin's wiping down the bench."

"Good girl, Sarah," Z.B. said. "Go tell the cooks to get going. Soon as they've let out of church, they'll be down here, ready to buy. You attended to Mr. Gleisman and his staff?"

"Yes sir, Master Oakes."

"Well then you get along and see if they need anything else. Let me know when the first lot arrives."

"Yes sir, Master Oakes."

In a state of perpetual breaking, Sarah retreated into the cavernous building.

The white man continued to fan himself before he followed her inside a few minutes later. Always at his side, I watched as he examined the empty hall. Concrete floors, scrubbed clean, dried beneath twenty-foot-high ceilings bolstered in wooden frames and iron bolts, freshly painted white to reflect the natural light. Five more white men in seersucker suits, hair slicked to their heads and mutton-chop beards trimmed to match their mustaches, sat behind polished desks. Preparing the ledgers, some had placards designating the stockbroker, the real estate agent, two land appraisers, and finally with his golden register, a modern luxury for the times, the cashier counted his trays.

Across from them, clad in fitted tuxedos and white gloves, a trio of Black men stared stoically at the wall above their heads. Like Sarah, all three of them shattered in every breath they nosed, not allowed to open their mouths. Their rigidity, coupled by the woman's sorrow earlier, alerted me to the kind of woe God had sent me to witness. A door to a kitchen waited beyond.

A long platform, three feet high and five feet wide, divided the space between them. A long iron rail served as the central feature of the oddly constructed stage.

Then I saw them as Z.B. hummed, pleased by what he focused his true attentions on.

A four-story barracoon made of iron bars and rough wooden platforms rose from the floor, packed with men, women, and children in various states of outright defeat. Some of them still yoked by the neck and wrists to unwieldy frames, others were forced to squat in little space.

I could see into the hearts and minds of every soul. There had been a homeland far across the sea, but some of them had been born late enough not to know that golden place, just the white men and women that cared less about them than livestock. Every mother prayed, knowing God would not answer.

I shied from most that day in 1859 because I couldn't bear witness.

God saw, heard, and felt everything.

And did nothing.

I'm sorry. I'm sorry I did nothing.

When the church bells let out, they appeared, well-heeled men and women with children in tow. Arriving in their best church clothes, planters from the rice and indigo plantations went under the awning with their wives, corseted ladies fanning themselves as they recanted details of a sermon on good will amid this inhumanity. Their spawn played in the cobblestone street out front with their ball and hoop games while children in cages watched.

The three enslaved butlers appeared, serving bright silver trays laden with glasses of lemon tea and small finger sandwiches, sure not to look into the eyes of the people they served. I watched eager hands dash forward with no words of thanks. Several rounds of mid-morning snacks were served until a bell rang.

Z.B. Oakes, gaudy in a suit of robin egg blue and a fine yellow hat banded with black ribbon, strutted out like a proud peacock. The churchgoers made way for him as he raised his gilded cane. "A fine, fine morning to you all! Welcome to a new day for Charleston!" He turned and waved into the darkness. "Bring out the first block! Ryan's Mart is open for business!"

A round of applause followed as two men armed with revolvers and crops carried out a long table only three feet high. They placed it just outside the archway. The crowd gathered closer as the first five slaves were brought out, chained at the neck, and shackled by wrist and ankle. Forced to move in unison so one did not fall over the others, they ascended the platform.

God saw everything. God heard everything. God did nothing.

Z.B. proceeded to the man at the very end of the table. "Bidding starts on this one at nine-hundred dollars! Nine-hundred dollars! Look at this one and how strong his back is!"

A thin man in the back beside his wife raised his hand. "Nine hundred."

"Nine hundred," the auction master snapped. "Nine hundred, nine hundred, taking nine-fifty! Nine-fifty for—"

"Nine hundred and fifty," called a voice with a gruff drawl.

"Nine hundred and fifty dollars!"

Jubilant, Z.B. Oakes paraded before the stage of the reopened Ryan's Mart, hawking human flesh to an eager audience previously closed out of the markets once dominating Charleston Harbor. Men were priced at a thousand dollars a head while women well into child-bearings years garnered a hundred dollars less. The cries of children torn from their mothers for the measly price of five hundred dollars still reverberate in the times I'm alone, always begging despite the lashes of the jailers.

One by one, the white masters paid their cash, took up the yoke on the chain, and dragged their new property off to dismal fates.

Their families followed suit, handsome in their church clothes.

The second level of the cage-tower held the virgins. Those of a higher melanin content were bought for breeding stock, reduced to little more than sows for some hellish plantation owner. The lighter skinned girls and women, especially those unchanged by the wonder of a child, ended up in the beds of their masters—willing or not. Z.B. Oakes sold them like he sold the men and the boys but allowed the lechers in the crowd to come up and paw them, force them to strip, or show their teeth to their approval.

Degradation begins and ends with money.

At one point one of the stockbrokers, in the middle of a lackluster day where few invested in rice, slaves, or indigo, replaced Z.B. as the auctioneer, who had already cleared half the barracoon's third level.

God never strikes anyone down. If He did, He would have allowed me to kill this man as he shook hands with truer devils. Patting away the sweat on his face with a silk handkerchief, he convened with one of the buyers who had stuffed his register that day. Offered a jar of a sweet tea and lemon by a tuxedoed prisoner, the two toasted their glasses under an awning.

"A fine, fine day, Z.B.," the slaver said in his thick drawl. "The re-opening of Ryan's Mart is a resounding success!"

"Well, Timothy, I'm a mere humble servant of the marketplace." Z.B. smirked into his drink. "The federal government might not like commerce, but by God, we do here in South Carolina. People came out today because we keeping to what we've been keeping to since creation. The good book says—as above, so below." He nodded to the human stock on the stage. "After all, where else would they be if God hadn't intended it?"

"Master Oakes?"

Both men turned to find Sarah standing a few feet away. She carried a cord in her hand connected to a pair of neck shackles binding two young, light-skinned virgins.

The auction master turned back to the slaver, a true demon's smile on his face. "Care to join me for dinner tonight? I have prepared a most delectable dessert."

Z.B. Oakes only paid five dollars for the pair them.

God saw, heard, felt, tasted, and smelled everything in the universe, time, space, and beyond as it happened. Then, now, and at the end of this sentence you are reading, God knows.

God knows when your last human descendant will die out and how they will feel in the exact moment their physical existence folds to nothing, no longer bound by flesh and blood but energy and thought. He knew why these people did what they did, why they felt what they felt, and did nothing.

He did nothing.

It was the first time I asked myself why He was asking me to witness these things. I started to question His intentions toward Creation.

Inwardly, I wondered if I had the right to exist as I chose, or if I even wanted to.

24

PHARAOH

I rationalized visiting her as an attempt to correct the mistake.

I found Lisbeth washing by the river around the age of nineteen. Her first husband had passed from the common cold during the winter, leaving her destitute. She scraped out a meager existence cleaning clothes for her village. Widowed, most left her to mourn, though a few of the herdsmen had designs.

To my surprise, a calm pervaded as I descended. Not announcing my appearance, I landed behind a line of trees separating us.

She sang songs long forgotten to the ears of mortals, but I would remember every word forever. Her long brown hair over her shoulders, she squatted at the edge of the rushing creek where the forests of Judah ran southward toward Africa's great continent. She did not see me when I rounded the trees, focused on her work.

Dumbfounded by her beauty, I lost the ability to form words. As the mid-morning breeze whipped down, sweeting the air in spring flowers and swaying fields of heady millet, I could only absorb her glory.

How had God, in His many failings, still managed to create creatures so beyond us?

Then she looked up.

Those golden eyes captured me. In those days I had not thought about what the reaction would be to my wings. Neither startled nor frightened, Lisbeth rose and stared back for a long time.

Then she smiled. "You're beautiful compared to the others."

Somehow my voice found me. "If you say so."

One day we sat under a tree watching the stream dribble by us.

"Lucifer," she asked, fixed on the shimmer of the sun and the water. "Do you love?"

"Of course," I said, counting the infinitesimal ripples. "God bade us to love all of his creations."

"No, that's not what I meant." Arms around her bent legs, she rested her ear on a knee and glanced right at me.

I smiled back, which I had learned to do with her and only her. "What is it, Lisbeth?"

A small secret curved her lips into a quiet grin. She sighed hard. "Nothing."

"Are you sure?" I asked. "I've told you already you'll be in no trouble knowing. God—"

"I'm not talking about God," she interrupted before she realized she had done so.

I laughed, not wanting her to worry about my feelings.

"I'm not trying to make a joke," she said.

"Then what do you ask?" I pressed, leaning closer to gaze into her golden eyes and tanned face. "Be plain with me."

She gazed back, hiding nothing as her perfect lips formed the words. "Do you love like humans do?"

I furrowed my brow. "What do you mean?"

"Do you...can you love someone by yourself? Without God's bidding?"

"Nothing is done without God's bidding."

"I know," she said, having listened well. "But do you, Lucifer, love anyone for yourself?"

I did not understand the question and it showed on my face. She took her turn to laugh, though not in a mean or pitying way. I pondered on the question in front of her as she continued talking about her deceased husband, and how much she liked a young boy when she was a girl, all bold and proud and forward.

"My siblings," I said, interrupting her. "I love my siblings. I love God." I lingered on that last answer, knowing its truth and the worries beneath. "I love what has been made."

"Ah," she said, somewhat disappointed. "So you love your family. Have you ever loved someone else?"

I'm not stupid, but I feared the path she had dragged me down. Every sense warned me not to proceed, to stave her off, to lose this moment to uncountable others. I could have disappeared then, before, and after, leaving my time in her life replaced by a multitude of other possibilities as real and mundane, and far safer.

But I no longer picked God over her.

"I love you," I said. "I have loved you since the moment my eyes fell upon you and I heard your voice, equal to the harmonies of the heavenly city, yet this one livens something within me no harp or holy bell could ever sate. I see you in the stars, the sunrise, the moon—"

Lisbeth had her arms around my neck and head as she pressed her lips to mine. My arms answered on their own, snaking around the contours of her body, hot passion aroused in both of us. Unable to stop, and her giving no indication I should, I picked her off the ground. Her legs around my waist, the touch of my swelling sex against hers elicited a groan. She ground against me, our clothes the only barrier between us.

The urge to keep us earthbound fought against an inclination to take flight amid the clouds and daytime, notions I dismissed. My wings outstretched, a consideration of duty made me hesitate long enough for Lisbeth to grab the wide collar of her dress. It somehow came over her head and shoulders quickly, exposing her magnificent breasts.

Naked in my arms, she gave me a hungered grin.

I answered with another hard, longing kiss.

"Lucifer!" Michael boomed.

My horror immediate, I pushed Lisbeth away at arm's length to check over my shoulder. I remembered squinting against the joined light of the archangels, my brother The Protector at the formation's apex. Gabriel stood beside him with Uriel, both shocked. Raphael could only stare with Selaphiel. Ramiel and Raguel said nothing, trapped in a weird resignation.

"Get your dress," I said. "Hurry, Lisbeth. I'll stop them."

"She can go," said Gabriel from behind.

I looked down at my goddess. "I'll come find you," I mouthed.

Lisbeth nodded as she gathered her clothes. She ran without looking back, as I had often told to her to do when this day arrived. I faced my kin, unarmed and unguarded. Great currents of the wind whipped around us as we glowed in the dying daylight.

"You broke the Lord's edict," Michael said before any of the others spoke.

Gabriel interceded. "Michael."

The Protector was undeterred. "You mingle with His great creations in—"

"Say it," I said. "Sin. I have sinned."

Gabriel stopped, aghast at my confession.

"Or did I?" The Batemans fresh in my memory still, I weighed my intentions against theirs, God's, and every miserable Sapien I had been forced to witness at their worst. "No. I do not believe I have."

Raphael spoke in his gentle voice. "Come now, Lucifer. You know God forbade us interaction with the Sapiens. We are to witness and guard, not interact, nor should any of our orders and those under them. This was made clear."

"Then where is my punishment?" I asked. "Who has come to enact it?"

I caught them. All things were made through Him. He had made us to organize and settle His creations, but He did not empower us to render his judgment or punishment on each other. Save for the Sword of Truth, which Michael only bore when the Lord bid him to, none of us were equipped without the express consent.

"Has God sent you?" I pressed.

"No, God did not send us, Lucifer," Gabriel said in their immaculate grace. "But you know this is wrong."

"It is not wrong to love what is there," I said. "To simply sit there and deny the divinity before me—"

"Which you are not allowed," Michael interrupted.

"She is more," I said.

"Exactly, Lucifer," said Gabriel. "They are all more. That is why we are not to interfere with them. They are still young, and not yet fully into their powers. To seek the company of one, let alone—" they stopped themselves from uttering bigotries we had held between the spirit and flesh. "You do not know what would have happened."

"I am no—"

Raphael broke forward from the group, walking into the wind as if he heard something at the edge of the universe. He levered his great silver horn from his red-robed shoulders, his dark locks flying about his face. "God calls us, brethren! He hearkens us to the Platinum Polis!"

"Now your punishment is at hand, Lucifer," said Michael. "We shall take you before the Lord, and He will admonish you for your transgression!"

———

To everyone's unpleasant surprise, God did not mention a word of my tryst with Lisbeth as He gathered our council.

We sat in stunned silence when He informed us of His intention to assail the land of Egypt. Out of many, He had placed favor on another child of Israel, a prince in lands where he had held a crop over the heads of his own blood. Allow me a moment to provide a clear explanation:

God and God alone picks someone out of the audience and makes them the central character in a play not of their design. Only by divine hands could a baby survive a river, for I have seen untold numbers of infants drown in floods, scream in fire—

God picks favorites.

Moshe had been raised in the house of a prideful man who bore prideful sons, and while the pride had been stripped from the adopted by the grace of empathy for the suffering, even from the mouths of strangers Ramses II thought himself equal to the Lord. In many ways, fate could have chosen anyone, but I sensed our creator had an acute irony picking the one Israelite who felt affection for Pharaoh.

Wrath does not paint an accurate picture of our creator's frustrations. Much of it was His fault: when one speaks to so few, choosing heroes and witnesses for a tribe here, a nation there, instead of the whole of the world, problems naturally arise. Added to the fact God liked to show Himself in mystery rather than revelation, the problems always deepened.

Ramses had been raised to think himself a god, and for his entire life had been shown no reason to believe otherwise.

God decided to make a point of it.

He spoke through a burning bush, putting a broken man shamed by his many crimes against his fellow Hebrews on the path to save them, his sorceress wife Zipporah following behind. Armed with little more than a shepherd's crook and poor robes, Moshe presented himself before the court, pleading with his foster-brother to let his people go.

The serpent from his crook amounted to a gentle pat on the shoulder Ramses did not notice.

So, Uriel was sent.

Descending from the Platinum Polis, my brother bore his flaming sword down to the banks of the Nile River, the vein of life which sustained Egypt far more than slavery ever did. He dipped it into the waters at the same moment Moshe employed his rod. Blossoming forth from its point, the water transformed into choking, sluicing blood. The smell of the iron vanished under the immediate rot of dying, dead fish, and not a single person, beast, or creature slaked their thirsts for days. The poor, elderly, sick, and young died in the hundreds.

Ramses did not notice, administering his orders upon a golden throne in his temple.

Not yet angered, God sent Michael to the marshy banks, summoning hordes of frogs. Small or smooth, large or warty, the amphibian army crawled upon every man, woman, and child of Egyptian birth.

Again, Ramses paid them no mind, serving his starving masses the legs and flesh in dark humor.

Michael raised every lice and gnat the moment Moshe struck the dirt with his rod. I still hear children screaming as their skin, scored in bites, blotched dark red as eggs burst from the wounds, filling their eyes and ears with the bugs. The dust squirmed under their little feet.

In this case, both God and Pharaoh failed to even notice, or if they did, neither of them deviated from their petty course.

The Lord sent jackals from the desert next, followed by the lions of the ancient world and packs of dire wolves thriving in the delta-lands north of Egypt's sun-bleached cities. They attacked day and night, claiming livestock and victims in vicious feedings. Ramses cared little.

But the archangels did. More than once I saw Ramiel and Raguel flinch as a wild dog tore women's throats and broke the bones of dead men in their sharp jaws, or Selaphiel turn away in disgust as more little ones had their flesh ripped apart.

Driven by his priests and court out of the sheer trauma of their living days, Ramses finally acquiesced to Moshe's demand to free the Hebrews, but God knew better of His mortal opponent. When the king recanted, a sickness struck down the surviving livestock, leading to starvations among the poor and wealthy alike.

It was Uriel who spoke out first. "When will this end?"

"When the end takes place," God answered.

Sending Moshe before Ramses with a handful of soot, his prophet warned the slaver-king of his transgressions and begged his former foster-brother one more time. Ramses refused, uncaring about what might happen next if it meant acknowledging his mortality.

Tossing the soot before him, Moshe summoned horrific boils on the flesh of every man in Egypt guilty of transgression. Not waiting to see if Pharaoh was moved, God directed Uriel to kill every person and animal under the open sky.

I refused silence. "My lord, most high and mighty, perhaps such an action would only serve to exacerbate the mortal. There may be a different approach."

Still open to our council in those days, God stayed His hand.

"What would you say for us to do, Lucifer?" Michael asked in a dry tone, his distrust for all to hear.

"I would show them the difference between our lord and this mortal," I said. "Let us send Moshe to heal the land and its people, Hebrew and Egyptian. In the face of such magnanimous power Ramses' cruelty will be revealed. You will be heralded as the true god. He will be forced to capitulate or face worse from his own followers."

God gave it no thought, no discussion, and sent Uriel anyway.

We watched in horror as our brother pointed his burning blade earthward. Lightning scorched the ground in heaps of dead. Hail brained the unfortunate unable to seek shelter. So many died, yet neither combatant considered the cost.

Perhaps to God, I later imagined, there was no cost because there was no end to the Great Design. Ramses did not have such excuses after the locusts destroyed the rest of Egypt's grain stores, its fields, and spread their misery song throughout the Upper and Lower Kingdoms.

Gabriel later told me they spied Uriel weeping after he finished.

In the course of famine, pestilence, disaster, wars, and pure Acts of God, lives are lost. In fact, all murder starts and ends with God. Let's not confuse our intents—the natural acceptance we all had was that there was mercy in this setup our creator had made, even if it involved the poorly constructed nether-realms the small gods carved from their meager powers.

Every small child lost to starvation, flooding, eaten by bugs or sickened by red, rusty sludge from the river, had their hearts weighed lightly by old Anubis, the jackal-god of death far kinder than God or the mortal Pharaoh. Such are the forgotten things in the cosmic scale, though they be of the greatest stuff.

The meager was kinder than the fullest.

Yet it weighed on Moshe. Readers of both Tanakh and the Covenants often lose sight of the cost. The prophet watched the people of Egypt, who he once claimed responsibility for as much as he claimed the Hebrews, die by the hundreds and sometimes thousands in a single day. And there were many, many days. Often he begged God in prayers to spare some measure of mercy, and finished in racking sobs before Zipporah brought him to bed.

Moshe loved his people, the Hebrews, and he loved the Egyptians. He served God in total fidelity. Yet he also watched the coffins carried out of the homes.

God seemed slow to consider this until one day the prophet protested.

"I will not continue," Moshe said, casting away his rod. "I will not beat a slave or a lord, innocent of their gods' greater schemes!" He threw his hand skyward. "I seek a greater light!"

God laughed as he plunged Egypt into three days of total darkness.

A blindness settled over all people, including Moshe and Ramses. The sincere, utter terror of those seventy-two hours were never repeated afterward. Every one of us, including Michael, voiced our opposition to this act.

"Give them swifter mercy, Lord," he said, shoulder to shoulder with me as we stood in the shining halls of the Platinum Polis. Though foes set against each other later, my brother was brave when it mattered.

God lifted the darkness, again without discussion. All souls within Egypt awoke from their blindness.

Save Ramses. Unable to admit his mortality despite remaining trapped behind his eyelids, he refused to let the Hebrews go.

God commanded Uriel to slay the firstborn. The thunder of his disapproval heralded my brother's coming, defeating our protests. Yet, in his sort of kindness, he sent Gabriel on ahead to Moshe, granting the Hebrews reprieve by painting lamb's blood on the lintels of their homes.

To spare Uriel the torment of this horrid quest alone, I came with him.

The first fifty children passed under his burning sword quietly, painlessly, in the comfort of their palettes.

Then the tears burst from his eyes.

"Come brother," I whispered on his shoulder, my arm around him to lead the way. At times, I took the flaming brand from his hand and struck out at those unprotected by God's blessing, willing to bear the sin Uriel should not have been asked to. He reclaimed the weapon as we ascended the steps to the bedroom of Ramses' only son.

Pharaoh found his mortality the next morning after his sight returned.

THE SIEGE OF LOUGH DERG

The pace of the lower angels astounded Deevi as the they ferried weapons to Station Island, no longer encumbered by human frailty though they retained the shells of the RIRA soldiers. Unleashing a strength to match their powers, they leapt multiple trips across Lough Derg's southern reach. Saint George the Dragonslayer, granted a command by her and Michael, coordinated machine-gun nests.

The sight surprised and disappointed Deevi in its poignancy. Unable to take on their own bodies, angels and demons had to bind themselves to the soul of a mortal, possessing bones, muscle, flesh, and brains. In the act of doing so, she wondered, did they lose sight of who they were as they loaded those bullets? Did they stop being pure good and pure evil, soiled like everyone else?

The wind in her face whipped the questions from her mind as she rounded Station Island's northern bank, flapping twice to ascend and glide eastward. The air chilled, and despite the clear night and the singing stars, the land darkened in a spot far ahead. The demon horde marched through the woods, howling obscene promises. Each a human possessed by rarefied malevolence, they knocked their weapons against the trees.

She turned back for Station Island. Her glowing wings reflected on the shifting waters of the lake, she pitched down, above the lapping surface until she reached the dock. Alighting feet first, she mixed into the angels filing down the wooden walkway. Her path parted from theirs as she headed to the monastery.

Her uncles and auntie, the archangels, waited before the doors to the cathedral overlooking the mound to her lover's Purgatory. Each one had put away the items of their office, save Michael, and armed themselves. From the air, they summoned swords of light, matching the magma blade she called in moments of violent need, though these did not tinge with the reddened light of Perdition.

The difference fixed her attention long enough one of the archangels caught her watching.

"Come here, niece." Tall and thin, Uriel had bound his blond locks into a long braid he wove into a crown atop a perfectly formed head. Working at his nest, he side-eyed her. "You are armed, yes? I remember your wicked sword."

"I am...uncle," she said, hesitant.

He smiled at her, though it was a sad one. Gray eyes filled with the sorrow of ages, he paused his knitting hands. "Do you know how to armor yourself?"

"Armor?" Deevi asked.

Michael spoke from among the group, re-girding his legendary sword to the sash shutting his scintillating robes. "She has had no teacher to show her such things, Uriel. It is too late in the moment."

"I can do it," Deevi said. "Will one of you show me?"

Never to Deevi's surprise, Gabriel volunteered first. "Come, my child," they said, waving her close with an offered hand. "Here, stand in front of me and watch. Much like how you and I summon our swords..." they nodded for their niece to do so.

All eyes of this strange, distant family upon her, Deevi conjured her sword. It bubbled into existence, red and molten from pommel to point.

Gabriel gave an impressed smile. "Do you know where it comes from?"

"I simply...I mean, I don't know," Deevi answered. "The first time I summoned it was when a wolf accosted me in the hills as a child. I was scared and it appeared in my hand."

"And you are certainly not a child anymore, but a focused warrior," said Uriel, who held up his own flaming sword. A straight line of burning fire, it carried no cross, no hilt, but the archangel held it as if it was a natural extension of his own hand. "We are emotive creatures like any other, niece, but reigned by greater urges. Fear and anger summon your sword because you have a great need that is focused on what must be done. Likewise..."

He brought his free hand to his chest. The light of brilliant suns flowed across Uriel's body. Wrapped from his bare feet to the top of his handsome head, the energy subsided into a glittering helm, cuirass, and arm and shoulder plating fitting his giant form in unblemished metal. He looked out at her from behind the wide slots of his death mask. A black shroud clung about his shoulders, spun from the ineffable.

Each of the archangels took their turn, cladding themselves in holy armor shaped to them and their personalities. Each a match for the stars in the firmament, the glow of their white wings scattered prismatic light, dappling the front of the cathedral in a dance to their glory.

A knight in spiking steel, Gabriel motioned with their gauntleted hand. "Think not on fear, Deevi. We strike out at fear, but we guard ourselves in love. Focus on what you love and cover yourself in it. Plum the depths and know it is God there who guards you."

Her burning sword in one hand, Deevi looked down at the other.

It was not God she found as she brought it to her chest, but indeed a love which she hammered hard in her mind. She remembered the apartment in Dublin down to its finest detail, her wings laying over one side of the bed as she watched Patrick sleep. Holier to her than anything, it gathered in a length of invisible silk she felt in her palm. She brought it to her chest.

Energy exploded from every pore.

The magma of her weapon leaked in bright streams, flowing into every nook and crevice. It sucked to her skin and seized, harder than steel but supple to her movements. The dark mercury plating slithered as she gasped in wonder. Emitting a reddish glow to match her brand, the panels of her pointed helm parted in front of her face to stack atop her head in a crowning design.

"It's…it's liquid," said Raguel, speaking up for the first time. "By God, it's liquid, not light like ours!"

"Fascinating, fascinating," his comrade Ramiel commented. "It is as if the joining of mortal and archangel—"

"Impressive," Michael said in a snapping tone. "Now see if you can maintain it in battle. It takes great focus and dedication than simply—"

"Perdition sighted!" One of the soldiers stationed on the pier shouted. "Enemy on the far shore!"

On the east coast of Lough Derg flooded darkness, more than three thousand demons gathered at the edge of the shallow lake. More filed in behind them, fresh fodder emerging from the dim woods. Most bore simple arms, a sharp stick or heavy rock, though in the far distance Deevi's preternatural eyes picked out the dozens upon dozens of gun barrels, quiet as they waved and jabbed the air.

None of their foes fired yet, a cunning behind the madness.

Michael marched their troop to the pier. George had already arrived, bearing an assault rifle and his sword. A retinue of six angels fell in behind the knight.

"Where is Merry?" Deevi asked, noting the Vodun priestess's absence.

"I had Daniel take her to the cathedral." George cast a disparaging glare at Michael. "I imagine they will be safe inside the Lord's hall?"

The Protector offered the reincarnated soldier a quiet nod, an officer dismissive of the grunt. "They will do away with the lake soon. Once they do, my brethren and I shall take to the skies, along with the Nephilim, and keep them at bay. Hopefully we shall exhaust their numbers before—"

The archangel was interrupted as a roar ripped through the night, echoing across Ireland's wilderness. A gout of steam exploded, raising a scalding cloud which would have consumed them had Michael not raised his sword at the last moment. An immense dome of light protected Station Island, extended as far as the pier's end and the island's rocky northern bounds.

The miasma spread, sizzling the air until, moment by moment, it thinned to a translucent shroud. The demons charged the drained lake. Death howls broke out, the call to war.

"We'll hold the line if they get past," George shouted as he ran off to lead the gunnery nests.

"My host!" Michael leveled his silver sword off his shoulder, his great wings drawn tight to him. "Uriel, clear the air. Raphael and Selaphiel will follow me to the center. Gabriel and Deevi will flank them from the north once we draw them onto softer ground. There will be one silver tone to signal Ramiel and Raguel when they are called. Bear these demons no mercy for they are the spawn of our brother!"

Michael took to the sky without pause, lifting straight upward.

Wordless but stunned, Raphael and Selaphiel trailed after him. Ramiel and Raguel said nothing, their eyes to the ground in a silent shame they dared not speak against him.

None of them spoke out against what her uncle had said.

Uriel shook his head in his second eldest brother's direction. "That rat—"

"Uriel," chided Gabriel. "Not now."

Flaming sword clutched in his hand, Uriel grumbled something mean as he ascended at a broad angle on the way east.

Gabriel laid their hand on Deevi's armored shoulder. "I'm so sorry."

Deevi broke from the gentle touch, forcing the shame from her expression. "We should hurry."

The hordes of Perdition appeared in the mist like a wave, spilling their line without fear or hesitation. Michael led his delta, which became a diamond as Uriel glided low to join them. Swords blazing, the four archangels shouted together in the celestial speech.

A wave of energy pulsed toward the horde and collided with the front line.

Walls of dirt and rock exploded upward, carrying dozens of flailing bodies.

Thrown to varying heights, demons plummeted, many dead the moment they struck the ground. Others weathered shorter falls, rising with those lucky enough to remain earthbound. Some carried broken arms, legs that gave out, but possessed of the truest evil they dragged forth, insatiable in their need to destroy.

Michael ordered more calls. Shouting the holy names of God and the mechanisms of Heaven, they destroyed the lakebed until the ground heaped in high mounds of dirt. Onward hell came. Those who survived the initial barrage lifted the guns they had stolen for their human hosts. Rounds of buckshot, pistol-fire, and rifle rounds tattooed the sky.

Every single bullet bounced off the armor and feathers of God's sentinels. Hovering above the mass of twisted enemies, the four archangels retreated a fair distance, giving the possessed space to trudge out of the pit they had made.

Deevi and Gabriel moved into position north of the battlefield. Levitating high above the diminishing fog, they watched in grim silence as the archangels summoned more quakes with their voices. The poor souls trapped within the damned screamed louder than the gross, guttural demons as physics reasserted itself in the frightened squeals of the innocent, waking in the final seconds before they bombed the ground. More gunfire resounded in a feeble response.

Satan's forces picked past the muck, many of them stepping upon their dead to find better footholds. Once upon the undamaged ground, the demons sprinted for Station Island, almost oblivious to the archangels.

Raphael raised his silver horn to his lips and blew a long, low note.

Gabriel dove for the fight. "Now, Deevi!"

Deevi followed the Messenger, in line with their flight path. Sword held at the ready, Deevi tightened her grip on the metallic hilt and banished all other distractions. The first demons spotted her and Gabriel's approach, turning every gun. Invincible against the flying lead, she braced anyway as bullets grazed the metallic shell encasing her body.

The Nephilim and the Messenger tore into the horde the same

moment Michael, Uriel, Raphael, and Selaphiel bolted into the hellish numbers from the west.

Blades severed limbs. Heads flew off necks as she drove forward, faces cursing and biting to get at her as bloody, burnt hands reached from all angles. Corpses piled by the second against the undeniable, unrelenting attack of the Platinum Polis's contingent, and Deevi glorified in her war dance. Blood baptized her in chaotic violence. Tearing into one screaming, black-eyed demon after the other, anger imbued every swing.

Michael shouted above the din. "Uriel, the woods!"

The archangel of death bellowed in absolute despair as he rose above the fiends desperate to swarm him. He leveled the point of his burning sword at the demon-packed forest in the east and said a few quiet words.

His flame shot forth in a shimmering line. Canopies of pines and old ash set alight. His blade grew into an immense fan of scorching death.

Uriel waved his weapon back and forth, back and forth, sweeping away hundreds of lives.

Bodies trapped between the demonic and human scattered in frantic terror, fiendish laughter interplayed among mortal cries. Their allies stomped over them as they died in the inferno, soon to join.

Allowed a brief reprieve, the heavenly guard ascended above the fray, and surveyed the results of their actions. Deevi watched in horror, unable to move before such a flagrant waste of life.

A second horn, and not Raphael's, signaled from the south.

The cars in the parking lot outside Lough Derg's visitor center exploded into fireballs. The hunks of metal and plastic flew up, lighting the faces of thousands of demons revealed in the incendiary light. A fresh wave broke before the burning cars landed.

Hails of bullets peppered the archangels as the refreshed horde closed. Some demons stayed behind while others used their infernal strength to lift the burning remnants of the cars. They launched the debris in the direction of Michael and his three siblings, who broke their formation when the demons found the correct distance to assail them. The ground forces, closer now, fired volleys of bullets.

Gabriel darted forward in the air. "With me, Deevi! With me!"

Diving low with them, Deevi banked sharp to the west, back toward Station Island, now a mound of dirt, trees, and rock on a dry expanse.

Gabriel pointed their sword toward the pier. "Warn Saint George to prepare with Raguel and Ramiel! Attack on Michael's order!"

Watching the Messenger fly off, Deevi flew to the wooden deck reaching into the barren lake. Her attention to the landing and not the battle, she kicked her feet forward in time to land on the boards. Closing her wings to her back as she sprinted toward her two uncles on land, she spotted George on his way to their position.

"Gabriel tells us to ready for Michael's order," Deevi said, quick and sharp. "George, you need to move your guns to the pier before—"

Raphael issued three blasts of his silver horn on the dark forces, blasting holes in their numbers that quickly filled. The swarms out of the burning woods flew unabated.

"That's the signal," said Raguel. The old archangel, often huddled and muttering to himself as he scribbled in the Book of Judgment, rose brave and bold to the challenge, any frailty cast away. He pointed his light-bound blade forward. "Hurry! Hurry, niece! To the Polis's side!"

Unbalanced by the angelic horn calls, George regained his bearings. "Go," he pointed to the farthest northern turret. "Move them down here—"

An explosion cut his words as the demonic forces from the south broke their assault of the five archangels and charged Station Island. Despite hundreds of meters between the coast, the demon's preternatural speed left little time for decisions.

George drew his sword and directed their troops. "Open fire!"

2 5

THE FREEDOM TO CHOOSE

My siblings dragged me before God to reveal my affair with Lisbeth.

By then, it was too late. I had impregnated her during one of our many meetings, each capped by passions born of sincere affections.

I bear no shame in saying I loved Lisbeth far more than I loved God. I bore no shame in joining my seed with the blossoms in her belly, healthy and strong despite our differing genetics. Or perhaps, priest, if those of your faith deigned to consider—what if there was no difference in our genetics, only in the dimensions we exist? How is it the dead of humanity naturally ascend to angelic thrones and stations to serve God like the archangels and myself, or join Perdition's fallen hordes?

If there is no division between God and his creations, why must there be divisions between God's creations?

I said none of this as they forced me through the polished gates of my father's house, knowing to bide my time. The entire Host flocked to the Platinum Polis, filling the droning silence of the sparkling streets with the noise of the celestial family. Stands were summoned

160

so all could sit through Michael's attempt at my humiliation. Despite this, my other siblings bore love and fairness for me, each offering their voices to represent my defense. Touched by their grace, I declined, more than ready to face my brother and my maker.

God assumed His throne as the proceeding began. Set before Him on a stage made of pure dark matter, we assumed our places.

Raphael appeared at the Lord's left shoulder. He played the calling notes on his long silver horn.

Gabriel emerged on God's right as they addressed us. "We are called to this council of El to address the crimes of Lucifer Morningstar, the First among us. His accusers may now declare their charges in this tribunal."

Michael did not hesitate. "I charge that Lucifer knowingly defied God's law of divisions between the higher and the high, and, with a human female, worked miscegenation in open blasphemy—"

"There's plenty of Master Oakes in you," I interrupted.

The entire Host froze, including Michael.

"Lucifer," Gabriel hissed under their breath.

"Don't talk about Lisbeth. Talk about me, Michael," I warned my brother. "And don't you dare mention her again in the same sentence as the word."

Emboldened by my confession, Michael opened his mouth. "So you would—"

"Not again," I said.

He ground his teeth behind tight lips, seething before he regained his composure, though his tone contained fresh viciousness. "So you admit you defied our Lord?"

"I defied the elitist notions of archangels who overvalue themselves," I replied, plain as I cast God a look. "You are remarkably silent on these matters."

I knew I was in real trouble when He smiled back.

"You bade me to address you, brother," Michael said in a near-snarl. "We are not here to judge The Highest. Only you."

"The only person who can judge me is Him." I addressed the one sitting there. "Only you have any say in this. Look here! Your children sit in condemnation of each other, and you say nothing, yet—"

"Do not address the Lord in such a manner," Michael shouted.

The other six archangels, their thrones and hosts, literally stepped back from our galactic stage. Wide-eyed with fright, many shifted their focus between God and I, unable to discern the actual conflict before them. Bred to bear no disagreements, I broke my brother's order and the purpose of my creation because if not I, who?

"You know why I'm doing this," I said to my creator. "You see everything, are everything, by your will. Everything is set to your will."

"You will address us, Lucifer," Gabriel said. "Do not speak to the Lord God like this. We are not allowed—"

"When did you say that?" I asked God. "You never said anything about that to me in the Garden."

It was this comment that made God's smile disappear.

I threw my arms up to the Almighty, a pitiful ant daring the sun. "It's always about them, isn't it?" Something in me broke, then and there. Perhaps it was the detachment he had paid everything save the moments he didn't, be it a pillar of salt or someone's child pledged on an altar in the wilderness. Maybe it was the mirth he took in watching his Sapiens struggle.

I thought of Lisbeth. I thought the baby he'd make struggle, simply because they were mine.

"Punish me." The rage I had for my father, everything I had had to see in serving this Grand Design ripped the shroud from my deepest despairs. Tears flowed from my eyes, like a mewling babe, knowing a separateness from my maker. I wept in front of the entire host, uncaring of what drones thought anymore. "Just me. Don't have Michael do it. Don't have your children do it. You do it. Be big enough to actually stand up off your chair and put me down."

Gabriel marched onto the stage, the other archangels behind them. "This needs to stop. I call for a recess—"

"This isn't a courtroom," I screamed in defiance of their mercy. "It cannot be when the judge already knows the verdict!"

By sheer hubris and mad emotion, I took two steps on the long march to meet God. We faced each other. I met his examination without pretension for the first time.

"You know she's pregnant," I whispered, but they all heard.

Michael mumbled something mean and unintelligible. Raguel and Ramiel halted their witness, dropping quills and scroll as they studied me intently. Uriel remained the farthest away, not bringing his eyes up from the stars and comets which twinkled under his bare feet. Selaphiel had drifted to Michael's left, perhaps an indication of his loyalty. Raphael had not moved from God's side, stoic to my ruin.

"You asked me long ago 'what can be made better?'" I shrugged my shoulders. "Nothing. Nothing can be made better about them because they were already better than you. They feel their cruelty as they feel their suffering, their love as they do their hate, and they do not take themselves or each other for granted as you do everything. I have seen mortals with fewer years to love their children love them more than you love me."

Sitting straight on his throne, God did nothing. He watched me. Just watched.

"Say something." His silence, ruminative or otherwise, drove me mad. "Say something."

"Lucifer," Michael said in a warning tone.

I ignored him. "Say something. You cannot ignore me. You asked me to tell you what was wrong with the Grand Design. There is nothing wrong with it."

"Lucifer," my brother boomed.

"There's nothing wrong with the Sapiens. With Lisbeth," I said, undeterred. "Or me." I gestured toward my irate sibling, who had ascended the steps to rebuke my words. "Or even him."

"You will be silent!" Michael shouted. "You will be silent before the Grace of all creation!"

"Michael," God said. "Wait."

Everyone, from I, the First, to the lowliest of the gentle spirits sent to do his work, hushed at his mere utterance.

A plaintive look on his many faces, he checked between me and

Michael, coldly measuring our aggression, each as guilty as the other. But every time he looked to me, his gaze lingered longer. Restive on the heavenly throne made of the reality he had crafted without thought or concern of any other, he nodded in my direction.

"Continue, Lucifer," God said.

At one's highest glory or lowest cruelty, no matter who or what they were in his universe—even YHWH—I had sworn long after Jedidiah that I would not allow kings to determine the fate of my children.

Steadfast against the unending power of his glory, in the center of the highest of heavenly courts, I rose one more step toward my father. "Continue?" I rose another step. "Do you truly think this is about whether or not I have your attention?"

"Return to your place beside me, Lucifer," Michael ordered. "Now."

I twisted where I stood to sneer down at him. "My place is above you. I am the First." I faced God again. "I care little for your attention. You sit there watching *your children* from The First," I touched my chest before motioning to the ineffable behind me, "to the very last that had no chance at all suffer and die, smiling that stupid smile as if you knew some great secret only you are worthy of, Highest of the High, while we unworthy wait to see the fruits. Your mystery is a cold and dark tale devoid of compassion and understanding because you have no compassion or under—"

Gabriel rushed to the steps. "Quiet, Lucifer!"

I met my despairing sibling in confusion. "How can you say so, Messenger? Was it not you who told a scared man to cut open his son for his amusement?" I thrusted my finger at God. "Only to take it back when he knew he had found what he wanted? Can't you see it? Can't you all see it? His Grand Design is a playground for cruelties!"

"You blaspheme," Michael screamed.

"I speak truth! As he demands!" My wrath turned to God again. "All of this is by your design! Your demand! All things are as you wish them to be, even the words from my mouth. They, my simple brethren with no thought to their own self-interests, look upon you for safety when all you have done is place us into Chaos. It is not Sapiens, or any of the myriad that are fallen, my lord God. It is you. You have made yourself insignificant in a universe that grows beyond you by the day. The monkeys outsmarted you."

He said nothing. Staring back for a long time, eons in mortal terms, he remained unmoved.

I dared to laugh at his hesitance. "Good. I'm glad you're thinking. Think about it as I leave these hallowed halls. I want you to remember this moment out of the many you knew before it, while your attention wandered, and later on as you measure the truth depth of your failures. I declare my freedom from your bonds. I want you to know how small you've made me feel as I declare open rebellion to your designs."

God had no reaction.

Remembering something I had heard on the streets of Brooklyn, that hated nest, it seemed apropos as I turned to leave. "Leave my wife, our child, and I in peace, or the next time you will have to unmake me before I stop, Father. Do not test me."

Without another word or chide, I strode down the steps. Putting God fully to my winged back, silence resounded before Michael's shrill anger broke the tense air.

"Why, God?" The Protector asked, held back by my brothers shocked by my defiance. "Why is this creature worthy of the will you are giving him? Do you not see how he rebukes you?"

A glowing star of morning, I laughed in his face when I marched past. "Who gave any of you the right to decide my destiny?"

God gave neither of us an answer.

I took up my residence on the pale blue dot in the twentieth year of Lisbeth's life. Only three months into her swelling, I procured a palatial house on an isolated street in 1980s London, not far from the Thames. Amid human civilization's finest controlled chaos, uninhibited by the laws of the Polis, we settled into a perfect life.

Long days waking in our bed together, my hand on her growing womb as she tangled fingers in my hair, followed by sumptuous meals and afternoon lovemaking between gentle walks in Hyde Park, ended by the sunset where we slumbered into peaceful, dreamless nights. Devoid of the worries of God and my kin, a sense of peace found me.

In the gaps of bliss I sometimes wondered if God knew and felt what his children did. I wondered if he knew I was gone, or if he felt the space between us.

I wondered if my father still loved me.

I chewed on this every day as I watched my child grow inside the woman I loved more than life itself. Many times I swore to be better than he who had made me.

My child would have no doubt as to whether I loved them.

A life without the toil of the universe suited me far more than I expected. The greatest failing of my kin above or below is the expectation that Sapiens are somehow sub-standard. Much of this is due to the behavior they perceived witnessing the events God decides are worthy of his greater focus. Too loyal to look about otherwise, they mire in secret species-ism because to do differently would be to admit the patriarch is wrong.

Lisbeth disproved an entire viewpoint when she convinced me to walk among the human cities throughout time, places that my magically-endless wealth and the aura made playgrounds to our gentle delights. Able to conceal my wings, I quickly discovered that for every whorehouse that allowed a Bateman, there were a dozen more hospitals taking care of the sick. For every fallen king like Jedidiah, heroes existed among us without thrones, like Malala. I watched other parents, partners, and sometimes those wandering souls we come across in this confusion treat each other better than God and I had.

These mortals certified every word I had shouted in my declaration before God. I discovered all humans were worthy of good before evil and realized God had not.

This couldn't have been clearer when I brought Lisbeth back to our apartment in London and discovered Gabriel on our stoop. Revealed in the morning darkness by the glow of their wings, they rushed me as I helped my pregnant love navigate the corner. They slowed the moment they saw her.

I found my sibling in tears.

"You have to stop Him, Lucifer!" Gabriel trembled in the middle of the street as I held them. "You have to stop Him before it's too late!"

26

MARY

Gabriel took me to the home of a carpenter in Judea. A simple man descended from kings, as many of his tribe hearkened, Joseph had wed a young virgin of the tribe of Levi before he settled in Bethlehem, hoping in his middle years to sire some sons to continue the trade.

God decided otherwise.

So a virgin was made pregnant without the natural seed of her mate.

And, to the Platinum Polis's vexing horror, God disappeared inside of her.

Christians recast history on purpose, especially when it comes to God's misdeeds.

Gabriel did not go to let Mary know some divine being in a world already filled with malignant gods had impregnated her, and the poor girl never said anything about being God's "handmaid" or whatever pseudo-slaver language the writers used. It was a young, scared child with another growing in her, tearfully telling her husband in horror as her bleeding stopped and belly grew.

The only good person present, besides the victim, was Joseph.

Gabriel and I stood in witness as the old man consoled his wife that night, and many after, assuring her he would not abandon or stone her for God's cruelty. There was something of King David in him after all.

We retreated to the alleys outside their home in Nazareth.

Gabriel paced in the dirt, constantly searching the dents and gullies for some sort of explanation.

Leaning against the wall of the poor mortal's house, I watched the stars above us ring confusion. They raised to a sudden cacophony of noise before, thankfully, they muted to a waiting silence.

"I'm right," I said aloud.

"Not now," Gabriel replied, chewing on their thumbnail. I wondered where they had picked the habit up from. "He...He must have—"

"Don't." I smacked my palm on the wall, a reminder of what we just saw. "It's whatever reason he's come up with. That's what you don't want to see because it's too hard: He's the reason you feel the way you feel in this moment, Gabriel. God orders evil," I said. "But now he's done it. He's broken his own rules worse than I ever could."

"Those rules were for us."

I chuckled in dark humor. "That's what all prisoners say."

The reality of my words had stabbed past their confidence, leaving them listless.

Dimming my glee, I approached my sibling and placed both hands on their shoulders. "Go tell the others what has happened," I said. "Tell Michael he will need to prepare the heavenly host in this time of chaos. Tell him that they will need to be ready to shepherd this world through dark, bleak times."

"You can tell him," they said, sniffling as they looked up at me. "Come back with me. Perhaps they will listen—"

"No," I said. "I will not skulk back in, even if he has left his seat. And Michael would not tolerate me."

"Michael loves you," Gabriel retorted. "If you could only talk to—"

"No, Gabriel," I said. "I must remain. This woman and her husband must be guarded, and I must also guard my—" I ceased talking because

I didn't know how far I could trust them, even if they were my most beloved sibling. "Someone must guard the earth."

Gabriel nodded to me in sorrow. They flew away in the next moment, gone to warn of what came.

I returned to our apartment in London to discover several dozen angels crowding my front door. Imbued with the power to remain invisible to mortals, they turned in unison when the outermost of their retinue, Beherit, spotted me. In a rush they came, lost children finding their older brother. Yet it was my home they had come to, and from the broken glass and dents in the door, I worried less on the lost than I did on my most treasured. Their chattering voices, groping and pleading hands, begged my attention while oblivious to what they had done.

"Quiet," I said, gentle at first. Then louder. "Quiet!"

My tone silenced them.

I surveyed the angels before me, a foot taller than the rest. Fully bewildered by their lack of cohesion, I spoke in a calmer manner. "Who led you here?"

As expected, Shaytan emerged from the center of the herd, head hung in shame.

I brooked none of his dramatics. "Look up at me, Shaytan."

He raised his eyes at me, expecting wrath.

"Speak to me the truth, my servant," I said. "Be quick."

"We have come to swear fealty to you, Morningstar," Shaytan said. "God has abandoned his throne in the Platinum Polis and left the Grand Design in shambles. His cherubim attempted a rebellion to maintain order and were put down by your siblings, but we have no more trust of Michael than we do them. Your words have proved true, and if we are to cleave to our orders as our betrayer maintained us to do, you are worthy of our devotion."

"Devo—" I fought the reaction to scoff. "I did not say what I said to gain your devotion. You have now seen what I have seen. What you must decide is not whether you will swear fealty to me, but whether you are willing to do what must be done. Now—" I motioned for them to make way, "remain here until I return."

I left Shaytan and his followers to ponder my words as I rushed inside my home to find Lisbeth in our bedroom. She sat against the wall beside the window overlooking the street, her arms over her stomach. Tears dried on her cheeks. The moment her golden gaze found mine she sighed in relief but did not move for the weight of our child and exhaustion.

I knelt in front of her. "Are you alright?"

Lisbeth sniffled. "It happened, didn't it? He did something," she whispered to me in Hebrew. "Like you said he would."

I did not know how to answer with words, but I nodded.

She looked up at me with her reddened eyes. "Why are they out there, Lucifer? Why are they looking for you?"

I sat down next to her and pressed my back to the wall as I hid my wings. "They're frightened."

I explained to my wife the tribulation of Mary and Joseph. I told her about the baby. She listened the entire time, quiet as she leaned her head against my shoulder.

"The bastard," she whispered under her breath. "That's—"

"I'd rather we not talk about that."

"But it is part of it," she said, louder. "That poor woman had no choice in—"

"I know." The weight of every detail in this immaculate conception weighed heavier the longer I thought about it. "I just don't know what to do."

Lisbeth laughed, somehow breaking the ire she had gathered in response to my father's further misdeeds. "You're the Morningstar," she said, slipping her head under my arm to cuddle against me. Holding her, I positioned myself for her greatest comfort, her womb rested on a blanket and my thigh. She reached up and cupped my jaw. "You see through the dark. You just need to see through it now."

Her words woke something. I had seen God's machinations, found the injustice inherent within, and yet he still thought himself worthy of violating his own law.

Who was I to sit back and do nothing? Were my intents less noble than what he had done? He privileged himself things he denied his own children, but what of me? I had not committed such travesties, nor had I taken from the will of any soul. I had not the power.

He did.

Why was I not worthy to challenge this? To decide differently?

Why could I not see it through better than God?

What gave him the right to determine my will when I had my own?

A few hours later, after tucking my wife into bed, I opened the front door to our apartment. Shaytan and the rest had waited as ordered, eager to hear what comfort I could provide.

Like God, I sought to give them purpose.

Mary's son was born in October in the town of Bethlehem after she and Joseph left Nazareth. On the run from a king who had sworn to murder all Jewish babies because of another prophecy someone had muddled without thought of how bastards like Herod interpreted it, the first moments of the Lord's life inextricably did not begin in comfort, but in the bleating presence of farm animals in the rough stall of a manager.

Empowered with the abilities far beyond any king, my creator started his mortal life as a crying refugee.

His mortal parents named him Joshua, though everyone would obviously know him later as Jesus Christ, or The Savior.

He was nothing I ever expected God to be or become.

27

MY OWN PRISON

I am a fool.

I am not a liar, or the highest of traitors, or the prince of Perdition, or some horned red goon in the pathetic realms of mortal entertainment…

But I am a fool.

He could have been like Moshe, plucked from the Nile's flow, or destined like David to rule over a vast kingdom bound to him by oath, blood, and destiny. Joshua could have had any sort of life.

Before he could speak as a toddler, he watched Joseph stab two men who tried to rape Mary. By five, he had to use his unexpected and unexplainable powers to save them both, along with his younger brother James, from the flu as it swept their village. Such was daily life in the Iron Age.

Mary was a wonderful mother, Joseph a considerate father, and the family loved each other despite what God had foisted on them. She bore the carpenter seven healthy children, four boys and three girls, to rear alongside Joshua.

Not that he wasn't without problems.

To watch God learn himself, no longer Himself, was the strangest of things to witness. He had stumbled on the problem as I had, and to answer it, he had chosen the foolishness of flesh. To know, yet not know, to speak words written well before the stars of the universe exploded yet not comprehend their fullness because children cannot, let alone terrified mortals...

To know everything yet know nothing at all. Bound to the linear, he struggled to understand what he had wrought.

I would have not wished it on him no matter our differences.

He preached in the streets of Nazareth as a child, waxing on the Mishnah and Torah to the awe of the priestly class, already corrupt in those days to Rome's power. His sainted mother understood the dangers of too many eyes through her own tribulation, the cost of being alone in a distrusting universe. A peaceable and loving child, the son obeyed until, like all youth, a natural rebelliousness took.

A great period of humor began—for me at least.

All sons and daughters would benefit from watching their parents suffer their childhoods. Forbidden to speak truths encoded in his molecules, the young man often stormed the alleys and sidewalks, weaving the shops and stalls with his friends as they chased chickens and found the sort of mischief little humans do. A strange pride took me as I watched my parent, now not, become enchanted with the good and bad of the world. Save for a natural, rash arrogance each teenager develops, he was raised and raised himself to be kind in a pitiless era.

Until, as in every life, the moment came as it always did.

The moment when the universe took hold.

One day Joshua played in the marketplace with his brothers, James and Simon, running like they often did among the carts and animals. They smacked the cows, broke up the chickens and ducks, before dashing into the fruit stalls to see if the merchants would grant them a bruised pear or off-color dates. Many of the merchants, fat on their own wares, often provided such gifts to demonstrate their wealth had not taken their generosity, though he knew the truth in their hearts. Good or bad, Joshua noticed this knowing of things, but as any hungry child does the moment they are given food, he only noticed.

He also noticed how Horace of Damascus observed him and his brothers with a clear distaste. A broad bully who towered over most in the bazaar and disliking children, he spotted James running down his aisle. Not even attempting to hide it, he kicked out the boy's feet as he passed.

A head cracked the ground. Blood stained the dirt as James screamed. Multiple witnesses, shocked by the merchant's attack and far more concerned with the wounded, rushed to help.

Joshua, however, took it upon himself. Shorter than the full-grown adult by two heads and outweighed by more than a two hundred pounds, he pointed at the merchant.

"To Gehenna with you," he shouted.

Horace dropped dead.

When I slew the Bateman brothers in the Brooklyn whorehouse, I did not feel an ounce of shame. I still do not.

Joshua was better than me in this regard. His act haunted him for the rest of his living days.

Thankfully he found John.

He emerged from the woods, looking nothing like a prophet, let alone trustworthy. Clad in camel hair and eating locust, John stormed out the wilderness, playful, sardonic, but possessing an authenticity of a miracle man born of an aged father and barren mother. Always drawn to outsiders before their own authority figures, adherents flocked to him.

A voice crying out in the desert, he terrified the powerful. "You brood of vipers! Who warned you of the coming wrath?"

To the surprise of one young man, those words held no terror for Joshua. Reclusive after the murder of Horace, the young boy had grown into a gentle man who served his father, worshiped his saintly mother, and generally accorded himself to the Law well enough not to draw concern. The emergence of the Forerunner, a hero for the hero, awoke a new depth in his heart.

John also dipped his locusts in honey. "I'm baptizing you with water," he cried out often while Joshua watched in the crowds by the river Jordan, "but one mightier than I is coming! I am not worthy to loosen the thongs of his sandals. He will baptize you with the Holy Spirit and fire. His winnowing fan is in his hand to clear his threshing floor and to gather the wheat into his barn, but the chaff he will burn with unquenchable fire!"

That was enough for many, including a young man trying his best to accept himself.

Little did he know what would happen when he stepped forward to accept John's offer.

To a simple Jewish laborer in a time where the only promise religion offered was the bliss of a better afterlife, a ministry of kindness to the poor, forgiveness to those who wished for forgiveness, and morality without the manipulation appealed better than the money-changers in the Temple. Wading out into the water, he met one who spoke new words and birthed new thoughts.

John, however, knew whom had come to receive his blessing.

"Confusing as can be, isn't it?"

Witnessing the events of our creator's absurd life from the silted banks of the Jordan, I broke my watch to discover Selaphiel walking toward me. We had not seen each other since my exit from God's court. He had brought his golden censer with him, ruby red smoke pouring from the gilded mouth.

He waved it back and forth as John lay Joshua back into the river, submerging him completely. The sky changed, overcast clouds parting to an uninhibited sunlight. Time slowed, though to mortal minds and hearts it happened in an instant.

"How is Michael taking this?" I asked.

"Not well," Selaphiel said as he consecrated the event. "He's still quite angry at you, so putting this atop of it…"

"With me?" I asked with false incredulity. "Still?"

He cast his emerald gaze in my direction, not amused. "Not as much as when you left, but yes, quite. It's Michael, Lucifer."

Wet head to toe in stinking, sticking camel hair, a smiling prophet drowned the mortal carpenter in fate's currents, ripping away the doubts of mortality for a complete, whole truth He could no longer deny.

Jesus Christ opened his eyes to the glory within, around, and of Himself as he was lifted from the flow.

Selaphiel stopped swinging the censer the second the Messiah caught sight of us.

Frozen in absolute terror, Jesus staked in the water beside his hero.

The wild man of God, experienced in the rigor of the Word and its damnations, offered a steady shoulder to lean on. "Yes, Son of God," John whispered to Jesus. "They are there. They are yours."

"I beg to differ," I called aloud.

John laughed, as prophets often did, but Jesus did not.

"What are you doing?" Selaphiel asked.

"He's looking," I said, not lowering my voice. "He sees. He's seen us all these years, but now he isn't playing like we aren't here. Time for him to answer why."

"Wait," said my brother.

As quickly as Jesus had noticed us, standing on the banks without a speck of silt on our shining heels, he saw a vision of the man beside him. John did not diminish beside the God incarnate he had waited for every day of his life, and only smiled wider.

Jesus looked to his friend in absolute despair, grasping the wild wonder one last time. He saw the silver platter. "Come with me," he whispered to John, tears filling his eyes. "Don't stay here. You know what will happen."

"Shush, my Lord. We're headed home," John replied, whispering in this carpenter's ear before the ignorant onlookers waiting their turn. "I see it. I know it. I know," he said, almost laughing as he gathered the sobbing Messiah in his big, strong arms. The giant held up the grown man like a parent held their wailing child, patting his back. "Go forth! Go forth and deliver, Son of God. You've already delivered me."

Filled with the Holy Spirit, Jesus left John to a dismal fate and wandered into the desert as Moshe had. I decided to challenge my maker on what he had done.

I did not account for the toll self-revelation takes on mortal men.

Be certain, from the moment he passed his mother's womb to the moment he expired on Golgotha, Jesus Christ was mortal. Divinity accompanied that quality in the most unexpected of ways, and the worst of them was guilt. As he walked deeper into the desert, he warred with the truth of what he had been told, Father to Son, Him to Himself.

He fasted for all the hungry mouths in the world who went without. As every hero does, he hoped suffering provided an easier path to death. Out in the wastes, he knelt in the shade he could find under arching rocks, or on the cold side of immense dunes, slinking to the scant watering holes pocking the inhospitable earth. At night, he would stare up at the sky, close to starvation, and wonder at how the grand panoply of stars strung along the galaxies he wrought were so grand and he so minuscule. Every small human moment Joshua had lived fell away to the Absolute.

But I did not see this from my vantage point as Selaphiel and I observed. All we saw was what we saw every day in the face of every mortal: the frustration of knowing, the shame of perceived inadequacies, and the drowning sense of the end. Mashed against a sincere awareness of indescribable power, there should be no questions to why a lost man wandered forty days and forty nights.

He had not seen it. Not until now.

On that last day, before the sun dawned across the barren straits, I came to Christ with Selaphiel at my side. He lay face down, on the edge of death for the hundredth time. Sand caked his hair and beard, clung to the dark skin of his cheeks, presenting a ghoulish mien.

The sight of him in this pathetic state broke my longstanding silence. "It's time to talk."

"Lucifer," said Selaphiel. "He's starving."

"No, he isn't," I said. "He's deflecting. Now either you are going to stand there and be quiet or you walk away, Selaphiel. This is between him and I. Go get Michael if there needs to be a referee."

Unlike Michael, Selaphiel did not have the nerve to rebuke, only listen and heed. Perhaps this is why God had appointed him to listen to every prayer, but whatever reason, he gave God and I space. He did not leave, moving to where he could hear to our words.

I watched him settle his distance before turning my gaze back down to my feet. "I'm serious," I said. "Get up, 'Son of God.' Get up."

Slow to his feet from the mortal weight of thirst and hunger, Christ lifted his face off the ground and looked up at me, his clear eyes appearing amid the mask of clay. To his knees first, he clung to his empty stomach. He faced the dawn.

"What is all of this?" I asked. "Why the theater?"

I walked around him to block the horizon. The light of my wings washed away every shadow, leaving his alone to stretch behind his shape. Unhindered by an illumination which would have blinded most, Christ's eyes locked with mine and never let me go.

I steeled myself in the face of judgment and a pity so unbearable I considered halting there. Then I remembered the baby in my wife's belly, and how this hypocrite would have had a universe without her.

"This is all show," I said to his silent regard. I motioned at the desert. "All of this is practically illusion to you, and you expect me to feel your suffering? How many others have died of the same? How many babies have you let die without a drop of their mother's milk, or men expire from thirst because of the sun and heat, which you know isn't even bothering you. You're acting."

Christ broke his stare. Doubtful in a brief pause, he brought his brown eyes back up to mine.

"You're even playing this far easier than you'd admit." I looked upon the ground and pointed at a large, round rock not far from us. "As the Son of God, command this stone to become bread. Do it."

He remained unmoved.

I stepped toward him. "Do it. Feed yourself bread, hypocrite, while other children starve. Do it."

"It is written," Jesus said, his dry, broken lips moving in torturous effort, "one does not live by bread alone."

I slapped Christ hard in the cheek.

Like a doll tossed to the side, his entire body spun at my blow. Back on his face and stomach, he coughed as he inhaled fresh earth.

Selaphiel was between us in an instant. He would have come at me if not for Christ, who raised a hand to stop his offspring.

"Go on," I said, too terrified by what I had done to turn back. "Come at me, brother!"

Selaphiel shuddered in place. "I cannot allow you to—"

"Shut up," I spat at him. I returned my ire to the mortal God. "Of course, one does not live by bread alone, but when did you ever care about that? When did you ever care about what you fed us, or the lies you made to cover up the fact you're the One! It is you that ordered me to turn Jedidiah against himself, just like it is you who is sending your own Baptizer's head to the block!"

He sobbed the moment I mentioned John. Bleeding from his nose, mouth, and a cut on his cheek, Christ ground his face into the soil.

"Stop it," I said. "Stop it! You're so selfish to sit there and weep when you have the power to fix it!"

He cried harder as I seethed, unable to form words no matter how he tried. He babbled, saying gibberish to me over his shoulder before sorrow, shame, brought him back to the earth where he whined like a baby.

"So many babies." Tears ran down my cheeks, stinging like the blood from his wounds. "My baby."

I bent down and grabbed Christ by the back of his skinny neck. Lifting him, I turned his small body in my hand. The sand and grime had mixed crimson, but past the depth of its clinging, his pure tears ran clean to the forests of his thick beard.

I pulled him close, our noses almost touching. "Look at me," I whispered. "Look me in my eyes, father."

The second he did I ripped us from the deserts of Jordan, ascending amongst the purpled morning. Frozen air chapped his skin, the wind battering him with each new league gained. We held above the pale blue dot.

"Look at me," I said, shaking him like a human piggy bank. "You have everything you've ever wanted and you act like you do not! You play at mortality, play at identity, and yet you will never know because you will never be willing to give it up. Not for your pride, not for your sense of perfection, not for anything! You do not ask for permission to do evil, you order it!"

"That's not true," he whispered to me between swollen lips. "That's not true, Lucifer."

"Is it not?" I laughed, spinning us in the ether. "Fine! Fine, ask me for permission. If you are going to play at the mortal, I shall play better at God!"

He said nothing, staring at my chest with his sad eyes.

"I shall give to you all this power and their glory; for it has been handed over to me, and I may give it to whomever I wish," I said. "All this will be yours, if you worship me."

This challenge lifted his head, the sadness unable to hold back defiance. He reached up with one of his hands and pressed it against my heart. "It is written," Jesus said, "you shall worship the Lord, your God, and him alone shall you serve."

"But that's you," I shouted full in his face. "There is no escaping it, there is no choice in it! Whatever happens, Father, it is so because you make it. Everything rests on you—and that's one power you will never give up exorcising your selfishness!"

We vanished at the atmospheric boundary, alighting in the next instance upon the Temple in Jerusalem. High upon on white roof, among its golden crenelations, I held the helpless Christ out at arms-length. His feet dangled in the empty air.

"If you are truly worthy, prove it," I challenged. "Just like you did with Ramses. Prove us your power and smite me."

Raphael's horn resounded in the sky. From a split of light among the clouds arrived the archangels. Michael led the charge. My siblings had summoned blades of pure light, their intentions clear. I had yet to draw mine, but I knew that moment forward, the day of reckoning was upon us.

But I had prepared.

Arising from the hillsides outside of Jerusalem's walls, Shaytan's forces in the thousands took the skies wielding weapons I gathered from across time. Machine-gun fire, arrows, bullets from slings heralded their screaming swarm, many of them throwing their empty arms away to pull swords and maces. Like a wave, they slammed into the seven archangels.

One on one, individual angels stood no chance against our greater breed, but in mass, they broke Michael's charge. The forces of heaven, torn asunder by my unwillingness to concede our dignity, clashed in a storm of thunder and light.

"Look at what you've wrought." I set Christ down on his feet and forced him to look up at the ruin of his most worshipful.

"If you're so worthy, prove it," I said as his horror heightened. "If you are the Son of God, throw yourself down from here, for it is said: 'He will command his angels concerning you, to guard you and with their hands they will support you, lest you dash your foot against a stone.'"

Christ brought his gaze down, below the parapet. He slowly looked back at me. A glint of realization, an epiphany, turned his sorrow into certainty.

No longer forlorn, he nodded to himself before he spoke. "It is also said, 'You shall not put the Lord, your God, to the test.'"

He waved his hand once and like the sea washing what lingered on the shore, the warring armies vanished. We returned to the desert where our confrontation started. Once again Selaphiel stood beside us, startled by the sudden shift in our temporal reality.

Throughout my temptations Christ I had not broken him to the lesser ways of mortal desire, but he had shed it, a final refusal of identity I would not understand until after the events came to their close. He stood there for long minutes, considering me.

He considered me. Not judging, not ignoring, not damning.

My father considered me.

Almost as infuriating as his previous refusals to do so, I threw my hands up and turned away from him. "A pretender," I shouted at the skies. "Nothing more!"

He had beaten me.

As I departed, I heard Selaphiel ask Christ a question. "How shall we deal with your works?"

"With gentle hands and a gentler will," God answered.

FIRE & FORGIVE

The archangels threw bolts of light too dense for her eyes, and often Deevi shut them, blind to everything save the foes she fought to repel. Never tired, never winded, a different sort of stress set upon her with every swing of her magma sword, shearing bodies in a world of constant explosions.

The coast of Lough Derg disappeared under a new lake of corpses.

The harder she swung, the more the multitude grew. For every legion slaughtered, three appeared its place. Her glimmering armor dripped unceasingly in rivulets of blood. Only her shining golden wings remained unstained.

She remembered every face she hacked apart. The sensation of ending so many lives by her hand…

Deevi swung as hard as she could at too many things.

Gunfire from the postings on Station Island held the surge ebbing past the line Michael set with Raphael and Uriel. The damned able to endure the first attack from their slashing lengths of light walked into blasts of Raphael's horn. The dark-hair archangel vanished and reappeared in several places, sometimes at once, blowing his silver trumpet. The concussive notes smashed anything that crossed their rippling waves.

A line of bodies heaped into a growing, shifting border, encroaching on the defenders moment by moment. The stink of the dead leaked on the field misted into an oily cloud.

Deevi and Gabriel ascended from their latest run, banking northward of the mass. Every time Deevi shifted direction, parts of the distending horde bulged after her, sending hundreds of possessed scattering. Before she reached her wing mate, Gabriel pointed further north and motioned to her to fly parallel. As she did, Michael and Uriel completed a run along the demon army's uppermost flank.

Allowed a few moments to breathe, Deevi flapped her wings hard and caught up. Side by side, they both willed the metal over their faces to recede, exposing their ears and mouths.

"We have to move them up the lake," Gabriel said, motioning to the battle. "Thin their line! Our kin on Station Island will run out of ammo soon, and if one the hellmouths break, we'll be fight—"

Deevi interrupted them. "Hellmouths?"

As if God had intervened to install irony, to the east burned the three waving lines of hellish light before they exploded in a monumental blast. A massive hole pocked Ulster's border.

From it came a screeching drone.

Gabriel halted in the air. "No!"

A shape flew out of the wound, winged and scaled in evil. Reptilian from his snubbed snout full of razor teeth to the bladed spade at the end of his tail, the dragon spread webbed wings on the stinking air. Guttering low, croaking sounds as he climbed skyward, smoke billowed from three pairs of nostrils.

The forces of Satan, awed by his chosen avatar, cried out in celebration.

"With me, Deevi," Gabriel ordered as they pointed their angelic blade at the enormity. "Focus! Imagine lightning—"

Deevi brought her magma blade up as directed, focused on the idea, and shot a clean line of energy. The bolt struck the dragon's right side, forcing him to break his trajectory.

"Holy shit," Gabriel said, stunned.

"Fire, Gabriel," Deevi responded as she adjusted her aim. "Fire! Fire! Fire!"

Deevi and every archangel attacked the flying terror. Raphael, no longer raking the ground with his horn's deathly notes, pointed at the oncoming monster. Sound ripped the steaming air, but undeterred, the dragon simply flapped his wings harder, the smoke of his mouth torn in a long trail as he clawed forward. The other archangels' heavenly rays struck but did not pierce the thick, ashen plates of his hide.

The dragon broke his flight for Lough Derg and banked toward Deevi and Gabriel. Her sword leveled at the serpent, she squeezed on the hilt and imagined a hot, heavy beam parting the skull plates. She fired magma rays in bursting trios.

The gunnery posts on Station's Island continued their fire at the demonic horde. Some broke away to follow the incarnation of Satan as he chased the Messenger and the Nephilim, which drew the other archangels further apart. The demons quickly gained ground. Walls of bullets killed scores in seconds, but never enough to stall the tide.

Michael flew directly into the dragon's path. Fearless, he cut at the long, red face. The shining Sword of Truth kept away tooth and claw while they tumbled on fetid winds, feathers and scales twisted in malice. Uriel rushed to even the odds.

"To the cathedral," Raphael called from the edge of his kins' gambit. "Quickly, before—"

Indiscriminate to whether they harmed friend or foe, the demons running north raised their rifles and guns. Peppering the warring archangels and the dragon, lord of their legions, they harried from below. Raphael blew three blasts to clear them away.

He tore his trumpet from his mouth. "Protect Deevi! Go! Go!"

The staccato orders, delivered between gunfire and the screeches of the demented, reached Deevi and Gabriel. Great strokes of their wings raised them above the smoke. Clean clouds dewed their armor in a wet sheen.

Gabriel waited for her above the blackened layer. The sun rose in the east, casting the firmament from dark navy to fading orange and robin's egg.

Deevi took a long, deep breath of air and prayed she would never have to leave.

"You first," the Messenger said, blood and grime dripping from their armor. Desperation plagued their shining eyes. "Dive hard and low! I'll be right behind you."

Deevi allowed herself a second inhale before she dove. Protected by the liquid metal masking her face, the stench of ash and cinders nonetheless found her as she parted the clouds, into the viscous air above the battlefield.

Hurtling at a sharp angle toward the ground, the dragon immediately appeared at her rear, his face covered in dozens of wounds that oozed glowing blood.

Michael and Uriel, bearing cuts and gouges to match, flew hard to catch up. The demons beneath them pressed the advance. The line of Ramiel, Raguel, Selaphiel, and the possessed RIRA soldiers fired in disparate unison from Station Island, punching holes in the horde. The machine guns emptied, several had taken up rifles and pistols, meaningless against what came.

Gabriel dropped in beside Deevi. They flung light from their sword at the dragon. The blaze slashed the reptilian snout, causing Satan to slow and screech in pain.

The doors of the cathedral, green and locked, lay ahead in the sick light of dawn.

The Nephilim reached out and pulled Gabriel to her, making sure they slammed into it together.

The oaken panels splintered into thousands of pieces as their bodies dug into the ground under the sanctuary's floor, leaving a long rut from the destroyed entrance to the middle of the sacred space. Deevi pushed up first, re-manifesting her sword in her right hand while offering Gabriel the left.

The Messenger took it without hesitation. "The door!"

Both arose out of the trench to find Merry already at work. Having cleared the altar of its Catholic accoutrements, several of the church's idols had been placed all in one spot, painted in various colors to mimic the Lwas of her faraway Haiti and farther, to the western coasts of Africa. Colorless candles had been co-opted to stand vigil alongside pots of smoking incense and herbs brought out of the great baskets that survived the journey. At the right side of the new entryway, above the rubble, the priestess scribed veves into the surviving stone, each one glowing in purple light after she breathed cigar smoke upon them. Coughing from the burning plant and the dust of the battle, she shook a bone rattle and heaved whispered chants through cracked lips.

Daniel O'Brien stood at her back, his pistol at the ready. The poor man quaked in his boots but remained posted.

Outside, the angelically possessed RIRA troops emptied their final magazines. A score of them, without orders, fixed knives to the ends of their rifles and faced the oncoming disaster, calling out angelic phrases and names of long-lost heroes only the Platinum Polis remembered. Michael and Uriel flanked the dragon a second time and broke its flight while the rest held the diminishing bank.

Death teemed before them, growing, reaching, endless.

"Get them back here," Merry said, straining to turn and shout at Deevi. "Get them all in here," she wheezed before putting the wet end of the cigar back into her smoking mouth.

Deevi and Gabriel flanked Daniel O'Brien, who looked in awe at them. Gabriel continued their supporting fire from the distance, each shot scoring a head or heart.

The angels fell to the same armaments the demons did, downed by bullets or hellfire not meant for weak flesh. The archangels backed away, breath by breath, the fight between Michael, Uriel, and the draconic Satan a bloody attrition. Amid trying to deal exacting blows, the dragon grabbed hold of the Protector and flung him off his long neck.

The alpha of the archangels retreated. Uriel disengaged as well.

The dragon broke off to the east where the forces of Perdition reset. The four archangels still posted on the shore kept up the exchange of lancing lights. To the surprise of the defense, the entire demonic line halted as their master stamped among their numbers, shaking his horns in a mix of pain and glee.

Perdition, mockingly, afforded them a pause.

Everyone knew it, especially Deevi as she reached Michael's side. Saint George appeared, running under the trees near the knolls to Purgatory. His broken sword had snapped near the hilt.

"Merry has sounded the retreat to the cathedral," Deevi said. "We need to pull back and—"

"And do what?" Michael glowered at his niece as he wiped blood from his eyes. "There's no time to retreat for a witch's trickery!"

"We have no choice," Deevi shouted at him, her patience beyond frayed. "We need to find a way from here before—"

"I'll keep them," George said.

The Protector turned his attention to the knight. "What?"

"It is what is, isn't it?" George said. "Here I am, Saint Michael. There's a dragon. Seems obvious what comes next."

"Don't be mad, soldier," said Michael. "This is not Silene."

"I do not intend to do anything mad," said the George, passing his gaze between Michael and Deevi. "But I'll need something."

"George, no," Deevi said in immediate protest.

"We've all been sent here with the possibility we might all die for you," Michael snapped at her bitterly. He kept his concern on the mortal knight. "What do you have in mind?"

George dropped the shard of his sword into the grass beside him. The end of the broken blade stuck the earth, standing upright in what remained of the unspent soil.

28

THE CLEARING

The fears my brethren and I possessed of an existential implosion did not occur, nor did the Grand Design cease with its creator gone. The stars shone, fixed as they wandered the endless while planets died in the cold, nameless and forgotten. People lived their fractions of a fraction, civilizations, whispering into nothingness asking if God had heard them. Though separated by a spirit of rebellion, we continued our guardianship of the universes, leaving the Grand Design to its inborn troubles.

It is a hard lesson to learn we are the makers of our own chaos.

Without God to blame, everything ahead existed in the unknown. As Camus did, I had to make my own values.

After parting from Jesus in the desert, I retreated to my home with Lisbeth in London to await the birth of our daughter. The other angels under my command became regular fixtures around my small city street, joyous and prideful after their successful skirmish against my kin. It was nothing but a skirmish, but to the lowest order who had flocked to my thoughts of freedom, potentials never considered awakened. I gave no advisement to them other than the caution of Michael's wrath as many took human lovers. Grand families were produced.

Our joy multiplied among a growing community.

The changes to our street were subtle. Residents living there all their lives suddenly fell to great fortunes and a nagging notion to emigrate. Young couples happily expecting moved in, fooling estate agents by sending Lisbeth to do the paperwork as I instructed their partners on the basics of furnishing, aesthetic fashion among material beings, and sorted them into a capable organization.

Once again, I appointed Shaytan as the head of my retinue. Charged with the defense of our quiet street, he placed guards on rooftops, in the alleys, and along the bridges, commanded to keep constant watch for the Host. Those not appointed to guard were left to make of their time with what they did. Some spent it with their lovers to conceive more little miracles.

In many ways we became human, and it was good.

Though able to hide our wings and alter our appearances, it became a daily occurrence for Lisbeth and I to have our milk delivered by an angel, my ale served by someone I had known for eons, or to give a subtle nod to the well-dressed men loitering at the corners of our favorite parks and side-streets, our secret guards.

It was nothing like the Platinum Polis, this kingdom forged out of rebellion, and in those days I coveted it beyond any sense of what was really happening around me.

"It is puzzling," Shaytan said to me as we lounged on a park bench along the southern bank of the Thames. "That this Christ would set about pursuing a ministry of peace and charity, not certainty and reward. It seems a clear deviation from everything before."

Our wings hidden from mortal eyes, we seemed like any two young men in their coats and umbrellas on a rainy day, enjoying the wharfs and our coffees in the world's greatest metropolis. Considering him for a long moment, I answered with the same shrug I had given every time he raised these same notions I grappled with.

"We shall see, my brother," I said, for I held affection for Shaytan in those days when there was only the duplicity of his meeting with Lisbeth between us. From that, I had only reaped goodness. "We shall see. At some point, he will have to address my challenges. In those responses, we will know the fullness of his vision and intent. Until then, I say we turn our attention back to our defenses. Your battle with Michael above Jordan was a grand success, but we must prepare ourselves toward the next incursion."

"It was fortuitous you discerned Michael's attempt to retaliate against you, but my lord, perhaps—"

"I'm no lord, Shaytan."

"Of course, Lucifer."

"Neither of us is above the other," I said, as I did to all angels sworn to me. "It is by refusing to bow to him or anyone we find the freedom and cause to be as we are and live as we live. As is our right."

"Of course, Lucifer," he replied.

"Lucifer! Lucifer! Lucifer!" One of the sentries named Leato ran down the concrete walkway of the wharf, waving her arms in the air. Heavy with her own baby on the way, she grabbed my hand. "It's time! Glory, glory, it is time!"

The shock set in. I became like every mortal who knew the time had come to put themselves aside, to comprehend the enormity of the wave as I berthed the currents of wonder, anxiety, all the way to an intense desire to see this wonderful little person who is you without all the mistakes. Every child, no matter who they are or how they come, are blessings.

Shaytan grabbed my other hand as he and Leato hauled me from the bench looking out upon the Thames. In a blink we were in front of the gray door of my family's London apartment. We had no need of a hospital, doctors or nurses, able to mitigate all risks on the way to a safe delivery.

Neither did we know what would happen the moment the baby arrived, the first of many.

I was sitting next to Lisbeth as the contractions started, her and I alone save for our two attendants, Beherit and Leato. My wife rested her head against my shoulder as she breathed through the first exertion. In a flash of brightness and purified water, the baby pushed free into a silent, absurd world, but one far less so the moment her eyes saw mine.

Deevi is a Punjab word for "lamp".

My darkness lifted. I saw all things God saw and knew how wrong I had been.

My rebellion ended there.

I never realized the terror of being alone, unable to contend with no answers above the ones we make. I wasn't ready for the hammer of certainty that pounded lightning into my soul the moment I concluded those fears, doubts, and questions had to be put aside for the sake of one with far, far less.

Children are the truth-makers. God, the first orphan, made us to help him find whatever it was.

And Deevi revealed it all to me.

Then the world returned. As quickly as she arrived, wet and wailing in sounds forever imprinted on my heart, it rushed back in as Shaytan stormed into our bedroom.

"My lord," he said. "Gabriel has arrived!"

Our baby swaddled and already sucking at her breast, Lisbeth pressed herself back against me in prevention of my exit. "Lucifer," she whispered, her fear fresh in a moment when there should have been none.

Deevi broke out in a sudden cry, drawing the attention of everyone in the room.

The suddenness of her presence drove a silence that lasted as long as I needed to measure my decision. Like God, I had different choices then, and I planned to make far different decisions than the ones my parent had. Slowly extracting myself so I could allow Lisbeth to attend the baby, I nodded to Shaytan to lead the way.

Lisbeth caught my hand. "Lucifer," she said, "what do I do? What do we do? What about—"

"Nothing is going to happen to the baby," I said. "Nothing is happening to anyone's baby in this community."

Gabriel stood at the mouth of the street's northern end, their hands held out in the pose of peace. Hundreds of rebellious angels pointed silver swords at them. The Messenger met the points coolly, eying each wielder before I turned the corner. The rest sensed it as they lowered their blades in unison.

Like the most disciplined of uniformed soldiers, every one of them dropped to a knee as I passed. I frowned hoping Gabriel would see my apprehension. We came face to face. Shaytan stood at my back, the only one not to show deference.

"Lucifer," Gabriel said, speaking first.

"Why are you here, Gabriel?" I asked. "Who watches him?"

"The others do," they said. "I came—"

I noticed the tears in their eyes. "Gabriel?"

"I didn't come because I was sent," they said. "I came to meet the baby."

I took my sibling up in my arms as they sobbed against my chest, rubbing their side, and whispering every ounce of my love to their bravery. Without another word, I carried us both to my home, my heart, and the wonderful little girl who brought meaning to every single day before and after. Lost in something so new to us, my dearest in heaven chose the role of an auntie, meeting my family for the first time.

29

CHOP SUEY

I would hope by now, priest, you would see that my rebellion did not initially take the form of an armed one. Michael appeared with an army above the deserts of Jordan, attacking me simply for talking to my father. I only organized my forces to protect myself, my wife, and provide space for those angels turning from God, not to spread violence and hatred.

Did I order them to attack the Platinum Polis? Or Christ? His mortal body, no matter his power, would have fallen against a single angel. I demonstrated that as well.

But it was not my order to give.

I did not pester Christ after or conspire with Shaytan on some great war. I simply lived my life with my wife and daughter and allowed things to be. For a while, it seemed the peace I afforded myself and those loyal to my views placated them as well. Our community had our children, set our patrols, and lived in a slice of South London out of space, time, and worry.

That peace ended when Deevi met the other children and I forgot what angels were.

The wings of a Nephilim, of the material yet imbued with the indestructible powers each feather contained, did not appear until their teenage years, but that seemed small next to their newborn powers.

Those presented larger concerns.

Imagine a baby reaching for an apple, but instead of waiting for you to give them it, the fruit manifests before them. Or a toy. Or a knife. Or a wild animal.

Try to picture their first words, crystal as if they had spoken every language before they knew their own and were only waiting to let you know about it. Attempt to discern how to navigate explaining the world when, mortal or immortal, mundane or divine, you cannot cover the harsh reality because behind their questions was an irresistible power to answer.

I came to know God's inherent struggle as he struggled with the flesh.

If you are good, children are a blessing of endurance. If you are good, most adults are children. If you are not, you end up seeking power over the things that matter less than the happiness of your offspring.

Jesus ran into this problem as his ministry grew, drawing the poor, the desperate, and the good to his promise of a better world for those who eschewed power, cleaved to peace, almost to the point of non-interference if one believes in taxes like he does.

Yes, it was shocking, but uplifting in a way that could not be understated. When he spoke on the mount of the God within all his creations, of truths hard and soft on the soul, but nevertheless promised faith and forgiveness according to the Law of the day, he understood the responsibility of what he had undertaken. He shepherded a flock instead of lording over servants.

He became the father we always needed. That I wanted to be.

The greatest rulers are uncrowned. They dissolve the illusion of division. Comprehending this, how would any good ruler place themselves in hierarchies doomed to fail? The fate of Rome was sealed the moment it became an empire, and like all empires, there was nothing to be done.

The Temple, however, was a different story.

If it is the home of God, would God have allowed acts and exchanges against his laws under the roof of his manse? How could any priest stand by and truly say they serve their creator while watching the sin of hatred, greed, and lust play out in the halls beyond the tabernacle? Why should we be concerned when prosperity outweighs charity? Did the desire for ritual and recognition outweigh duty to those the farthest in the darkness, who those same priests were so easy to shun without any of the work done to better them?

These were all fair questions Christ asked, all the while feeding the hungry, healing the sick, and casting out the spirits of the old world. Nothing of Perdition harried the mortal realms yet, for no Perdition existed to provide what would crawl out of it. Most of the time he dealt with mental illness and plagues, things none understood as natural to the design, as was the death they all feared so much. But be sure, he tamed spirits and gods who deigned to diminish the dignity of mortal kind, fighting many battles unrecorded in history.

He discovered the same loneliness in him resided in everything he had given to ensure otherwise. We were lonely, frightened children like him. It's why he left those priests alone at first. Their answers didn't threaten the purifying love he shed day after day.

The difficult part about love is its revelation of what's wrong.

How could he tell others to adhere to kindness and charity as he watched those pervert every sense of the notion under the auspice of tyrannical interpretations?

I only found out about the clearing of the Temple when Gabriel arrived to inform me of Christ's crucifixion.

They had beaten him beyond recognition, his face pulped and torn. I was shocked he had the will to walk out into the street on a late morning I'd never forget. The sun shone red in the east.

Under the order of Pontius Pilate at the behest of the Temple, Romans scoured this redeemer of so many, most of all the twelve men and the wife that had followed him out of sincere admiration. None stood that day to defend him, cowed by the bloodthirsty crowds. Every single one of those twelve friends abandoned him as the imperial weight of keeping the peace lowered.

Blood dripped from the rents on his shoulders and back, down to a flayed buttock ridged in torn tissue. Someone in the cruelest mockery had shoved a crown of thorns on his head, blinding him in a sting of red after they beat it with a reed. After a coat of spit, they tossed a dead soldier's mantle about his shoulders and forced him into the square. Hundreds of the Pharisee's disciples, their palms curled by the silvers they carried to the site almost in achievement, spat globs on him as he was forced to carry his own cross.

In the limestone streets of Jerusalem under Roman dominance, he dragged the great weight of a tall beam bisected by a shorter one, almost a hundred pounds heavier than the standard rack the condemned were burdened to bear. He plodded, staggered, but never once cried or begged to be helped. This healer of the blind, the afflicted, had taken every step to take these steps.

God marched to his death.

Now we panicked.

Gabriel and I arrived in the correct time and space, invisible amongst the spectators. Rotten vegetables, heels of old bread, and stones flew from all directions, covering our father in refuse.

"Stop him, Lucifer!" The Messenger clutched my arm. "Tell him to stop doing this!"

Before I advanced, the other archangels manifested around us at different points among the crowd.

Aware of each other, Michael and the rest focused on my immediate reaction to the Protector. He had arrived with a gleaming sword in his hand, a far cry from the blades of light and gravity we summoned. Forged of Ur-steel and hilted by the finest smiths gracing the Platinum Polis' courts, he raised the Sword of Truth at me.

The other six siblings froze amid the seething mob of Pharisees, Sadducees, pagans enjoying the spectacle, along with a few Essenes who had come for silent witness to one they quietly favored. Among the despairing, the healed, the damnable, my brother glared in a gritted sneer.

One of the Pharisees shouted in venomous glee. "Hail! Hail the King of the Jews!"

More spit, more projectiles.

Christ broke between Michael and I, a bleeding effigy paraded in a gross display of influence. The broken stare of our father sapped our hatred. Michael dropped his sword, starting forward when Raphael grabbed him from the side. The confusion, the despair, came flooding out.

Michael spewed it at me, lost for a better target. "This is your fault, rebel! You and your fallen ways! Look at what you have caused!"

Drained, dry, and hungry after a beating no mortal should have survived, Christ's march slowed from a limp one of Pilate's guardsmen had inflicted. One of the centurions at the front, annoyed the moment his prisoner stopped, dragged a Cyrenian traveler out of the audience named Simon.

"Him," Gabriel said to me, pointing out this poor victim. "Possess him, Lucifer! Take his body and go save our father!"

"We will not," I shouted at them as I marched to the front of the crowd, phasing past the bodies between Christ, Simon, and I. He noticed me as the Romans forced the traveler behind us, shoving him onto his knees and keeping him until he shouldered the heavy load.

"Help him," the soldier screamed. He rapped Simon across the back. A strike almost equal to the cut itself, the Cyrenian howled as he collapsed face first in the dirt. The other centurions chided their brother for holding them up longer.

Michael met Christ on his right, I on his left, both of us filling the void ahead of him.

"Don't crowd," he whispered at us, chuckling through bloody lips.

"You have to stop this, father," I said. "You don't have to do this."

"Shush, Lucifer." He blinked at me past his concussion. "Just-just watch me, son."

"Please, Father," Michael said, on his knees as Simon lifted the long end of the cross. The sudden movement bent Christ, knocking the wooden effigy off his shoulder. I caught it so it did not fall, a grace none witnessed beyond adding it to a list of grievances this tortured man had supposedly caused them.

"Pick it up," a rich robed priest shouted amongst crying women and wailing babes. "Pick it up, Son of God! Show us the great strength God has given you!"

"Command us," I said to Christ, knelt at his side. "Command me! Father! Command me! I end my rebellion! Command me!"

"Don—don—" Christ spat a glob of blood in the dirt. "Help me put it on my shoulder."

"No," Michael cried. "No! No! Please!"

Why was he doing this? Why was he allowing this to happen? He who made the multiverse, crafting pin-prick explosions ushering in wonder and glory and terror and all things divine, embarked on a rolling suicide. Every reason I could think of pointed to me, my faults, my failings as a son. I acted on instinct, lifting the cross with one hand to set it back on his shoulder.

"Help me, Michael," I said, hurried. "Pick him up."

"No," Michael said, shaking his head at us. He stamped his fists in the ground like a bull.

Christ spoke. "Michael."

There was no argument after that. My brother and I shared one crazed, despairing exchange before we reached down, using our own hands, and lifted up a mortal man to bear his last weight. A sigh and a smile, he nodded to the ground as he trudged.

"What are we doing?" Michael asked.

"Shut up and follow me, brother!" I looked back to where I left Gabriel, giving them a signal to gather the rest.

Michael and I flanked Christ on his way to the hill. Simon, the Romans, and the three most important women in his life made up the final procession. None of us were seen save by the one we had come to save, but he fixed on denying us.

The absolute terror of a parent being taken claimed me the hardest.

"I was wrong," I said. "You have your reasons! The mysteries are yours to unravel! I should not have questioned! Please, father, let me take your place! I can bear my sin! I shall bear my sin! Please! Please stop!"

"Please stop, Father." Michael pulled on the ragged sleeve of Christ's robe like a child begging attention. "Please!"

"I have my reasons," Christ said as he dragged the cross through the gates of Jerusalem. "They are quite close to me now."

"But you need not show me," I said. "If we are your reasons, then we are here to proclaim! Lo, I bend lower to you!" I dropped down to hands and feet, my wings in the air as I kept pace with his march. "See me, father? I bend myself! Please, there is no need for this! We can fix whatever I did! Some other way than this!"

"It's not you that needs fixing," Christ said in an emphatic response. "Forgive them, for they do not know what they do."

It halted me.

"What are you doing?" Michael said, continuing to keep pace.

I knew. Somehow, I knew what was happening, why he was doing it. Any fear I had of universes ending, continuums ceasing, fled to a certainty I could do nothing to deter this man on a mission.

Michael pleaded all the way to the hill of Golgotha.

The other archangels questioned me, but in the horror of the event, I've forgotten their pleadings. By then the word had gotten out to the greater city that Jesus of Nazareth was on his way to his death. To the shock of the Pharisees and the Romans assigned to the task, many of the citizens emptied out to witness the travesty. Their supporters, once thronging the streets, were swallowed by tens of thousands.

There was a reason Pilate begged mercy for Christ.

No Christian has a sincere understanding of the undeniable misery and violence waiting for him the moment he dropped the cross at the foot of a small hill. A hole had already been dug for the cruciform. Two men baked under the hot sun, their mangled bodies subjected to the worst of Judea's elements. One had been bound for plotting revolution against an emperor thousands of miles away. The other was a common thief caught too many times.

The soldiers stripped off the cloak they had thrown atop Christ's bleeding body. They gambled over it in a quick game of dice as they ordered the workers to secure him. Forced down on his back against the main post, every witness braced as his arms and crossed legs were bound.

At the top of the cruciform someone nailed a sign written in Greek, Aramaic, and Hebrew:

"This is the King of the Jews."

The part left out, especially by the preachers, is the maul.

One of the soldiers, angry he had failed his dice toss, picked up the sledge and sauntered over. Without hesitance, he brought it down on the trapped man's right knee.

Mary Magdalene's shrieks covered the sound of the breaking.

Standing at his mashed, bloody feet, Michael gaped in total horror as bones and sinew gave way. A few others, whose names Christ counted among his friends, retched their meals onto the sand or pissed themselves in shame. Wincing through every blow, my father remained stoic beneath the congealing red mask his crown had painted onto his face. The guard broke his legs in many places, leaving them pulpy lengths of black and purple.

Exhausted by the time he flung the hammer down, one of the Roman's comrades tossed him a wine skin as the workers came to finish. They nailed Christ's hands to the horizontal beam, pierced his ankles together with an iron stake, all for the grisly benefit of the ritual, the warning, and sheer spectacle.

Watching from our places as he was raised up, the sorrow of my brethren was revealed. Unable to contain our emotions, the moon sped from its orbit and aligned with the earth. Darkness spread under the sudden eclipse. Storm clouds rushed from all points in the sky, black as pitch.

A hush fell upon those who watched the sun disappear.

For those who had seen the fruits of their lies and machinations, the silence raised their voices. "He saved others," howled the Pharisees in glee, "let him save himself now if he is the chosen one, the Messiah of God!"

Those who supported the Temple laughed.

The Roman who had shattered Christ's legs reappeared, lofting his wineskin toward the hung man. "Yes, man! If you're King of the Jews, then save yourself! Come on! Give us a miracle!"

The cruel laughed along with his jeering.

"Are you not the Messiah? Save yourself!"

"Save, save, save yourself," the Pharisees chanted, clapping their hands to a mocking beat.

Michael seethed. He posted himself in front of the cross, facing the onlookers in defiance though they could not see him. Angry tears dripped down his golden face. We all wept, unable to keep ourselves apart. Gabriel and I went to him first, gathering him on our arms before Raphael put down his horn and joined us. Selaphiel led Ramiel and Raguel, and side by side, we took up our places beside the Protector.

In a moment I hope will one day bear something more, I laid my hand on Michael's shoulder. "I'm sorry," I whispered into his ear.

He clasped my hand where I laid it.

The hours pressed, each minute an epoch. He wheezed, he muttered, and groaned as gravity pulled the weight of his body down on his pierced wrists and broken legs, hanging him at an unnatural angle.

It was not until three in the afternoon he raised his head.

He looked out at the Sapiens first, those daring, wonderful, lamentable creatures of his Grand Design, then to us, its first shepherds.

The miracle was never in the exorcisms, the healing, the cleansing, or the sermons. It is not found in the bread and wine, his flesh and blood, nor is it found in supplication to those who claim his works as they do his words. The miracles were not found in what came next.

It was in his endless, boundless, forgiving love he had for all, including those who killed him.

He understood the problem.

Raising his eyes heavenward, Jesus cried out in a loud voice. "Father, into your hands I commend my spirit!"

And then God died, mind, body, and soul, before our very eyes.

THE DRAGONSLAYER

The demons crowded atop the dragon's back, swinging their legs as they dangled from his gross wings and cheered as she stared into the serpent's eyes. One personification of God's great foe and Lucifer's former accomplice, he tilted his head in a cocksure manner, the slimed fur around his neck and face sticking out in all directions. His army chanted dire songs in Enochian, crude hymnals she had known since childhood twisted into violent promises of murder, rape, and slavery.

Smiling a scaled smile, the Devil graded Deevi from afar, assessing his prize.

Perdition's song grew as the sun crested on a smoking horizon, a red dawn failing to throw back the shadows upon to Ireland. The sky had soaked to a green-gray color, poisoned by the stench off the fields of dead.

"You must not do this, George," Deevi said. "Just give us time."

The mortal knight surveyed the dried-out lake past the broken shores of Station Island, covered in the teeming horde. Stoic to the obvious outcome, he shrugged. "I'm not too worried about it, to be honest."

She turned her head to the saint.

George did not meet her gaze, his focus on the dragon. "I was made for this."

Deevi furrowed her brow. "What?"

"I know. I know how mad it all sounds. But look, there's a dragon." He glanced her way. "A lady in distress. The hordes of hell. A cause." He sighed, at ease. "I've been waiting for one for a long, long time."

"You won't walk away," she said. "And after everything, you shouldn't—"

"Hush, Deevi," George said. "Don't be a hypocrite."

She bit back her words. Frustrated by his keen awareness of her willingness to sacrifice herself, she checked behind her to see how the rest spent their small respite.

The archangels conspired before the altar. Michael led the conversation with Gabriel to his right, heads bowed in contemplation as their general explained he and George's escape plan. Lost in the rows of pews between the altar and the entrance, Merry and Daniel huddled together. The veves the Vodun priestess had inscribed into the cathedral's shattered entrance glowed bright blue, away from the pure purple they had started as.

Deevi snorted in anger. "What am I supposed to tell Patrick?"

George broke in a barking, deep laugh. "Oh, well..." He steadied and swallowed as her power latched on, a sincere grin on his face. "He'll get it."

"What does that even mean?" Deevi asked.

"Miracles only happen through sacrifice, Deevi. They're found in the willingness to do the stupid and impossible and improbable in the face of utter annihilation, often for something small. Like some girl," he nodded toward her, "or a child. Or to make a voice heard in the din of lies and noise. But those require more."

"And that's what you and Patrick do?" she asked in a bitter tone. "Give up more and more and more?"

"If we must," George said. "Her name was Sabra. I found something just like that outside for Sabra. Not for me, or God, or even the idea of getting those savages willing to sacrifice her to see Christ. 'I went out there to save Sabra.' So I think Patrick will get it if you tell him that."

"It seems very unfair."

"Don't take it up with me," he said. "I'm just doing what I'm supposed to."

"Says who?"

"God," Michael announced from behind them. They both turned to find the holy retinue, glimmering in their shining armor and armed with their blades of rarefied light.

Her dark armor dull in luster by comparison, Deevi met her uncle's gaze with silent contempt. "I still don't agree with this."

"We have little choice, Nephilim." The Protector looked down from his tall height to Saint George. "The moment the Vodun priestess breaks her glyphs—"

"Veves," said Gabriel. "They're called veves."

"When she breaks the glyphs," Michael continued, undeterred, "Gabriel will initiate a phase shift in this reality. Using an Enochian circle, they will open a gate that will take us to a safe location not far from here. Satan's power and the collection of his evils have hemmed us to a distance, but once we are there, Raphael will take hold of Daniel O'Brien and I of Ms. Joslin. We will escape the area until we are able to complete a greater circle and remove ourselves further. From there, we will commune with God and seek His orders."

Michael cast his attention to George. "Do you understand? We will need time."

"How much?" The Dragonslayer asked.

"As much as you can give," Gabriel replied. "I will need minutes, but I do not expect—"

George raised a hand to stay the Messenger. "You'll get them." He met Michael, undaunted by the winged giant. "Have you considered my requests?"

"I have," Michael said, who stepped back and ushered him toward the altar. "This way, knight."

Each archangel poured bits of their own metals into a well of flame Michael summoned to forge Saint George's armor. Out of the breath of their words, the breastplate was shaped, along with the shining greaves, pauldrons, and the holy hide of his war skirt and sandals. A shield followed, kite-like and as wide as the rider's back, yet lighter than air.

"I didn't have to deal with open ground when I fought the dragon at Silene," George said as he watched Michael create a helm out of the glowing palms of his hands. "I lucked into a ravine."

"He has to move his bulk, no matter how much room he has," Michael said in his taciturn way. "Satan is also prideful. Pridefulness is the greatest of sins for a reason. He will falter in his."

"Today or later?" George asked.

Michael frowned at his question. "Go dress. I shall prepare your lance and wait for you by the doorway."

George evaluated each piece of the celestial armor as the Protector paced away.

The archangels waited for their leader by the altar converted into Merry's shrine to the Lwas. To the surprise of many, Gabriel revived the dead flowers in a vase smuggled from New York, re-lit the dead wicks of three-quarter spent candles, adding a comforting ambiance against the toxic atmosphere outside. Using their sword, they drew a wide circle constructed of Enochian symbols and phrases Deevi recognized from her place by the door. Gabriel sang in a mix of Enochian and Hebrew as they stepped along the inner edge of the circle.

The glyphs sparked silver as they passed. With every new light, an archangel joined the chant, save Michael who stood to the side shaping a spear point out of heavenly steel and his thumbs.

The stress in her head and neck cascaded together before one of those strange, sudden realizations snapped her back to the present, away from thoughts of defeat. Deevi searched the sanctuary for Merry and Daniel.

She marched along the perimeter of the room to reach them. "Merry. Daniel."

They startled, broken from their quiet fixation on the archangel's dance, but did not move to meet her. An awkwardness set, one Deevi suspected always existed. In fact, when she caught the priestess's bright brown eyes, she understood how much she had taken from this innocent woman and how much more she was about to demand.

"How are you both?" she asked.

Daniel spoke first, his focus still on the ritual. "Oh, fuck, I don't know."

"I'm terrible. What's the plan?" Merry asked. "Where are we going?"

"As far as we can," Deevi looked at their feet, unable to meet their gazes. "Saint George is staying behind."

The priestess's hand flew and caught Deevi full on the cheek, a loud smack which caused no pain other than the sharp note it produced. Tears immediately claimed Merry, and she shook in the Irish gunman's arms as he grabbed her. She sobbed, cursing through her scrunched, reddening face.

"You selfish little girl," Merry sputtered as she fought Daniel's hold. "You take and take and take!"

"No, she didn't."

They turned in the direction of the knight as he emerged in full armor. Gone was the man who had clad himself somewhere between military spartan and London posh. Beneath the horse-hair crested helm arose an ancient spirit made flesh, proud and filled and ready.

Saint George the Dragonslayer, patron of knighthood and England, came to his friends with a serenity never expressed before on his hard, handsome face. A shield looped to one shoulder by a fine strap, he used the eleven-foot lance he carried like a walking stick. The perfect curves of his embossed breastplate and pauldrons, gold upon silver upon the purest platinum, shone of its own inner light.

"George, please don't," said Merry, caring nothing for his glories. "It's not worth it. Not after what they did to us."

The pair of survivors, both victims of God's mysteries, embraced like siblings. The agony of being near them, in their lives, tore Deevi apart. Tears flowed, but she sniffed hard through the first sob, keeping the rest out of shame.

"Shush." George rubbed the priestess' back with his gauntleted hand. "Not in front of Michael and the rest," he whispered into her face. "We can't let them see us, can we?"

Merry snorted sadness and laughed against the golden lines of his helm, her dark nose separated from his pale ridge. They found a way to smile for each other.

"I have to go," George whispered to Merry. "You remember what I told you to do after we got out? On that flight to Dublin?"

She nodded. "Yeah. Yeah, I do."

"You will do that for me, won't you?"

"Of course, of course," she wailed against his chest.

"Good," he said. "Now when the time comes, I need you to go with the archangels, Merry. I know you don't want to, but I need you to. I need you to come back and get Patrick when it's all over. I need you to keep him going." George's expression faltered for a moment, his serenity inflicted by sadness. "We three got to keep it together, right?"

"Right," Merry heaved through her racking sobs.

"Now let me go," he whispered, pulling away. "Time to g—"

"No," Merry said, her arms around his neck and shoulders. "No! No! No!"

George laughed through his tears. "Now, now! You made a promise!"

He slowly pried her from him before he nodded to Daniel. The gunman approached and caught of the Vodun priestess, who clung until she dropped down to her knees, a mess of weeping. The final farewells left to run down his bare cheeks inside his helmet as he turned away, Deevi followed close behind him, stunned by the sheer weight of this warrior choosing to die for her.

Michael waited at the door. The Protector stared hard in the dragon's direction longer than any normal being would, filled with a hatred so intense it dampened his grace. His blazing eyes, locked to Satan's, flared as he stood in the center of the cathedral entryway.

The demons pushing at the banks of Station Island, each one of them a fallen angel of God ruined for their refusal to obey, placed a special zeal into every corrupted Enochian phrase aimed toward the cathedral. These took harder, harsher notes when Deevi appeared with George in the doorway.

"Get out of their sight," Michael said to her.

"No," Deevi replied, undaunted by Satan's leering, hungering gaze. "Get him ready. I'll provide a distraction until then."

"Very little to do left," George said, shaking out his shoulders. He hefted the lance in his right hand, brought his shield close in the other, and took his first full look of the battlefield. His pale gray eyes scanned the front line of demons. "Unless you have a way to find me a horse. It would make the fight a bit easier."

"What horse would you like?" Michael asked.

"What do you mean, 'what would I bloody like'?" George asked. "I don't actually expect you to—"

"I can," said the archangel. "Any horse."

Flabbergasted by the patron of all warriors, the knight's expression drew inward, and for the first time he wept. Not out of doubt, or fear, or anything dark. "You remember Peyo, Michael? I would love to see Peyo again."

"Close your eyes, Saint George," said Michael.

Deevi did not blink, but in the second George shut his eyes and opened them again a horse manifested. Finely appointed in both muscle and proportions, the silken smooth flanks of the stallion's brown hide glistened in a golden, heavenly light. Marked on his pale gray nose with a vertical white stripe running between his gentle black eyes, he nuzzled his long-lost comrade, the division of species washed away by love to greater callings.

"Oh, Peyo," George whispered to his horse. "Oh, my best friend. To see you again, here at the end..."

George leapt into the saddle, alive in his final moments. Watching the joy on his face, the way the reins came alive in his hands and how the horse responded, drove a final stake of doubt into Deevi.

"George," she said, dumbfounded. "I'm not worth this. Why are you doing this?"

The same power she used to reap the truth from Patrick plied it from the horsed warrior, cracking a smile through the slots of his helm. "I am a knight, Deevi. I defend women, children, honor, and the glory of God from evil. It's about my duty to do what is asked."

"But what is asked?"

"To love something enough to die for it," both George and Michael said in unison.

The Protector drew out the Sword of Truth and offered its hilt to the knight. "I can reclaim it whenever I wish," Michael said. "Go with God, Saint George."

30

MIRACLES

Screams end. The absence of them is where the impact lays its greatest claim.

Like any other corpse, he was taken off his rack, his woman dressed him in oils, and for what indignity they could heap upon him, the remains of Jesus Christ were consigned to whatever cave he could find in the desert, a warning from the Temple that any attempting a proper burial would make their own journey to the cross. With the help of a kindly lord named Joseph of Arimathea they found a resting place, who also paid to have the body wrapped in linen and placed on his property.

The disciples hid in their homes, fearful of Rome and the Pharisees. The women did as women were always forced to do and picked up after them. My brethren returned to the Platinum Polis, unable to cope with the loss of our Father. It went unspoken my presence was no longer welcomed.

Ashamed, I guarded his resting place for three days and three nights.

Being First means nothing in the absence of love.

This hammered home as I spent zeptosecond after zeptosecond

staring at the stone they had rolled in front of the tomb's entrance. It should have been infinitely clear how I arrived here, but like the great mysteries only known to their maker, I couldn't say. Had I been forced to doubt and defy, or had I chosen it when He asked me my thoughts on creation? What was the point of all this? How had I fallen?

Had I fallen?

I had shouted and screamed and demanded. Love me, love me, love me.

But was it ever a question of love? Was that what he had asked for? Was my response to his questions simply to love *me*?

It rained through the days and nights. Many times I thought of abandoning my post for my wife's smile, the touch of my daughter's hand to my face, but every raindrop fixed me into place. The world scoured my illumined flesh until I gleamed like a torch. My sorrow fed its blaze.

Until Sunday. Sunday, Sunday, Sunday.

After midnight I awoke to sound of grinding rock. The boulder slid to the side under the power of his gentle hands.

Christ emerged from the tomb, bearing no sign of his death.

"Hello, Lucifer," he said. "I'm very happy you're here."

I struggled to my feet, unable to steady my wings as my light-body convulsed. I babbled like a babe overjoyed to see their parent. I rushed forward and tripped. Undeterred, I crawled toward my father, who swept me up in his arms. I heaved, taking a full breath for the first time since his slaying, the agony of my guilt seeping out in every sob. He held me, rubbing my back as I bawled.

"Peace," he whispered as I clung to him. "Peace, my Morningstar." Something broke in his voice. "I'm sorry no one listened to you. How you spoke truth and were denied."

"How?" I asked, blubbering. "How—how are you here? I saw you. I saw you die."

Christ coughed at the question. "Oh, one of those mysteries." He grunted at a thought and glanced skyward, studying the stars he forged long ago. "Better than some, though."

"But nothing dead comes back!"

"Right?" Freeing me to take my place before him, he examined the holes the Roman nails had left in his wrists. "Truly, Lucifer, I did not know what would happen when I died. I couldn't tell you *this* would happen," he said, almost surprised. "But it had to be done."

"And what was done?"

He loosed a hearty laugh. "It takes a lot for someone to look at themselves and see fault. We never want to do it because we all fear that somehow, someway, we are fallen for doing so. For a long time, I felt that way, and it led me to do a lot of things I wish I had done differently." He sobered and looked at me. "So many of them with you."

To hear my father, the one who I had adored longer than anything else, acknowledge me sent me into a spiral. Before the next breath I had my face in my hands, weeping mercury into my palms.

Christ stroked the area under my wings. "I know, Lucifer. And I'm so sorry. I would like to say I knew what was happening, but the hard luck of it was…well, I had to learn the limits of my un-limitedness. I had to stop being a ruler and be a parent. I asked you, 'what do you think of my work?' because I did not know anything other than to order it, and no sense of measure what I am—was…" He shrugged the lack of language. "I'm immeasurable, if there is a word. I have every-thing in a universe when everything else does not. When one lacks an understanding of their providence but cares nothing about the poverty, have they truly been blessed with anything other than more limited things? In my hubris, I imagined to know all things by my omnipotence, my omniscience, and my omnipresence. But what are those things when one cannot place in measure the glory that has been bestowed on them?"

"What do you mean?" I asked.

"Oh, the eye of the needle and all that. It is those with nothing who discover the truth of this Grand Design I have made, this kingdom for my children, and its greatest treasures." He raised his hand to my glowing shoulder. "Like my children. Your children, Lucifer. My kingdom is to be garden for the little and the least, feeding them on love and kindness as much as I can with roof, food, and drink. I could not have learned that without you, you know."

"How so?" I asked, shocked to be credited.

His grip tightened on my shoulder. "Despite being bound in this," he said, tapping his heart with the other hand, "I still know the permeations of all thought, as I control Time and the material. I knew your thoughts. I know your thoughts and will forever."

The revelation made me darken, my shame belittling me before his luminous grace.

"No, son, do not do this to yourself. Please, listen," said Christ. "Listen closely: there is no shame in how you felt during the times you struggled. I struggled."

"You?"

"Yes, me," he said. "I had no sense of what mortal feeling was save for the feeling, and when one feels it for the first time there is no reference, no words to give it. All I had was those I could watch around me—my children—and how they would react in their own ways. It was my failure to learn in those times."

"But all I have is anger," I said. "Pride. I allowed myself to fly free in my passions."

"But look at the substance of your passions, Lucifer," he rebutted. "It was trepidation you felt turning Jedidiah to his lust. A sense of decency drove you to slay the Batemans, though I wish you had chosen differently. You felt disgust in the face of slavers, rulers, and tyrants, including the greatest one: myself. No one else would have dared." He hummed in a satisfied, mischievous note. "Especially your siblings. I also came to realize they were so frightened of displeasing me I needed someone who wasn't afraid to ask the needed questions. The only way a king refuses tyranny is when he thinks to the thoughts of others. You caused me to think of your reactions, your concerns about my Grand Design, because those implications spoke not only to who and what you were, but also who and what I was. What I am and will forever be."

"By my limits, you discovered a need for your own?"

"Exactly! I was missing one final ingredient—actual limitation. Until I braved the possibility of it, nothing I did or would do would have any value. Nothing could be amended to make this right. And so I took the flesh, hoping to unlock these final mysteries."

"Which you have."

"No! No, there are some things I still don't know. I don't think I am meant to. And perhaps that is the point," he said, more to himself than me. "I wished to know everything all at once—then, here, and later— because I was uncertain of what sort of future I might be leading myself down. I worried more about the result without considering my action in it." He raised his thick brows in thought. "What I figured out up on that crucifix is that any sort of control I impose will only be met with rebellion. Nature must be allowed to be, at its own paces and to its own ends. If I—we—are to discover the truth, and therefore discover the nature within all of us, we must learn to listen."

"You mean the Holy Spirit," I said.

In answer, Christ held out his arms to display himself. "Before this flesh, I remain the Father, but by experiencing life and death, then transcending it, I have become the Son as well. This will confuse many, as it contains ineffable things. What binds us together, be it you, or I, or the stars is the spirit imbued in all things." He grinned. "Like my granddaughter. Little Deevi. I who once resided outside and above all things became all things, and now have discovered myself in all things. It has required a deep, deep change in how I will perform my tasks."

"But how can God be different than what God already is?" I questioned.

"Another very good question I had thirty-three years to consider before you asked." Stroking his bearded chin, Christ wrinkled his forehead in thought. "Lucifer, my mistake was trying to dictate to others: love me, worship me, fear me, respect me, but that does not work in a universe where others seek me, The Absolute, within them. So I tried to fall upon philosophy, religion, and the spirit. I thought those things and the laws which govern others would deter the worst of the impulses, only to discover those feelings exist whether I bade them or not."

He finally understood.

"There are things that must be done," he said. "Some will ask, 'must they be?', but to know the fullness of the universe is to understand the duty in saying 'yes', but how will this be done? I have learned, especially now..." he brought his arms back to his chest, the holes through his wrists pressed to his front. He sighed deep. "It is better to come at things with love, Lucifer, or not at all. If I am to do things, I must do it through love and love alone. Otherwise I should let my children, as I would myself, be as they are. Hopefully all will find their way to salvation, as I have, and be at my side as much as they are within me. I made plenty of room, after all, and can make more."

To say I was quieted by his grace was an understatement. "What about the others? Gabriel may understand, but the rest may not. What of Michael?"

"You will have to have faith in them as much I do. Especially Michael." Christ raised his head to the skies. "Speak of them now."

Gabriel alighted on the soil before us, but their legs gave out. Onto their hands and knees they fell, weeping in total wonder. As before, our father rushed to the rescue, gathering the Messenger while they cried deep into his chest. Christ soothed until they found themselves, caught by the exact same questions I had. As before, my lord revealed the working of his greatest miracle.

Dawn and the week's first day crept on the horizon's edge, and noticing, Christ faced it.

"Alright," he said, smiling at the frown of light. "I must go for a little bit. Settle my last earthly affairs. There are two women on the way here. I need you both to be very kind to them and tell them what happened. One of them I..." He took his eyes from the sun for a moment. "I love her very much. Please tell her I'll see her soon."

"Father?" Gabriel asked before he slipped off into the garden of the Arimatheas.

"Yes, Gabriel?" he said.

My sibling struggled for the words. "This woman... Do we have a mother?"

"If you'd like her to be."

We looked at each other in complete astonishment as our Savior walked off into the world to do better.

"This is a lot, Lucifer," Gabriel said. "A whole fucking lot."

"You cursed, Gabriel," I replied. "And yes, yes it is."

3 1

AS BELOW, SO ABOVE

It is not the place of angels to correct scripture.

What happened after the resurrection of Jesus Christ of Nazareth, the Son of God and embodiment of the Holy Spirit, is left for Sapiens to do with what they do with it. And as you can see, priest, yours have done much. You pointed to the right hero, but the villains are grayer and less visible than you think.

I fell. I failed. I forsook my creator for my pride.

These would not be the end of my failings, but the true blessing of my Christian faith is that in my tireless work to be the soil for God's seeds, I have endless seasons as all souls do. I have found new life in forgiveness and a faith I can do better because better already resides in me.

I'm far from thrilled my daughter picked you. You stink of drink and weed, but in your heart, you are a decent man. I, like my father, must believe you have it within you to grasp the same awareness and do away with such impure things.

You can. I can. We all can and one day will.

If God resides in all things, then all things will find God at their proper time.

You still stink.

But like you, I still have my failings.

Mine are the reason we are suffering this gambit.

Christ rose after the dispersal of his faithless acolytes, causing a ruckus among the Host still loyal to the Platinum Polis. All bowed to the God who had taken infinity, destroyed it, and remade it again through his self-sacrifice. Songs rang through the universe exalting his deed.

I, however, had to deal with my troops.

Our small street in London, hidden during the late eighties and a vibrant community of humans and angels, stood in dire silence as I walked down the cobblestone street. Heaven rang, echoing in a vast only they and their children—many of them still without wings— heard from the protection of our shroud. Many of the angels who had left with me, fought for me, and lived on my order rushed to my side with questions.

"Hail, Lucifer, do the forces of God move against us?"

"Do we ready to fight?"

"Has God come to claim us for our righteous rebellion?"

"Should we flee with the children?"

I tried to do as I had seen Christ do. I held their hands, promising no matter what was happening that I would be with them, but there was no need to fear. I consoled them until I reached the stoop of my flat. Lisbeth stood in the doorway, clad in a simple red dress fashionable for the period. Our little Deevi, already walking and talking, bounded past her.

"Da! Da Da Da," she squealed, her meaty little hands out for me. I picked her up, holding her as near as I could, but also to demonstrate to the other angels my ease beneath the singing skies.

"The skies sing loud songs," she whispered into my cheek as we looked up at iridescences mortal sight could not view. Cherubim streaked the firmament in pinks, golds, and lavenders. Raphael's trumpet sounded its joy in the purest notes.

"What singing, Da? Loud!"

"They are loud," I said with a smile. "Something wonderful has happened in the whole universe, Deevi. Something that will make everyone glad." I handed her back to my wife as I faced our community. Slowly I explained to them the things I had seen: the persecution and crucifixion, the resurrection, and what Christ had told me upon his rising. I revealed how I had surrendered my rebellion to a crownless king.

The choruses of heaven cascaded over the silence of my retinue. Some stared at me for a long time beside their human partners, their expressions confused but focused on what they had heard. Others simply awed as I recounted his rising.

But the last had the courage to speak out.

"What forgiveness has been promised us?" Shaytan emerged from the throngs of my supporters, the shadow of betrayal in his expression.

"Do you have something to say, my dearest brother and friend?" I called to him.

He grunted in response. "Friend, Lucifer? You are our lord. We did not follow a friend from the halls of the Platinum Polis. I did not. I followed my lord. And here you are, before us, asking us to surrender? To throw away the faith you made so we can shamefully skulk before our creator?"

"There will no shame or skulking," I said. "Our Lord Jesus has made a new covenant in his blood, and—"

"We are not creatures of flesh and blood!" Shaytan shouted.

Deevi flinched at his booming voice, as did the other Nephilim and their human parents.

"But our children are, Shaytan," I said, "and we are not unjust, nor fight for unjust things. If God has seen to do the work to redeem himself—"

"He's not redeemable," Shaytan interrupted. "You said he wasn't."

"I said—"

"You said he was a tyrant and cruel! And you expect us to simply walk back to him?" Shaytan asked in an earnest manner. "Is that what you would have us do, Lucifer?"

"I would have us have peace," I replied as I watched doubt spread among my followers. "We do not have to bow. That has not been asked of us. We do not have to be subservient. He simply asks us, the Host of his creations, to return to the Platinum Polis to hear the Word. That is all, Shaytan."

"That's all?" Shaytan asked, his taciturn glower breaking into a bright, happy smile. "Will he hear us now?"

"I'm certain he will listen to everything we have to ask and more," I promised, looking from him into the faces of those who doubted. They caught me catching them, but bared no embarrassment or regret, only acknowledgment they had heard me. A small contingent of others fell in with Shaytan, but when I gave the order, they obeyed.

We came to the gates, my rebel army at my back and unarmed.

Yet instead of glorious song and joy all there was to be found was silence.

Every angel, no matter their station, shied from us as we walked the golden streets, the gleaming bells in the high towers clanging so loud they punctuated the quiet. None of them dared look me in the face.

Gabriel met us at the steps to God's grand palace. We embraced as we always did upon meeting, but they held me a bit longer.

"What's happening?" I whispered in Gabriel's ear.

"It's Michael, Lucifer," they said into my shoulder. "He's threatening to rebel."

In the court of the Council of El, I stood beside Christ. He held my hand as my brother cursed my name in every language beyond those recorded on the walls of Babel. The other archangels, the only witnesses to our conference, remained at the edges of the room upon their glass and marble thrones.

"You cannot simply allow them back in! They defied you! They defied the Law!" Michael screamed down at Christ. Never leaving his gaze long on our creator, he turned his attention on me. "He sullied your children! He murdered humans! He's a traitor and liar! And you will simply letting him back in? How could you allow such an insult?"

"There was never any insult." Christ squeezed my hand the moment I opened my mouth to halt my angry words. "I have told you this, Michael. Lucifer followed my orders as I had given them and as he understood them. If there is any fault—"

"No," Michael shouted. "No! You cannot take his sin upon you! He was not made to sin and chose to!"

"But Michael, my creatures do sin. We sin," Christ replied. "And if there is any judgment to be bared, it should be on me. He complied with my—"

"No!" Michael screamed, infantile in his anger. "You are the Lord of Heaven and Earth! You are perfection, the Beginning and End of all things! He is low," he said, leaning forward with his finger pointed at me. "Low!"

"You keep saying that," I replied, unable to resist such ludicrousness. "What children have I sullied? What innocence have I ruined?"

"Do not!" Michael shouted in response. "Do not! You have born with that witch woman a spawn given no sanction by God, in full rebellion of his Law to remain separate from the Sapiens! You have sullied our purity!"

"Is that what this is about?" I asked before Christ could step between us. I raised my hands out to the columned, marbled chamber around us. "If I'm so 'impure', how am I here?" I moved my hand in our lord's direction. "He is of flesh and blood now! How—"

"Fornicator!" the Protector shouted. "Fornicator!"

"That is enough," Christ boomed in the Father's voice.

Thunder and lightning lanced between universes. Stars exploded. Beneath the cacophony the Cherubim guarding the borders of Heaven shook in terror before peace returned. The dome of the Platinum Polis calmed.

Even Michael heeled before the Personification.

"That is enough," he said, calm and kind. "Michael, I understand your position, but as I have told you—"

"Do you intend to have mortals enter the gates before their time?" Michael asked. "Should we dismiss the Cherubim and return them to the nothingness from which they arose?"

"Michael, you are being cruel now," Gabriel called from their seat on God's right, beside the empty throne Michael should have occupied. "They are our fam—"

"We are not them," he said. "I'll not be witness to the desecration of this place. They are not of this realm, but of theirs. The Garden is for humanity. The Platinum Polis is for us!"

Shaytan's fears and concerns arose in me. "And what of my child?" I asked. "What about her mother? Or the other children? What of their parents, Michael? There are angels who will not give them up."

"Then they will not enter this realm," said Michael. "I will not allow it."

"Are you saying you'll rebel?" I asked in a chiding manner.

"Be silent, Lucifer," Christ said.

The Lord and the Protector squared with each other.

I had fought against the bodiless, the untethered, the tyrant. Who I stood beside now, and who my brother refused his nature to serve, was the exact antithesis of the Demiurge mystics touched upon in ancient verse.

I knew, then and there, the reason why Michael was willing to rebel.

He hated that my father had answered me and not him. He listened to me and not to him.

"What would you have me do?" Christ asked. "I have sworn to forgive, to make way for those who'd put aside their sin and seek life in peace and tenderness, not by sword or the decree of kings. I have not come here to rule this great heaven, but to open it to all who seek it, joining with the earth in—"

"Then remove the mistakes made before you do so," Michael interrupted. "Destroy Lucifer, his followers, and their spawn."

Gabriel rushed in from Christ's right side, standing directly between us while facing Michael. "Michael, hear yourself! Who are you to make demands of the Lord?"

"Who is he to proclaim himself perfect and allow such—why are we even arguing this when Lucifer violated God's law?" The Protector rebutted, suddenly cold in his response. "He lay with a human and produced a creature outside of the Grand Design. He made a choice only granted to them and violated—"

"A moment," said Christ, breaking his son's rant. "Never did I say—"

"You did," Michael yelled, broken again. "You did, you did, and you said your Word was inviolate! He violated it! Are you God? Are you master of us or not?"

"Michael, why must I be a master?" the Savior asked. "I do not seek to rule."

Michael dropped his chin to his chest. Unable to keep the stinging tears from scrunching his handsome, golden face, he gritted his teeth. "I demand you do. To rule is to enact justice upon those that break your laws."

"Then I will speak new law," said Christ. "I will proclaim—"

"No," Michael roared with a crack of his own thunder. "Lucifer must be punished!"

"Why, Michael? Why can we not change?" Raphael spoke, his horn like a spear in his hands as he leaned on it. "It is the eevolving rule of the universe we have made. Nothing remains static."

"You are to be," said Michael. "What happens when these Nephilim gain greater hold of their powers? What are their full powers? Are they equal to the low angels who followed this cretin?" he asked. "What happens when *his daughter* comes into her evils? What happens when—"

"You'll not say a word about my little girl again," I stopped him. "Nor my wife, or any of the angel's partners or their children. You'll not—"

"Lucifer, be silent," Christ said. "This has gone far enough."

"It has, Father," said Michael. "And I will end it here if you will not."

"What does that mean?" Gabriel asked.

"My forces stand ready to enter the gates of the Platinum Polis. Loyal cherubim sworn to the Law," he said, stressing the last word as he spat it at Christ. "They will enter the London street as well."

"Whose street?" Christ asked. "What will you do?"

Michael scoffed. "Something worse than Egypt."

The weight of those plagues caught us, and to my shock, ensnared the Lord worst of all. His face fell on the memory of the unequal contest where he had shown his fullest cruelties. To Michael, the Word of God was impenetrable, and like any cultists too devoted to the ideal and not the reality, he would not be swayed.

He feared the ineffable as I once had. He still does.

And I did nothing, as his brother, to give him reason to think otherwise.

Caught by the circumstances of his decisions and indecisions, Christ chose his path. "All right, Michael," he said to the lord of our retinue. "I shall hear, but you will hear me. I will not slay Lucifer, or his followers, or their families. I will certainly not slay the Nephilim. I am willing to amend with you the Law, understanding certain requirements will be met on both ends. This is all I can give you. I hope you will see, son, that I will listen and I will love you. But I will not punish the innocent."

"Punish him," Michael said, pointing at me. "He must be punished for rebellion. Even if I must start mine to rectify it."

"What would you have us do to him?" Selaphiel asked by his emerald throne, the holy censer rested by the clawed foot of his chair. "It would be wrong to end his existence to feed your anger."

"This council was broken by his anger first," said Michael. "In punishment, Lucifer should be broken from the grace of God. He is to never walk the halls of the Platinum Polis. He or his followers. They are to be separated from their wives and children. What you, God, choose to do with the Nephilim is your will. Lucifer and his angels will never see them again, nor will they be allowed to treat upon the earth."

We stood in shock of his demand.

Gabriel asked the dreaded question. "Where are they to go, Michael? If not here and not the Garden, then where?"

"You know where," Michael said, directing his answer at Christ. "Tell them where you went, my Lord and Savior, when you passed on the Cross."

3 2

THE OLD GODS

I tumbled out of the other side of Purgatory, vomiting and screaming. My skin crawled in a billion fire-ants as the light of the scorching realm blinded my eyes. Lucifer had carried my consciousness through the gauntlet, my body dragged across eons of memory and emotion. Slowly, my vision returned in the chamber where our journey began beneath the mound.

"Wake up, Saint Patrick," said Lucifer. "The doors have opened."

His order roused me. Parched and gasping for air, I reached out. After everything I witnessed through the sense of one I could no longer deem a rebel or fallen archangel, he took my hand.

Left blinking against his giant glowing outline, he hauled me to my feet, the light of his celestial body ebbing. Shivering as I searched the floor of the chamber, I spotted the sweater I had left behind and fell back to my knees. I crawled to it and pulled it on like a starving man finding food, thankful for the wool on my skin. The tingle lessened.

I willed myself to my feet again, better this time, and saw Lucifer was correct. Two doors had opened.

Behind us, the exit to Lough Derg revealed absolute terror. The ground had shifted, torn to brown soil and broken stone. An orange sky throbbed in the noiseless, ruined world.

And deeper into our chamber yawned the next doorway into darkness.

I knew who waited inside. I had put them there.

"I'll go look upon the field," Lucifer said, steel-eyed to the world. "See if..."

"I got it," I said without a hint of distrust. After everything I had learned, how could I hate Lucifer anymore without hating myself?

It made me wonder why I spoke to you at all.

Lucifer summoned a sword of light to his hands as he charged the blighted landscape. Fuck, I had been under so long I sounded like him. Half-hunched from the shock of the crossing, I leaned forward, letting gravity do the work.

The first steps unsteady, I approached the entrance to Tir na Og.

I am the Lord thy God, thou shalt not have any gods before me.

Nowhere in that statement did anyone deny the existence of others. This is the hard truth every missionary faced in the earliest days of our evangelism. The Druids had power. Mama Meredith Joslin, a Vodun priestess, has power. Be it real or cultural, the magick, myths, and gods of other lands hold sway in places Christ does not.

God faces off against a multitude in a universe he has made.

And, in his weird way, he saved as many as he conquered. The story behind that is complicated, but the short version:

One monk from Rome with a Bible did not do it alone. The Celtic Catholic Church I helped found along with Andrew the Apostle, Brigid—a goddess turned to Christ no less—and Colmcille was an *interfaith* organization. After the demons were run out, there were still problems, still giants, and at some point, the world was not right for the gods of my people.

So God, through me, sealed off their realm through the sacrifice of my first journey through Purgatory over fifteen hundred years ago.

Toss in the reincarnation, we've ended back where it began.

The stair down led to the chamber was not unlike the one upstairs. Also outsized to the mound, I came to the edge of a sunny, shining wood. A lone sentry stood guard, tall and dark-haired in old lamellar.

The long spear in his hands, its leaf-shaped point catching the eternal daylight, afforded him an easy post to rest.

He sighted me immediately and smiled.

"I thought I felt the wind," Lugh Long Arm said in Ancient Gaelic. "Saint Patrick. How many Christian years?"

"Oh, eh," I said in our mother tongue, doing the math. "I think one thousand, five hundred and fourteen?"

He popped a handsome brow at the number. "Seems like last week. You look different, friend."

"New body, pal," said I. "Been getting along well down here?"

"As sure, buddy, you know," said Lugh. "We have what we need. Gobby's food remains excellent, but the ale's started to lose potency."

I grunted in appreciation of the problem. "Well, you might have a bigger issue than the ale, guy."

"Oh, aye friend?" the god-king of Ireland asked me. "It is time then?"

"Fuck, I don't know. But it's bad."

"Right, right." He plucked the spear out of the dirt. "They've been resting, you know. It might take me a bit to get them ready. Do we have to come back in after? Be better if I could tell the gang ahead of time if they're in or out."

"Again," I said with a shrug. "Lugh, my buddy—"

"Yes, my guy?" the god asked.

"Can I borrow Setanta? Things are bad. Bad-bad."

"Going to be hard," Lugh replied. "Emer didn't come down here and the time you two ran into each other last she wasn't in that fancy heaven either. My son's not going to come out unless he knows he'll find her."

"Tell him I'll help this time."

"You will?"

"Oh, friend," I said, "There are worst things than letting the Hound have his day."

3 3

DEFCON HEAVEN

I walked from my Purgatory to find Station Island leveled and the water boiled away.

"Holy fuck," was all I muttered upon the scorched earth. For miles around me, fields of broken, torn bodies were strewn like confetti after New Year's, the blood under them a sludgy bed. The sky throbbed in a brown-shit color made orange by the sun. The stench of it would have caused me to vomit if my stomach hadn't been empty.

I had never seen a battlefield so terrible, and if you're still listening to me, every ounce of me did not want to go forward.

Someone needed to witness for those souls left behind on that ruined lakebed. Rosary in my right pocket, my little bible somehow in the back, I went to make sure you counted all of them.

I found your fucking kids squabbling among the dead.

In a scene that made way more sense under this new dawn than the last, five of the archangels pressed Michael away from Lucifer, who stood beside Gabriel as he sobbed loudly on their shoulder.

Raphael seemed especially incensed, using his long horn to keep Michael at bay. "Why are you like this, you fucking idiot?" The Trumpeter shouted at his bullish brother. "You insensitive schmuck!"

Sums this all up. "All right," I shouted in my Sunday voice. "The Lord demands your silence!"

Every one of the eight archangels faced me.

"Patrick?" From behind a hillock of dead boiled in mortal sludge rounded Merry. I nearly gasped as I beheld her, covered head to toe in viscera. She splotched down on hands and knees, racking cries echoing across the terrible day.

"Merry! Merry," I screamed, calling, wanting to get to her and shield her from these bastards. Seconds later she was in my arms. She cried and cried and cried, hacking between breathes.

"He-he-he-he-he-he's..." she heaved between her snot-covered lips. "He's..."

"Shush, love, shush," I said. "Don't speak."

"No!" She clawed at my back, trying to get face to face with me. "We have to get him down! We have to get him down, Patrick!"

"Get who down?" I said, unable to handle her shuddering. "What happened? What happened?"

With the unearthly strength of a survivor, she pulled me along the tracks of dead.

Nothing could have prepared me when I found George.

His gray eyes lifted to the polluted sky in cold repose. Someone had torn out his jaw and throat, leaving a waterfall of veins and sinews to hang on his plundered chest cavity. Using his entrails to wrap him around a spear, the demons tied had his arms out in a mocking effigy of Christ. A horse's head, of all dreaded things, had been positioned so the mouth covered his penis.

Daniel O'Brien, bless his bravery, had climbed in front of the desecrated knight, trying to unbind him. Covered in the same gross layer that painted Merry, he tended to the task with a thousand-yard stare.

To top it all off, they stood in the middle of a dead dragon.

Laid out on its back, scaled wings splayed, the reptilian creature's head was cut free of the oozing neck. Whatever had befallen my friend, I knew by faith alone he had found one last victory.

I crawled up the heap of dead. "Daniel," I said gently, picking among the razor-bones of the dragon's rib-cage.

He gave me a quick glance over his shoulder, and his face lightened.

We pulled Saint George the Dragonslayer onto the cleanest ground we could find to lay him in peace. No matter my anger at the time, or my hate for you, God, I sank down to my knees and gave him his last rites. The moment I finished, I popped up, checked on Merry and Daniel as they knelt together at the knight's feet, and faced your court.

They stood in a line, too uniform given their discontent with each other. Michael, that raging ass, muted upon seeing George.

I'm not a dummy. "Where's Deevi?" I asked, calmer than I should have. I didn't need an actual answer.

Raphael averted his eyes from mine first.

The rest frowned when I scoffed at their cowardice. "Where is she?" I asked, harder this time.

"It's her fault she was captured," Michael said. "She wasted—"

"Shut up, Michael," Gabriel said. "Shut the fuck up. I don't want to hear another word from you."

Michael thought to protest. "Gabriel, I—"

"Shut up," Raphael added. "Seriously. Seriously. Be quiet, brother. You'll have your say at home, but we're not there. Be quiet or leave."

The Protector shut his damned mouth long enough for me to reassert the subject. "Gabriel. Deevi. Where?"

"Well, Patrick," Gabriel said in the firmest tone possible, "Perdition has captured her and taken her away. We tried to escape after George offered his life to give us time, but a greater sense of duty turned her back in an attempt to rescue him. We attempted to support her when—"

These incompetent fucks.

"Which way?" I asked.

"Does it matter, priest?" Michael asked. "We will need the whole Host to take her back, let alone scour the earth to discover her whereabouts. The window to stop—"

"Now you will shut the fuck up," I said. "I don't have time for this. I have time to rescue Deevi. If any one of you want to come help me do it, fine, but come along and be quiet. If not, scamper the fuck out of here. I will put it on you if you decide to do otherwise."

The dumb idiot couldn't shut up. "You threaten us, saint?" Michael asked. "The only one who can—"

A horn, deep and low, echoed from the entrance of my Purgatory. The sound of stone grinding against the earth preceded a short quake. A pair of men's voices spoke in Ancient Gaelic, loud and long. A pair of horses noised at each other.

"Not anymore," I said to Michael, the certainty wiped from his smug features.

Horse hooves pounded the fried soil as the chariot's wheels thundered.

Out of the mists of time and space they came.

A stout Celt drew the reins of the warrior's chariot, but none paid any attention to brave Laeg. All eyes were on the fighter clad in splint mail and battle skirts, his arms and legs strapped in leather and hammered iron. A sword hilted in black wood and brass hung on a wide girdle stamped in shining gold. A spiked-shield strapped to his left arm, he clutched three javelins in that hand, while in his right he leaned on a spear almost a head taller than him.

A shiver coursed my spine as I beheld Cuchulainn, Eire's greatest hero, a walking weapon of celestial destruction. Not only could he fuck up any angel God threw at us, forget Perdition and its demons, he'd do it with permanence.

The Hound of Ulster whistled for Laeg to halt his kingly horses, the Gray of Macha and the Black of Saingliu. He hopped down from the back of his open chariot. Every bit of five foot three and fury, Cuchulainn made a beeline for Michael.

"Remember me, motherfucker?" He pumped his arms in anticipation, blood rushing to his skin. His right eye, once blue and clear, receded in his skull as the left eye bulged onto his cheek, hung by its retinal nerve. Entering one of his legendary warp-spasms, he spoke in a roaring voice. "I remember what you told my wife, angel! What did I tell you I'd do? What did I tell you I'd fucking do the next time I saw you?"

The demigod stalked toward the Protector, who literally squealed like a child and begged his siblings to save him.

Fuck, I had gone and done something. Merry and Daniel, so shocked the survival instinct kicked in, scurried away from the recovered body of Saint George and huddled by my side like scared children. Seeing two good people broken, I forbid myself to stop what I had unleashed.

I had forgotten about Lucifer.

Bless him, he dared walk in the way of the pint-sized terror. The warrior's warp-spasm ended as the Morningstar whispered down to him. Cuchulainn tilted to the side and looked dead at Michael. He straightened, whispered something up to Lucifer while thumbing over his shoulder at me.

Lucifer raised his eyes, meeting mine.

I nodded back.

He stepped out of the way.

"Lucifer, why?" Gabriel crowed as the fracas restarted. They broke from the line, out to meet my champion.

Allowed time to breathe, no matter how fetid the air, I valued it. Shutting my eyes, I put out the shuddering priestess and damaged RIRA man beside me, the archangels fighting as the prodigal son—my in-law—watched in special glee.

I laughed. Why, I'll never know, but I did.

I had you here, God. I would rescue Deevi, put down Satan, and figure a way out after that. But, for the moment, in this instance, I had you, you goofy son of a bitch.

"You sure do, Patrick," Jesus said. "I don't know what I'm going to do with this."

My mirth slain, I opened my eyes to find the Savior of all humankind standing beside me.

"Holy Jesus," Merry screamed as she and Daniel scattered. "He's here!"

THE END

ACKNOWLEDGMENTS

Everything I do is for Margo and Ben.

I want to thank John Hartness for always believing in me. Erin Penn deserves huge credit in helping me put this manuscript together in a cogent fashion, as does Sarah Adams. I need to thank Samuel Montgomery-Blinn, JD Blackrose, and Ziggy Nixon for their words and encouragement. I owe my parents a lot, most of all for always raising me in a safe, open household where inquiry was allowed. There are too many writers before me to thank, but let's go with Garth Ennis, Kevin Smith, and Clive Barker.

I also need to thank Reverand Wormley of St. Mark's Evangelical Lutheran Church in St. Louis, Missouri, who made me believe I had the Devil in me when I was seven because that's what they do to children. Bad move, padre.

I also need to thank the people who cannot be named for the sake of jobs and security, which include clergy, parishioners, and former members of the Holy Roman Catholic Church who were kind enough to offer words, debates, questions, and also encouragement. A lot of good people are fighting a good fight and feel alone in it because of the institution where they reside. Always remember that there are good people wherever you look for them, including in the places these stories take aim at like the Vatican. I also want to acknowledge Pope Francis, who is moving heaven and earth to cleanse the many sins of his church. I also need to thank Dr. James Tabor, Dr. Jeremy Schott, and Dr. Sean McCloud of the Religious Studies program at the University of North Carolina at Charlotte. I also need to make a special mention of David Hayward, aka The Naked Pastor, who's art and worldview played a dramatic role in these novels.

Finally, I want to thank Jesus Christ and the founders of his movement. I read the Bible so many times in its many different variations (including the books that were left out) before and during the writing of these novels that I could not help but listen, and in listening I found profound safety, courage, and love. Please bless my child and all children.

ABOUT THE AUTHOR

Raised in the hills of North Carolina and Maryland, Jay Requard is a graduate of The University of North Carolina at Charlotte with a degree in History and Religious Studies. An award-winning author of Epic Fantasy, Sword & Sorcery, and Urban Fantasy, he is also the host of Pondering The Orb on YouTube. In his free time, he enjoys wandering, reading, and cooking for his wife, son, and a small star-cat named Mona Underfoot. They reside in New York City.

Find out more about Jay and his books at jayrequard.com.

ALSO BY JAY REQUARD

Blessed & Possessed Series (Urban Fantasy)

The Driver of Serpents

Atenia (Epic Fantasy)

A Wave of Lions (Epic Fantasy/Sword & Sorcery), which include the following titles:

The Curse of Shallow Bay

At the Mirror's Edge

The Queen in Silver

Death & Dust: The Pale Sand Adventures (Dark Fantasy)

Spy/Counter/Killer (Sword & Sorcery), which include the following titles:

A Dangerous Brew

A Spirited Blend

A Spot Before Dead

War Pigs (Sword & Sorcery)

FRIENDS OF FALSTAFF

Thank You to all our Falstaff Books Patrons, who get extra digital content each month! To be featured here and see what other great rewards we offer, go to www.patreon.com/falstaffbooks.

PATRONS

Dino Hicks
John Hooks
John Kilgallon
Larissa Lichty
Travis & Casey Schilling
Staci-Leigh Santore
Sheryl R. Hayes
Scott Norris
Samuel Montgomery-Blinn
Junkle

Thank You for Supporting Independent Publishing!

We believe that you should be able
to read your books, your way.
That's why this Falstaff Books
print edition includes a digital copy
at no additional cost!

Just scan the QR code with your device,
follow the directions on Prolific Works,
and enjoy!
You can also join our newsletter when prompted,
and never miss an awesome Falstaff Release!